# Family Binds

Holly Ash

Published in association with Cabin in the Woods

Editor: Alana Joli Abbott

Cover Design: Maja Kopunovic



ISBN-13: 978-1-7325740-3-8

To my parents, for everything

# Chapter 1

Sirens echoed off the glass dome of the colony. The sound would have been unbearable without the oxygen mask covering most of Crystal's face. Stapleton Farms was losing oxygen at an alarming rate. The colony should have had enough oxygen to last roughly four hours—plenty of time to safely evacuate the eight hundred people that called Stapleton Farms home. Or it would be if whatever had shut down the atmosphere generators that provided breathable air hadn't also locked down every docking port and the escape pods.

Crystal's team had been forced to make a hard dock, physically cutting a hole in the colony's base, in order to get in. There wasn't a direct path to the town at the center of the dome, so Crystal's team was forging a path through rows of tilled soils and freshly planted crops. They were still a half mile away when the cart carrying the reserved oxygen tanks got stuck for what felt like the thousandth time. Crystal hadn't factored in these delays.

Even with the extra oxygen they were carrying, they were going to be cutting it close with the evacuation. She glanced down at the computer strapped to her wrist and cursed every salad she had ever eaten. Only sixty-five minutes until the colony was out of breathable air. She reached below the cart and pulled several large heads of lettuce from under it, freeing its wheels.

"Flint, any luck yet?" Crystal asked into her headset as she ran. The two combat teams had split up as soon as they had arrived. Their greatest chance of success was to attack this problem from two fronts: evacuation and restoration. It was a race to see who could complete their mission first. Personally, Crystal hoped Flint's team would be able to bring the atmosphere generators back online long before she had completed the evacuation.

"We just reached the command room for the west fields," Lieutenant Desiree Flint's voice rang in Crystal earpiece.

"As long as the computers there are connected to the main network, like I think they are, I should be able to get into the atmosphere programing," Tyler's voice replaced Flint's over the headsets. Tyler sounded confident, and Crystal believed him. He was the best programmer LAWON had and it wasn't like they would have to deal with the crops getting in their way.

"Good. Keep me posted." The computer on Crystal's wrist started to vibrate. She had already used a quarter of her oxygen reserve. "And Ty? Work fast." Crystal knew that small breech in protocol would be enough for Tyler to understand everything that was running through her head. Even though they hadn't grown up together their bond as siblings had always been strong.

Her team started moving faster once they were finally through the fields. She had read the colony's emergency plan and knew that the escape pods were located in the basement of the Community Center. It was standard set up for a bubble colony. It was easy to build the pods into the colony's platform, which usually rested at least ten meters above the ocean floor.

They carried the carts up the three steps into the Community Center without breaking stride. The sound of the sirens was muted now that they were off the street. A steady hum of voices filled the large open atrium even though the room was empty. "Find the entrance to the basement," she told her team.

There were at least fifteen doors in the circular room. She rushed at the first one only to find it led to a supply closet. She glanced down at her computer and shook her head. More time wasted. She moved to the next door leaving the supply closet open so they wouldn't accidently check it again. Every second mattered.

"Over here," Justin yelled from the other side of the room. She shot him a smile, even though he couldn't see it through her oxygen mask. Justin never let her down.

"I want four people to a cart," Crystal ordered as she ran across the atrium. Her team quickly arranged themselves, and a few seconds later, she was leading them down the stairs. A fluttering sensation grew in her stomach with every step she took. She couldn't explain the sudden onset of nerves. Even with the high level of civilian lives at stake, this was a simple rescue mission. No one was even shooting at them. She could have led a mission like this in her sleep; still she couldn't stop her hand from resting on the butt of her gun.

Chaos crashed around her as soon as she entered the basement. It looked like a few of the colony's engineers were attempting to get the airlock to the escape pods open, but were having a hard time given the hundreds of scared citizens crowding them. Crystal tapped a button on her wrist computer to get an atmosphere reading. The oxygen levels were dangerously low compared to the rest of the colony. It wasn't surprising given how many people had crammed into the small space. Unfortunately, only a handful of them were wearing oxygen masks. She had expected them to be more prepared. It looked like they had never even run a simple evacuation drill before.

Crystal turned to her team. "Grady, set up two oxygen tanks on opposite sides of the room." Grady nodded and left. "Anderson, coordinate the distribution of masks. I don't want any delays once we start moving people." Justin quickly squeezed her hand as he moved past her to carry out her orders. He could tell she was on edge, but his touch never failed to calm her.

With her team immersed in their orders, Crystal turned her attention to the man standing on a box in the middle of the room, attempting to restore a semblance of order to the situation. Crystal assumed he was the colony's leader. "Everyone please, give them some room to work. We'll figure this out!" he yelled through his mask. It had no effect on the people surrounding him, but his voice sent a shiver down her spine. She knew that voice, even if she wasn't sure where she had heard it before.

Crystal pushed the feeling aside; she had a job to do. She needed to find a way to calm the pandemonium that had overtaken the room. Crystal's team was dispersed throughout the basement, trying to hand out supplies. The colonists were so wrapped up in their fear, they hardly noticed what they were being handed.

"Ladies and gentlemen, please remain calm." The mask gave Crystal's voice a robotic quality that was easily lost in the panic.

"Everyone shut up!" Grady bellowed. He had pulled off his mask so that his voice carried over then noise. The room feel silent, except for the faint echo of sirens. Grady returned his mask before Crystal could reprimand him for breaking protocol.

"Ladies and gentlemen," she started again. "I'm Lieutenant Commander Crystal Wolf from the LAWON ship *Journey*." Crystal noticed the colony's leader dissolve into the crowd. She could only assume he wasn't thrilled about LAWON's presence at the colony. Stapleton Farms was not a member of the Lands and Waters of Neophia and had been adamantly against joining every time they had been approached. In Crystal's opinion, they were a little overprotective of their farming technology, but given their importance to the planet's food supply, the brass at headquarters didn't hesitate to divert *Journey* hundreds of miles off course to respond. In fact, they had only been able to pick up the distress call because of a new booster she had installed on the ship's antenna last week. "As we speak, there is a team working to bring your life support systems back online. In the event they aren't able to restore the systems quickly, we are going to begin a complete evacuation of the colony."

"Our escape pods are down! How do you suggest we evacuate?" yelled a man from the control panel for the pods. He wasn't wearing an oxygen mask, so Crystal was clearly able to see his eye roll. She knew the people here didn't have any faith in LAWON. She let it slide off her back, reminding herself that despite the tough guy act he was putting on, he had to be scared. They were farmers; Crystal doubted any of them had ever been in a life or death situation before. She murmured a quiet

"Anderson" into her comm, audible only to her team. When Justin looked up on the other side of the room, Crystal nodded to the man that had yelled at her. Justin started to make his way over, his arms weighted down with oxygen masks. Crystal hoped people would start to calm down a little once they each had their own oxygen supply.

"We were able to create a hard dock on the west side of the colony," Crystal explained, keeping her voice steady, showing she was unfazed by the colonist's doubt. "I have shuttles standing by to bring everyone to *Journey*. My team will come around to break you into groups and will pass out oxygen masks to anyone who doesn't have one. We have set up a few oxygen tanks in this room to temporarily bring levels back up to a safe range."

A pressing calm filled the room as the first of the tanks was released. The citizens might feel like they had been saved, but Crystal knew better. Moving eight hundred people half way across the colony would be no small feat. She looked at her computer. Forty minutes of breathable air left.

Rescue missions were not Desi's strong suit. There was far too much planning and not enough action to keep her attention. It wasn't that she didn't care about the lives they were trying to save; it was just hard to get overly excited when all she had to do was get Price to a computer and let him work his hacker magic. The countdown to suffocation did add an element of tension to the mission, but honestly, it didn't really faze her. Price was the best programmer in the military. She was confident that he would have the systems back up long before they were in any real danger.

It hadn't taken them long to reach the command center from the west field after helping Wolf's team unload the oxygen tanks. Wolf had insisted that it was their first priority, though Desi wasn't sure why. She had bet Justin twenty bucks that they would have the system back online long before Wolf's team even reached the center of the colony. Standing outside the command center with the rest of her team while Price worked at the computer, she was confident she would win.

"Flint to Wolf switch to channel five." Desi quickly switched from the open channel to the private channel she shared with Wolf.

"What's wrong?" Wolf's panic cut through the line.

"Calm down Crystal, I just thought you'd like to know that Tyler's working on the computers now so this mission should be wrapped up any minute now. Have you even reached the Community Center yet?"

"Don't get cocky, Flint. I'll have the first group of evacuees moving out in two minutes. This isn't over yet. Now switch back to channel one. Wolf out."

Desi switched her comms back to the open channel then stuck her head through the doorway of the command center to check on Price. "I told Wolf you'd have this wrapped up any minute, so you got this handled right?" Price's fingers didn't stop moving. She admired his focus.

"I'm connected to the main network. I should have a better idea of what caused the malfunction soon," Price said without looking up from the monitors.

Desi walked over and stood next to him. Numbers scrolled over the screen so fast she wasn't sure how he could even tell what he was looking at. Price had started to teach her some basics of computer programming, but there was no way she could follow what he was doing. She only gave herself a headache.

"This doesn't make sense," Price said under his breath.

"What doesn't?" Desi stared at the screen harder, hoping she would be able to spot the problem, but it was useless.

"It's fighting me."

"What do you mean it's fighting you?" Desi half expected to see pictures of warriors flash across the screen, but the freight train of numbers and letters continued.

Price stopped typing and ran his hand through his hair, causing Desi to worry for the first time since arriving at Stapleton Farms. "The virus attacking the system is blocking my attempts to send data from this computer to the main server."

"So you can't bring the life support systems back online?"

Price sighed, finally looking away from the screen. "No. Not from here anyway. I need to get to the central computer system."

"Let's move out." Desi took off running toward the center of the colony with the rest of her team trailing behind her. "Flint to Wolf," she said into her headset as she ran.

"Go ahead Flint." Wolf's voice played in Desi's earpiece.

"We are unable to restore systems from the field command center. Heading your way now," Desi said as carefully as she could over the open channel. There were no secrets during a mission on Neophia. It was still something Desi was getting used to.

"Do you have a plan?" Wolf asked.

"Price needs to get to the central computer system."
"I'll find someone who can get him access."
"We'll be at your location in five."
"Understood. Wolf out."

Crystal scanned the room quickly. She needed to find the colony's leader. She was sure that any number of people in the room could tell her where the central computer system was, but if she went around asking random people, she was afraid she would only cause another wave of panic. She finally spotted him toward the back of the room. She pushed her way through the crowd, which was still overwhelming despite the fact that Grady had already left for the shuttle with the first group of evacuees.

She was halfway across the room before she realized she was clenching her hands. Something about this man put her on edge. Crystal wished she could place him. She stopped a few feet away from him. He was arguing with a woman, a young girl was clinging to her leg. A teenage boy was standing next to her with his arms crossed in defiance. Crystal watched them closely while trying to relax the muscles in her hands.

"Take Gina and Leo and go with the next group," he said.

"Dad, let me stay and help," the teen said.

"No Leo, you need to go with your mother. I need you to help look after Gina until I get there." Part of Crystal wanted to turn away and find someone else to show them to the server room, but she couldn't tear herself away. Something about this man was so familiar. She just stood there watching as time ticked by.

"I'm not leaving without you," the woman said.

Crystal could hear the tears in her voice, even though the woman's face was covered by an oxygen mask.

"Yes, you are. I need to stay behind and make sure everyone gets out. I can't do that unless I know you're safe. I'll meet up with you as soon as I can. I promise." The colony leader reached out and gently squeezed his wife's hands. Crystal's heart throbbed at the sight. She remembered her father doing the same thing whenever he and her mother were sent on separate missions.

The family interaction blocked everything else from Crystal's mind. Her parents had never entered her thoughts during a mission before, but now she found herself wondering how they would've acted had this been their colony. Would they go with her, or stay behind to help? She wanted to believe they would have gone with her, though all the evidenced pointed in the other direction.

The computer on her wrist started to vibrate, breaking her from her trance. She glanced down at it to see a message from Grady. The shuttle had just left with the first group of evacuees. Crystal did a quick calculation. More time had passed than she realized. Flint would be here any second.

Crystal forced herself to move again. "Excuse me," she called out as she approached. He turned toward her, hesitantly. "Are you in charge here?"

"Um, yes I am." His voice faltered. She could only assume the pressure of the current situation was getting to him.

"I need you to come with me." Crystal didn't wait for an answer. She relied on her perceived authority over the situation to motivate him to follow. Justin was at the bottom of the stairs waiting to lead the next group to the shuttles. "Alister, take over here. Anderson you're with me."

There was no logical reason to pull Justin off his job, but Crystal's gut was screaming at her not to trust the man trailing in her wake. She had learned to trust her instincts while working counterterrorism and those instincts were telling her to bring back up. Alister was the better fighter, but Justin had become her rock in the month they had been dating. She hoped having him with her would help put her nerves at ease, even though it went against everything she had made him promise when she agreed to give their relationship a chance. Who would have thought she would be the first one to break the relationships-can't-affect-the-mission rule?

"Is everything all right?" Justin asked as he followed her up the stairs and out to the street.

"I'm not sure." Crystal glanced over her shoulder at the man following them.

Crystal didn't stop walking until they had reached the middle of the street outside of the Community Center. She had to make sure they were far enough away so that they wouldn't be overheard by the groups of evacuees heading for the shuttles. She turned to the colony leader, who finally caught up with them. "We were unable to stop the virus attacking your life support systems from the command center in the field." There was no use beating around the bush.

"So, we're all going to die here. Is that what you're telling me?" The man's shoulders slumped and he ran his hands through his hair. Just like Tyler did when he couldn't solve a problem.

"No one is going to die if I can help it, Mr…"

"Martin, Ben Martin." The words tumbled out of his mouth.

"Mr. Martin, what I'm telling you is that plan A didn't

work, so we are moving on to plan B. We have the best computer programmer in LAWON here. If anyone can fix this, it's him." Crystal's voice was calm, even though a quick glance at her computer told her that only a quarter of her air supply was left.

"How can I help?"

"We need access to the central computer system." Crystal glanced over Ben's shoulder as she talked. She could see Flint's team at the other end of the street.

"Of course. Where's your tech guy?" Ben looked from Crystal to Justin, who shook his head so adamantly Crystal had to really focus to keep herself from laughing.

"He's there," Crystal answered, pointing at Tyler, who stopped just behind them, slightly out of breath.

"Follow me." Ben took off toward a building at the end of the street. Tyler and Flint followed after him while the rest of Flint's team went to assist with the evacuations.

Crystal was about to follow when Justin asked, "Do you want me to stay and help with the evacuation?" There was new level of concern in his voice that hadn't been there before.

"No. I need you with me. Something feels off, and I want to be there in case Flint needs backup." Crystal was glad Justin couldn't see her face through the mask. She didn't want him to worry about her needlessly.

"You're the boss."

They hurried down the street. When they arrived at the colony's control room, Tyler was already at work. Ben was talking to two people in the corner of the room. Crystal assumed they had been attempting to fix the issue when Tyler showed up and pushed them aside. They left a few minutes later.

Crystal was trying hard to pay attention to what Tyler

was doing, but she couldn't shake the feeling that Ben was watching her. Even though every time she glanced in his direction, he was looking at something else. She couldn't be imagining it, could she? She looked to Justin for support, but he was standing guard at the door. He was taking her suggestion of backup to heart. Instead she looked down at her wrist computer to give her something else to focus on. She had about twenty minutes of air left in her mask, and the colony was down to ten minutes of breathable air. "How's it going Price?" she asked.

"I'm working on it." Tyler didn't look up from the computer. "Every time I get close to killing this thing, it launches a new attack. The coding is incredible."

That wasn't the reassurance she was looking for. She turned away from the computer and connected to the open channel. "Grady, status update."

"The first shuttle just left. The second shuttle is making its approach. We should begin loading the next group in less than five minutes," his voice echoed in her ear.

"Jim, children first," she said quietly. She could feel Ben watching her.

"I got this, kid. Don't worry."

She closed the link to Grady and turned her attention back to the computer screens in front of her.

"We got a problem," Tyler yelled over his shoulder. She noticed he was flexing his fingers. She had never seen his hands cramp while coding before. She hoped the low oxygen levels weren't affecting his circulation yet. They needed him.

Flint was by his side in an instant, though Crystal knew she wouldn't have any idea what she was looking at. "What is it now?"

"The virus was planted manually. The colony was sabotaged from the inside." Tyler turned away from the computer.

Crystal's hand shot up to her ear and instantly opened the link to Grady back up. "Stop the evacuation." She couldn't risk sending the person who had sabotaged the colony to *Journey*. It wouldn't take much for them to plant another virus on the ship. Then they would have access to countless highly classified LAWON databases, or worse, the ship's weapon systems.

"You can't stop the evacuation. Innocent people will die without your help," Ben argued. He started to move toward her, but Justin stepped between them.

"Repeat the order," Grady's voice rang with desperation in her ear.

"Stop the evacuation."

"Are you sure?" His voice was softer this time. He rarely questioned her orders. She could only imagine the panic her order would cause, but she didn't have any other choice.

"I am. No one in or out without my permission and make sure the shuttles that have left don't dock with *Journey* until I give the all clear." She glanced over at Ben, who was still trying to get around Justin. He looked like he was about to explode. She couldn't really blame him. "But keep everyone in a holding pattern in case things change." She needed time to figure out the best course of action. Unfortunately, time wasn't something she had.

"Yes, ma'am." Grady's voice was filled with reluctance, but she knew her orders would be followed.

"What gives you the right?" Ben had managed to get around Justin.

"As the commanding officer of this mission, I have

every right." She tried to remind herself that he was just scared, but she was having a hard time being understanding as he moved closer, in what she could only assume was an attempt to intimidate her.

"There are children here and you're condemning them to death." Ben swayed slightly. Crystal looked down at her wrist computer. The oxygen levels in the room were dangerously low.

Crystal was about to respond when Tyler stepped between them. "If you would stop arguing for a second none of this will matter."

"What do you need Ensign?" Flint asked. At least one of them was still behaving professionally. Crystal took a step back and tried to get her emotions in check. What was it about this mission that had her so on edge? She usually had no problem remaining professional, even with someone screaming in her face.

"The server room," Tyler said.

"Down the hall on the left." Ben pointed in the direction as he spoke.

Tyler sprinted past them. By the time Crystal got there, he was already searching the panels in the room. "Life support, life support," he muttered to himself.

"Over here," Flint called.

Tyler was at her side in a second. He pulled the panel out of the server, quickly looked it over and removed a small chip. The alarms stopped the second he returned the panel to the server. The silence was deafening. Crystal hadn't realized she has been yelling over the alarms since they had arrived at the colony. Now that she could speak at a normal volume, she noticed a dry scratching feeling in the back of her throat.

They waited in stiff silence. "Atmosphere generators re-engaged." The automated messaged played over the colony's intercom system. Crystal looked down at her wrist computer. The oxygen levels in the colony were slowly starting to climb. It would take a few hours to completely replenish the system, but they were out of danger now.

Crystal pulled off her mask and flexed her jaw to loosen the muscles in her cheeks. She should really try to come up with a more comfortable design. As she glanced around the room, she saw that everyone had removed their masks except for Ben. After a few seconds hesitation, he pulled his mask up. He maintained eye contact with Crystal the whole time.

It was as if Crystal was looking into the face of a ghost. She recognized him at once, even if her mind couldn't make sense of what she was seeing. Maybe she was still feeling the effects of oxygen deprivation, because this simply wasn't possible. Yet here he was, standing an arm's length away from her. Part of her wanted to run to him. To fling her arms around his neck and cry as he held her. Another part of her wanted to sprint from the room and never look back. It didn't matter, though, as it seemed her feet were glued to the ground.

"Commander, is everything all right?" Justin asked quietly. Out of the corner of her eye, she saw him standing next her, but she couldn't force her eyes away from Ben. There was nothing she could say to make him understand anyway.

"Crys." Justin gently grabbed her hand. His touch gave her strength.

She finally pulled her eyes away from Ben and fixed them on Tyler. The resemblance was incredible. She was surprised she hadn't noticed it before. Tyler was looking at her with growing concerned. He hadn't pieced together what was happening yet. Crystal wasn't surprised; the two men had never actually met in person.

"Tyler," Crystal said finally managing to find her voice, "I'd like you to meet our father."

# Chapter 2

The only sound was the hum of the servers. Crystal felt the room shrink. Tyler looked like she had punched him in the gut. She couldn't blame him. What she had said should have been impossible, and yet here they were.

"Your father." Flint's voice finally cut through the silence. "But I thought..."

"That he was dead. So did I." There was an underlining anger in her voice that she hadn't intended to be there.

Crystal couldn't move. So many thoughts raced through her mind, it was almost like her brain had been wiped clean. She couldn't focus on anything. She couldn't even make her body follow the simplest commands. Not that she had any idea about what she should be doing. Where was her fight or flight instinct when she needed it?

"Did she say '*our* father?'" Ben, formerly Jedidiah Wolf, a man she had given up as executed, turned to look at Tyler. Of all the things Ben could have said, that's what he had decided to go with? The absurdity of it as enough to kick start Crystal's brain.

"My mother is Susan Price," Tyler said by way of an explanation. His voice was flat and his face unreadable. It was so unlike him. Crystal's mind flashed back to the day Tyler showed up on her grandparents' doorstep, holding a picture of her father they had never seen before. After the execution, the military only released his official portrait, which honestly barely resembled him. There were very few other pictures of her parents accessible to the public. They had to protect their identities in order to do their jobs after all. But the picture Tyler had was different. A candid shot of her father looking completely relaxed and happy. Exactly how Tyler looked most of the time.

"I didn't know." Ben voice was laced with guilt, which only increased Crystal's anger. If he had known about Tyler, would things have been different? Was it ok to abandon one child, but not two? He had been able to walk away from his daughter; would it have been different with his son?

"How are you still alive?" Crystal was only vaguely aware that anyone else was there. She had been dreaming of being reunited with her parents her whole life, but it had always been just that. An impossible dream. She should be happy now that her father was standing in front of her, but happy was the one emotion she couldn't seem to find. It had been killed by the anger and betrayal building up inside her.

"It's a long story," Ben said, taking a small step toward her. Crystal backed away instinctually. She could feel the heat coming from the server cabinet through her uniform. She had never felt more trapped in her life.

His words brought forth a memory of her father

putting her to bed as a child. She would beg him to read her book after book—anything to spend a little more time with him. It had gotten to the point that he would have to tell her to choose only one book. She would agree, as long as she could choose a long story. Crystal fought to push the memory back down. She needed to keep it together.

"Is mom?" She couldn't find the strength to finish. She regretted the question as soon as she asked it. Either way, the answer could break her.

"No. Your mother is gone," Ben said.

The confirmation broke Crystal's heart, but there was some relief in it too. At least she had only been abandoned by one of her parents. She relaxed the muscles in her hand; it was only then that she realized Justin's fingers were intertwined with hers.

"Why don't you and I go talk in private?" Ben reached out his hand to her.

Crystal side stepped, putting Justin between her and Ben. "I'm not going anywhere with you. I don't know you." She tried to focus. They were still in the middle of a mission. If she could push everything else out of her mind, she had a chance of staying in control. She took a deep breath, desperately trying to get her anger to subside, and turned to Tyler. "Ensign Price, can you please confirm that all life-support systems are fully operational?" Tyler didn't move. "Ensign," she said with a little more force.

Tyler shook his head slightly, as if he was rebooting his brain. "Yes, Commander."

"Please run a diagnostic check on the colony's life-support systems."

"Yes ma'am." Tyler turned to the small computer station in the corner of the room. He seemed to relax a little the moment his hands touched the keyboard.

This was good. Maybe she could get through this after all. As long as she focused on the task at hand, she could push Ben to the back of her mind and deal with the fallout of her father's reappearance once the mission was over and she was alone.

"Dad? Dad, are you in here?" A young voice echoed in the hall. With a fleeting look at Crystal, Ben left the server room.

Just like that, any semblance of control Crystal had over her emotions shattered. Ben had a family. One that didn't include her. The anger came back with vengeance. She knew she wouldn't be able to keep it under control this time. "I'm sorry. I can't do this." She threw her hands up as if to surrender. In a way she was.

"What do you mean?" Flint asked.

"I can't be here with him." She took a deep breath. She had never envisioned a time in her career where she would have to do this, but she couldn't see any other way. She could already feel herself breaking. It wouldn't be long before she would be completely shattered. *Hold on just a little longer,* she willed herself. Crystal forced herself to focus. This had to be done according to procedure. "Lieutenant Flint, I'm formally relinquishing command of this mission to you. I will inform my team to report to you for the duration of the mission."

"You don't have to do this." Justin took her hands in his.

"Yes, I do." She stared deep into Justin's eyes. She had to make him understand. Could she find the words to explain it?

Tyler had turned away from the computer. Crystal didn't think even the threat of a painful death could make him do that. Of anyone here, he should understand what she was feeling in that moment. Too bad she didn't get the normal understanding Tyler she had come to depend on. "They'll have to put it on your record," he said. "It will follow you around for the rest of your career. Are you really going to risk everything you've accomplished over him?"

"I'll find a way to live with it." Crystal could see the disappointment on Tyler's face.

"I don't have to accept command," Flint countered. Crystal thought she would have jumped at the chance to take the lead. A lot had changed in the month since *Journey* had set sail.

"If you don't, I'll transfer command to Grady." Crystal paused. She knew they were trying to help. They didn't want her to make a quick decision that could derail her entire career path. The military didn't give captain positions to people who gave up command at the slightest hiccup. Still, Crystal knew it was the only option she had. For the first time in her career, she was compromised. There was no way she could make rational command decisions with this hanging over her. Couldn't they see that she was doing this for them? They needed a strong leader to finish the mission successfully, and she couldn't be that anymore.

"Please Desi," she finally said. Crystal's voice cracked as her emotions threatened to break through. "I'm asking you as a friend."

Flint hesitated. "If you're sure this is what you really want to do?"

Crystal nodded. "It is."

"I accept command," Flint said with a resigned sigh.

"Thank you." She felt the knots in her stomach begin to loosen. She tapped her earpiece and opened the channel to Grady. "Lieutenant Grady, be advised that

I've relinquished command to Lieutenant Flint. Please inform the rest of the team that they are to report to her for the duration of the mission."

"Is everything alright? Are you hurt?" There was a sense of urgency in Grady's voice that she wasn't prepared for.

"I honestly don't know." What could she say to make him understand? "I'm not injured. I'll explain it to you later." She closed the connection before he had a chance to question her further.

Instead, she turned to Flint. "With your permission, I'd like to return to *Journey*." The last order she had given to the team at the shuttle was no one in or out without permission. Now that she had given up command, that authority transferred to Flint. Not that she thought anyone at the shuttle would actually refuse her, but Crystal wanted to show her team that Flint was in charge.

"I'll make sure the shuttle is ready when you get there," Flint said.

Crystal nodded and turned toward the door. Tyler took a step toward her. He opened his mouth, but said nothing. They locked eyes. After a few seconds, he ran his hands through his hair, and turned back to the computer. Crystal knew this couldn't be easy for him either. He never had the chance to meet his father. She assumed he had made peace with that a long time ago. Now that sense of peace had been destroyed. She knew she should go after him, maybe try to convince him to pull himself from the mission too, but she knew he wouldn't. He was just starting his military career. His reputation couldn't afford to take the hit that hers could. Instead, she turned and walked out of the room without saying a word.

True to her word, Flint had a shuttle waiting for Crystal when she made it back to the hard dock. Her team was in the process of unloading the colony's citizens evacuated prior to Crystal's hold order. Crystal tried to stay out of the way as her team worked. She was hoping to slip onto the shuttle and back to *Journey* relatively unnoticed.

Unfortunately, Grady was waiting for her at the shuttle entrance. She should have figured he would be here. She really was not thinking clearly. He made his way over to her the second they made eye contact. Crystal tried to read his facial expression, but she couldn't tell if it was concern or anger behind his eyes.

"I don't need a lecture." Crystal put her hands up to stop him.

"Will you please just tell me what happened?" Grady stopped a few feet away from her.

"I'd rather not. Now if you'll get out of my way, I need to get back to *Journey*." Crystal tried to step around him, but he moved to block her. "Do you have a problem Lieutenant?" Crystal's anger toward Grady was irrational, but she couldn't stop it.

"Yeah I do." Grady took a half a step forward to close the gap between them.

"Then spit it out. I don't have time for this." She put her hands on her hips to emphasize her annoyance.

"My problem is that there is clearly something wrong with my best friend, and she's refusing to talk to me about it." Grady's voice wasn't laced with anger like Crystal expected it to be. Instead all she could hear was concern. She hated that she was being so hard on him; it wasn't like any of this was his fault. She just needed an outlet for all the emotions shooting to the surface. Feelings she had locked away years ago and, now that they were resurfacing, didn't have any idea how to control.

Crystal reached out and gently grabbed his forearm so that she could pull him farther away from the few remaining team members hanging around at the shuttle's dock. She was going to have a hard enough time telling Grady what had happened; she didn't need anyone else to overhear.

She took a deep breath. "Do you remember that guy who was trying to take charge when we got to the basement?"

"Yeah, what about him?"

"He's the colony's leader and um..." Crystal didn't know how to tell him. Part of her didn't believe it herself.

"Did he do something? Did he try to hurt you?" Grady looked her up and down as he spoke. She knew he was checking her for an injury. Too bad her wound wasn't one you could see.

"No—I don't know. He's my father."

"He's your what?" Grady took a step closer to her and lowered his voice as he spoke.

"I don't know how, but it's him. My father's alive." Crystal put one of her hands over her mouth. She felt her emotions surfacing again. She focused all her energy on pushing them back down. She couldn't fall apart yet. Not here. Not where anyone could see her.

"Crys, I don't—"

"I know." Crystal cut Grady off. The last thing she wanted was his sympathy. If he lost faith in her, she knew she wouldn't be able to ever come back from this. "He's alive, and—here's the kicker—he has a family. He got a fresh start, while I've been left to bear the burden of everything that happened to him during the war. I just can't deal with it right now." Crystal turned and looked longingly out of the colony's dome. The dark outline of *Journey* hovering just over the kelp fields beckoned to her. Her sanctuary was so close.

"Tell me what I can do. How can I make this easier for you?"

"You can't protect me from this one Jim. I really wish you could, but you can't." Crystal fought back the tears she felt forming in her eyes. Not yet, she told herself, not here.

"There has to be something I can do," Grady pressed.

"I need you to help Flint. The colony was sabotaged from the inside. I left her to figure out who did it. I know she doesn't have the training to deal with something like this on her own, but I left her to do it anyway." The guilt of what she was doing sank to Crystal's stomach. She knew her team needed her, but she was leaving. She simply wasn't strong enough.

"Commander Wolf, the shuttle is ready to leave if you still want to head back to the ship," Collins said.

Crystal turned to look at him. He seemed slightly uncomfortable having interrupted them. "Thank you. I'll be right there." Crystal tried her best to smile, though she didn't think she succeeded. "I should go," she said, turning back to Grady. "I don't want to keep them waiting." She started to turn but Grady reached out to stop her.

"Are you going to be ok?"

"Eventually." Crystal walked over to the shuttle with her head held as high as she could. She didn't want to worry the rest of the team. She knew she was leaving them in a tough spot, but she felt her defenses breaking down with every step she took.

# Chapter 3

Desi had to find a way to regroup now that Wolf was gone. She and Wolf had been alternating the lead on missions over the last few months, but they had never had to change command halfway through. She really should have paid better attention when Wolf was prepping the team. Though to be fair, it had all seemed pretty straightforward when they were back on the ship. Get into the colony, start evacuations, and get Price to a computer to restore life support. A nice easy in and out. They hadn't prepped for anything like this. It had never even crossed Desi's mind that this could have been an inside job, and that she would be the one responsible to figuring out who did it. Sabotage was something that happened on Earth, not Neophia.

Desi took a deep breath and started to think through the situation. Sure, this was outside of her comfort zone, but she was always game for a challenge. Who knew? Maybe she had some untapped talent for investigative work she wasn't aware of. She had certainly watched enough crime dramas with her mom to pick up a few things. She was excited to prove herself in a way the U.S. military would never have let her. They preferred soldiers to simply follow orders instead of actually thinking for themselves.

She needed to break the situation down and solve one problem at a time. They had eliminated the immediate risk to the citizens, but if life support shut down again, they would be right back where they started.

Desi looked over at Price. He had retreated to the computer as soon as Wolf had left. It might look like he was simply focused on the job at hand, but Desi knew there was so much more to it than that. He had to be hurting, though his lack of emotion caused Desi more concern than if he'd broken down. Price was always very open with his feelings. She probably should have sent him back to *Journey* with Wolf, but Desi couldn't risk losing him, too. Not when he was the only one with any shot of getting the computers back up and running,

She thought about going over to him and trying to comfort him, but what could she say? Sorry your dad's not dead? No, she would give him a few minutes on the computer to get himself together, and then they would move out.

Desi walked out of the sever room to find the cause of all of her problems. Discovering Ben's true identity had affected her more than she expected. She didn't even know who her father was. She could have passed him on the street a thousand times and never have known the connection between them. From time to time she would see an older man with the same dark complexion or curly hair and would wonder if maybe he was her father. She had asked her mom a few times when she was younger, but her mom always sidestepped the question. After a while, Desi stopped asking. It wasn't uncommon on Earth for kids to only have one parent. In fact, if there was a family anomaly in her neighborhood, it was Justin's picture-perfect nuclear family.

She found Ben at the end of the hallway with his young son. She couldn't help but wonder if he had told him about his newly discovered siblings. She guessed not, as she watched Ben send the kid away as she got closer to him. It was probably a smart move; Desi couldn't guarantee she wouldn't blow Ben's cover if given the chance.

"I need someplace that's big enough to hold the colony's entire population," Desi said as soon as she was within earshot of Ben. She could have introduced herself, but she didn't bother. She had no respect for the man she was addressing, so why should she show him any kind of common courtesy? She would do her job to the best of her capabilities, but that didn't mean she had to be nice to the guy.

"The school auditorium," Ben said without hesitation.

Desi didn't respond. She turned her back to him and activated her headset. "Grady, I need you to get everyone to the school auditorium. We will join you there as soon as Price is done."

"Sure thing, but I'd try to make it fast if I were you. These people are likely to start a riot any minute."

Desi had a hard time hearing him over the background noise.

Price and Justin slowly made their way down the hall. "The servers are clean," Price said once they reached her.

"We're in route," she told Grady, then closed the link.

They left the building in silence. Desi led the group with Justin at her side. He was clearly distracted. She knew that he would much rather be back on *Journey* with Wolf, though Desi wasn't sure there was anything he could do for her right now. Desi's main concern was that Ben had fallen into step next to Price. She strained to hear what they were saying. She needed to be ready in case she needed to intervene.

"So, Susan Price is your mother?" Ben's words were carefully measured as he spoke.

"Yes," Price said. There was absolutely no feeling in his voice. Desi had never heard him like this before.

"And you're sure that I'm your father?"

"I know that Crystal is my sister." Price's words were short, and there was a harshness in his voice that Desi didn't recognize. Maybe it was for the best that he was keeping his emotions in check.

"I didn't know. Susan never told me," Ben said.

"Would it have made a difference?" Price asked. Desi would have cheered for him if she could. There was nothing Ben could say to defend himself.

As they reached the town center, a steady stream of people was heading down the street to what Desi assumed was the school. "The escape pods are in the Community Center basement, right?" Price asked without looking at Ben.

"Yes," Ben said. Price took off without another word.

"Anderson, go touch base with Lieutenant Grady. Let him know that we will be along in a minute," Desi said to Justin. She wanted a few minutes alone with Ben.

"Yes, ma'am." Justin took off down the street, absorbed in the sea a people a moment later.

Ben took a step forward, but Desi put out her arm to stop him. "Not so fast. You and I need to get a couple of things straight. I don't like you, or respect you. I will do everything I can to figure out who tried to destroy this colony, because it's my job, and I won't let the rest of the people here suffer because of you. In exchange, you're going to leave Wolf and Price out of this. You deal with me. Is that understood?" Desi put as much authority into her voice as she could.

Ben's puffed out his chest and took a step close to Desi. "Here's a few things you need to understand, Lieutenant Flint. I really don't give a damn if you like me, and I don't need your respect. Now, I agree that there is a job that needs to be done, and while I welcome the use of LAWON's resources, let me remind you that we are not a member nation. You have no power here. You can't so much as walk into a building here without my permission. If you push me, I won't hesitate to revoke your welcome here. And while I do wish things with Crystal and Tyler had played out differently, you can be damn sure that I'm not going to let some twenty-something with a rank and a false sense of authority stop me from getting to know my children now that they *are* here." Ben turned and walked down the street before Desi had a chance to respond. She felt her hatred grow for him with every step he took.

Crystal's shuttle arrived back on *Journey* fairly unnoticed. The crew in the launch bay seemed surprised to see her, but none of them said anything. She told them to send the shuttle back and started to make her way to her quarters. She didn't bother to drop her gear off in the combat team room. She would have to walk directly past the officer's mess hall to get there, and she didn't want to be questioned. It was hard enough trying to make it to her quarters without any of the other eight hundred crew members stopping her. Fortunately, since they were still in the middle of a mission, the corridors were almost deserted.

She needed some time alone to try to process everything that had happened. Her father was alive. How was she supposed to deal with that? If he had been out there all this time, why hadn't he come home? Why hadn't he reached out to her? She only had good memories of her father. Why wouldn't he want to come back to that? Was it possible they weren't the happy family she remembered? He had cheated on her mother, so maybe their relationship had never fully recovered. If she wasn't enough to make him come home, then what about his parents? Crystal had experienced her grandparents' pain first hand. Her father had to know what he was doing to them by allowing them to believe he was dead. How could he put them through that? They would never know that their son had lived through the war, but maybe that was for the best. They wouldn't have to deal with the betrayal she now had to shoulder.

"Commander Wolf." Reed's voice reached her just as she was about to open the door to her quarters. She couldn't tell if it was anger or confusion that laced his voice. It didn't really matter. Anything he had to say to her would pale in comparison to what she had already told herself.

"Yes, sir." She turned to face him, trying to act like the officer she was, but her words lacked any real conviction and her posture was slumped. It was the best she could manage.

"I received a call from Flint saying you had pulled yourself off of the mission. Would you care to explain to me what is going on?"

The disappointment she heard in Reed's voice was almost worse than finding out her father had abandoned her. A fresh wave of guilt crashed over her. What was there to say? She had deserted her team when they needed her. There was no justification for it. She was supposed to be better than that. She watched two crew members rush past them, the echo of their footsteps on the metal grating calling to her. She wished she could go with them. Anything would be better than having to put into words what she had done.

"Well?" Reed prompted.

"My father is alive." Crystal's words were robotic. Her mind was shutting down her emotions one at a time until she was numb.

"Jedidiah Wolf is alive?" Reed grabbed the metal railing for support. Crystal had forgotten that Reed and her father had served together early in their careers. She even had vague recollections of Reed mentioning that he'd been at her parents' wedding, though she couldn't be sure if that was true or not.

"Yes, he's alive. I saw him. I spoke to him." Crystal felt like she was reciting stats on an unknown target instead of talking about the man who should have raised her. "He's been living under the alias of Ben Martin and is the leader of Stapleton Farms."

"Do you mind if we talk in your quarters? I think I need to sit down," Reed said as he moved to open the door.

"Of course." Crystal couldn't refuse him. In some ways this would be easier. She could set aside her own emotions and help Reed work through his. Maybe then she would have some clue how to do it for herself.

Reed moved through the room as if in a trance and took a seat at the metal T-shaped desk that divided her side of the room from Flint's. She took a seat across from him, pushing a tray containing the remnants of her lunch out of the way. She had been reviewing the latest growth data for *Journey's* bio-skin hull when they received the distress call from Stapleton Farms. Crystal's eyes wandered the room while she waited for Reed to speak, though she made a conscious effort to avoid looking at the picture of her and her parents on the shelf next to her bunk.

"So, Jed's alive." Reed didn't look at her as he spoke. "Did he say anything about Kendra? Is your mom alive too?"

"No. He said that she was dead." Crystal's voice was small. She felt like she was seven years old again, talking to the military officers who showed up at her front door an hour after her parents' public execution. Only, it wasn't both of her parents like everyone thought. It explained why the man's face was covered while her mother defiantly stared down the camera. Did Rank know he hadn't really captured both of the Wolf spies?

"Did he say how he survived? Your dad always was resourceful. He got us out of more than one sticky situation over the years. I was sad to lose him when he took his first undercover assignment, but his talents would have gone to waste if he had stayed on the destroyer." A small smile crossed Reed's lips as he spoke. Crystal envied him. "Did he say why he never came back?"

"I didn't ask." Crystal couldn't help but feel like she had let Reed down. Of course, she should have asked. There were a lot of things she should have asked him. If only she had been able to put together a coherent thought.

Reed looked at her for the first time since she told him the news. His face softened. Crystal felt like a child under his concerned gaze. "I'm sorry. I'm sure that was the last thing on your mind when you saw him. What did you say to him?"

"I introduced him to Tyler. I couldn't think of anything else to do," Crystal said.

"I'm sure that shocked him," Reed said raising his eyebrows.

A small smiled crossed her face. "It sure did, but then his new son showed up, and I couldn't handle it. I got so angry."

"You have every right to be angry."

"So angry that I abandoned my team." The smile vanished as quickly as it came. She looked down at her hands so she didn't have to meet Reed's eye.

"Let's get one thing straight," he said sternly. "You did not abandon your team. You saved eight hundred lives today before passing command onto a competent teammate. You have nothing to be ashamed of. In fact, I'm proud of how you handled the situation. A lot of officers in your position wouldn't have the courage to do what you did."

"Thank you, sir." Crystal looked down at her hands. She knew that was what she was supposed to say, even if she didn't believe it.

Reed gently cupped her chin and tilted her head up. "I know it might not seem like it right now, but this is a good thing. You have a second chance to get to know your father. It's just going to take time to come to terms with it. I have to get back to the Bridge. Are you going to be alright?"

"Yes sir, I'll be fine." Crystal nodded, not sure if she was trying to convince Reed or herself.

Reed stood up and patted her on the shoulder gently before leaving the room. She wasn't sure she really wanted him to leave. Once she was alone, she would be forced to face her emotions, and she didn't think she was ready for that. Instead she pulled her computer over and began poring over the bio-skin data with a renewed vigor.

# Chapter 4

"That's him isn't it," Grady said to Desi as soon as she arrived at the school. His eyes locked on Ben at once and followed him until he disappeared into the auditorium.

"I take it you saw Wolf before she left." Desi could feel the outrage emitting from the open doors. She wasn't in any rush to go in there and try to calm things down. She wanted to make Ben sweat a little.

"Yeah she filled me in," Grady said, his gaze still following Ben.

Of course Wolf had talked to Grady, Desi had never seen a stronger friendship than the two of them shared. If Wolf could talk to him, maybe she wasn't as far gone as Desi thought. "How was she?"

"Honestly I've never seen her like that before. She seemed almost broken—though I'll deny it if you ever tell her I said that." A hint of smile crossed his face.

"That's what I was afraid of." Desi's hand rested on her holstered gun. A nervous habit she had picked up while fighting on Earth. "You weren't there when she first realized it was him. She just completely shut down.

Like, I know she's probably the least emotional person on Neophia, but this took it to a whole new level."

"How's Price taking the whole thing?"

Desi paused to let the last few people pass them on their way to the auditorium. "He's holding up, I think. I'm not sure how much more he can take before he breaks too."

"Where is he?" Grady scanned the school's entrance for him.

"He's working on bringing the escape pods back online. I suppose we could let the colony's computer programmer handle it though." Desi looked to Grady for reassurance. As much as she hated to admit it, Wolf's departure had shaken her. She needed to get her confidence back.

"No, I think you're right to have Price on it. If Wolf's right and someone from Stapleton Farms planted that virus, then we could be giving them free access to the colony's computer system again. I for one," Grady said placing his hand on his chest, "would really prefer if the atmosphere generator stayed online while we are here."

"You're right. I just hope Price can handle it," Desi said with a sigh. She needed to figure out the best way to move forward. On Earth, she would be allowed to use whatever means necessary to get the information she needed, but she was pretty sure the same techniques wouldn't fly on Neophia. She needed to start thinking like an investigator. Anyone with access and motive could have planted that virus. She needed to figure out a way to start narrowing down the suspects from the eight hundred people in the colony.

"He's stronger than you give him credit for," Grady assured her. "Besides computers are his drug. He'll probably find the whole thing therapeutic."

Desi nodded. "Hey what happened to Anderson? I sent him here to help you." She looked around the hallway, even though they were the only two people not inside the auditorium.

"I sent him back to *Journey* to recharge the oxygen masks and tanks in case we need them again." Grady didn't speak with his normal confidence. Desi knew the oxygen was just an excuse. It had to be killing him that he couldn't go check on Wolf himself. Was he afraid she would be upset that he had sent him back to the ship without permission?

"Good thinking." Desi said. She wasn't going to call him out on worrying about Wolf. She was worried too.

Angry voices erupted from the auditorium. "We better get in there." Desi patted Grady on the shoulder before making her way to the doors.

Ben stood alone on the stage. His demeanor radiated control, despite the fact that the citizens looked ready to rush the stage.

"Why are they still here Ben?" one of the citizens yelled.

"We aren't members of LAWON! We don't have to listen to them."

"Why are they keeping us here?" The voices came at the stage from every direction.

"I asked them to assemble everyone here," Ben called into the noise. Desi was amazed how he was able to lie with such ease and confidence. "If everyone would take a seat, I'll explain everything."

Desi scanned the room. Her team was gathered near the entrance of the auditorium. No one had made a move to try to calm the crowd. Desi caught the eye of Cortez and pointed to the stage. They worked their way through the crowd until they formed a perimeter around the stage. No one had their guns out, though several of them were keeping their hands positioned over their hips. If Desi didn't do something soon, things could get out of control fast.

She and Grady made their way to stage. Their presence only increased the anger in the room. She had never gone from hero to enemy so quickly.

Out of the corner of her eye, she saw Grady pull out his gun and fire it into the ceiling. She whipped around and glared at him. She hadn't expected him to do something like that. Desi was used to being the most unconventional person during a mission. The shot had been harmless, but the look Grady was giving Ben was not. At least he had gotten everyone to shut up for a second.

"I know everyone must be scared," Desi said before the citizens had a chance to regroup, "and I'm sure you have a lot of questions. If you would please take your seats, we'll explain what's going on." She turned to Grady while everyone was taking a seat. "If you see anyone acting suspicious," she said under her breath, "detain them."

"Gladly, though I feel I should remind you that we don't really have the authority to do that yet," Grady said without taking his eyes off of Ben.

"Let me worry about that." She turned back to the rest of the room. They had all sat down and the yelling had calmed to a dull rumble. She could work with that. "I'm Lieutenant Desiree Flint, stationed on LAWON's peacekeeping submarine, *Journey*. My team has been able to restore your life support systems, and we are in the process of reenergizing your escape pods."

"And we are grateful for your assistance, but your job here is done. You don't have the authority to keep us here," yelled a man in the front row. His words received a round of applause from the rest of the auditorium.

"They might not, but I do," Ben said. The applause died down slowly. "Let's show these people a little respect. They risked their lives to save us when they didn't have to. There are downsides to not being a member of LAWON. They didn't have to spend their resources to respond to a distress call from a nonmember colony, but they did it anyway. These are good people."

Desi was a little taken aback by Ben's support. She expected to have to fight him on every little thing. She couldn't help but wonder if it was all an act for his people though. A way to save face.

"Believe me, there is nothing I want more than to return to our ship and leave you in peace. Unfortunately it's not that simple," Desi said to the crowd. "It wasn't a computer error that shut your systems down. Someone planted a virus to target your atmosphere generator and escape pods." Desi was ready for the gasps that followed her declaration, but she wasn't done yet. "We believe that the virus was planted by someone at the colony."

The room exploded in outrage. Several angry voices reached Desi's ears at once. She glanced over at Grady to see if he had picked up on anyone acting suspicious, but he shook his head. She had been hoping whoever planted the virus would give themselves away when she made her announcement. She should have known it wouldn't be that easy.

As the anger in the room slowly died down, one voice came through loud and clear. "They can't possibly think it was one of us." It belonged to the large man in the front row who had spoken up earlier. Everyone around him went quiet the second he spoke. It spread through the room at an alarming rate.

"That's exactly what they think," Ben said, staring down the man. "Based on what I've seen, I agree with them," Ben said starring down the man.

"Then we should be conducting our own investigation. We don't need LAWON meddling in our business." The people closest to him cheered. Whoever this man was, he had power here. A lot more than Ben appeared to have at the moment.

"You're not thinking rationally, Shawn. We can't do this on our own. We're like a family here. It would be too hard for anyone to remain impartial." Ben remained calm despite the growing outrage in the room. It felt unnatural and was precisely the reason Desi didn't trust politicians.

"Everyone here would do whatever it took to protect this place," Shawn shouted to another general round of applause.

"Well, not everyone," Desi couldn't help herself from saying. Thankfully, she was pretty sure Grady was the only one that heard her.

"That's exactly my point," Ben yelled over the noise. "You're too invested. Your emotions would get in the way. Everyone's would. We almost died today, and that's a lot to deal with. We need outside help to find the person responsible. I'm going to consult with LAWON to determine the best course of action. Until then, I'm going to uphold the ban on leaving the colony that Commander Wolf enacted."

"You can't do that," Shawn yelled.

"Yes, I can. You elected me to run this colony, and that's what I'm going to do. I will not risk a repeat of what happened today. Now everyone, go home. The sooner we can get back to normal, the better off we'll be." Ben's tone made it clear that he wasn't going to answer any more questions. The room slowly started to empty.

"Did you pick up on anything?" Desi turned to Grady, who was studying the crowd as they filed out of the auditorium.

"Other than the general feeling that we really aren't welcome here, no." Grady turned and looked at her.

"I want to start questioning people. The more time that passes the harder it's going to be to catch the person responsible."

"We still need to get official permission from Ben before we can begin our investigation." Grady looked thoughtful. "He was very careful about the words he used. Saying he would consult with us doesn't mean he will step aside and let us do our jobs. I get the feeling that he wants something."

"Three guess what that is," Desi said with a raised eyebrow. Grady's body tensed again. He kept his anger very close to the surface. She made a mental note to keep an eye on him as they moved forward.

Desi and Grady were the last to leave the auditorium. Ben had gone to check on his family—at least the part that he acknowledged—and hadn't returned yet. Desi wanted to find him and get his permission to begin the investigation. The sooner she could get started, the sooner they could leave. She was about to exit the school when she heard voices coming from a classroom down one of the side hallways. With a glance at Grady, they diverted their course. It didn't take them long to locate the room.

Desi peeked through the small window in the door. She was surprised by the similarity to classrooms on

Earth, rows of desks filling the room with a large screen taking up most of the front wall. Ben and Shawn squared off in front of a model of what Desi assumed was DNA—biology was not one of her best subjects in school. She cracked the door so they could hear the argument better.

"You can't seriously be considering allowing LAWON to investigate us?" Shawn protested. He was towering over Ben, though the colony leader didn't seem fazed.

"Of course, I am. I'd be a fool not to." Ben was calm, and his words were even. Given where the argument was taking place, Desi couldn't help but picture him as a tired teacher dealing with some know-it-all teenager. Not that she had any experience with that.

"You know they are going to use this as an excuse to force membership on us. We've managed to hold them off for years, and now you are rolling out the welcome mat for them!"

"What would you have me do? Send them away and have one of our computer engineers trace the virus back to its source?" Ben squeezed the bridge of his nose as he talked.

"That's exactly what I want you to do."

"And if it was Erin or Jordon who planted the virus? What then? I'm not putting everyone's lives at risk to protect our technology," Ben said.

Desi liked what she was hearing. Maybe Ben wouldn't be the roadblock she expected him to be. She felt her confidence come back. If Ben cooperated, maybe she would be able to pull this off. Too bad her gut was still screaming at her not to trust him.

"So, you're going to sit back and let LAWON slowly take over," Shawn accused. "You saw what happened when Terra Farms joined LAWON! They were completely displaced by LAWON appointed personal within two years. Is that what you want to happen here?" Shawn's arms were flailing as he spoke.

"Andrea and I built this colony from nothing," Ben said. "I have no intention of handing it over to LAWON. If they try to force our hand, we'll stop selling to them. Their members won't put up with that for long."

Desi's dislike for Ben flared into hatred. She had a big problem with people using food as a weapon. She had seen it done too much on Earth. Her hand came to rest on her stomach as she remembered the year the rest of the world had turned on the United States and set up food embargos. She had watched several of her friends waste away to nothing, until only two-thirds of her fifth grade class was left at the end of the year.

"That all sounds great, but it's just words. Your actions are telling a different story. You were pretty quick to defend them." Before Ben could interrupt, Shawn pressed him. "Don't kid yourself. I've known you long enough to know that despite what you said in there, you aren't the one making the decisions here. You're just going along with whatever they tell you to do. I was there when they stopped the evacuations. I saw the fear in everyone's eyes. They didn't hesitate in condemning us to death. You didn't see Andrea trying to console Gina as she asked if they were going to die. It wasn't some computer virus that did *that*. It was LAWON." Shawn's anger filled the room. Desi was tempted to close the door to keep it contained.

"Don't use my family to try to manipulate me. You don't know what was happening, what choices I had to make. They were able to bring our systems back online before anyone was hurt, and that's all that really matters. I had faith they wouldn't let anyone die." Ben's face was turning red. His calm teacher like demeanor was starting to crack now that Shawn had made things personal.

"What makes you so sure of that?" Shawn took a step closer to Ben. Desi put her hand on her sidearm out of habit, though if pressed, she wasn't sure whose side she would be on if a fight broke out.

"Because Commander Wolf is..." Ben's voice trailed off. Was he about to give away his big secret?

"She's what?" Shawn pressed him.

"She's one of the most well-respected officers in LAWON. She has made a career out of saving people. I had to trust that she knew what she was doing." Desi almost believed that was what Ben had intended to say.

Shawn snorted. "For a guy who claims not to want anything to do with LAWON you sure do know a lot about them."

"There's not a person on this planet that doesn't know who Commander Wolf is. That doesn't change the fact that I want this colony to remain independent just as much as you do Shawn." Ben seemed to be a little flustered, but he recovered well.

"I'd be careful Ben. You barely won the last election. It won't take much for everyone to lose faith in you. We don't need a leader who folds to LAWON at the slightest threat," Shawn said, puffing out his chest as he spoke.

Desi had heard enough. She carefully closed the door and motioned for Grady to follow her. She stopped when they reached the front door of the school. "I think we found our first two suspects."

Grady turned and looked back down the locker lined hallway. "You really want to start by investigating Ben?"

"You can't tell me you trust him."

"Of course I don't, but if we go after him guns blazing, he's likely to kick us out of here pretty fast,"

Grady said.

"So, we start with that Shawn guy." Desi waved an arm in the direction they had come from.

"After we get approval from Ben."

"You know, just because you're Wolf's second doesn't mean you have to act like her." Desi put her hands on her hips. "Where's the guy who used his sidearm to silence a crowd? That's the guy I want to work with here."

"Don't worry, he's always nearby," Grady said with a rueful grin. "But we need to be smart about this."

"Fine. We'll ask permission first," Desi said reluctantly.

Crystal tried to work on analyzing the bio-skin data, but she couldn't focus. Her mind kept connecting the data to Aquinein skin saturation rates. She had trained hard in order to achieve her max submersion time of sixteen hours, starting when she was young. Her father had been the first one to take her out swimming in the ocean. It was one of the most thrilling experiences of her life. He said it was important to honor their heritage. Too many Aquineins didn't bother anymore. She wondered how much stronger she would be if he had come back to teach her more. She felt her anger ratchet up a few more notches. It was bad enough that her father's sudden reappearance had forced her to walk away from the mission, but now it was affecting her other duties on the ship.

She took a deep breath and tried to focus. She read through half a page of data before she realized she had already been over it three times. She slammed her computer closed in frustration. She was useless, and it was all Ben's fault. She grabbed her gym bag and headed out the door.

Ten minutes later she was changed and working the heavy bag in the combat team room. Since everyone was still in the middle of the mission at Stapleton Farms, she knew she wouldn't be disturbed. Crystal worked the bag hard, alternating between punches and kicks, but her anger hadn't dissipated. Every time she found a rhythm that was working for her, the image of Ben removing his oxygen mask played in her head, and she would lose focus again.

She pulled back her arm to start another round when someone grabbed the bag. She stopped her punch short, leaving an unsatisfied buildup of kinetic energy in her arm. "I could have hit you." She pulled her headphones out of her ears, leaving a whisper of rock-n-roll music in the air.

"I've seen you work out enough to be able to anticipate your punches," Justin said from behind the bag. "I knew I was in the clear." The sparkle in his brown eyes melted away some of the anger inside of her.

"When did you get back?" She wondered if the rest of the team would be filing in soon too. Maybe she should leave while she still could.

"Not long ago. Grady thought it was a good idea to refill the oxygen tanks and masks incase the atmosphere generator goes down again."

"That's smart." It made her feel a tiny bit better about pulling herself from the mission. At least Grady was thinking along the same lines she would be. Stapleton Farms was in good hands.

Justin walked around the bag so he had a clear view of her face. "How are you doing?"

Now that the bag was clear she could finally release

the energy in her muscles. "I've been better," she said as she punched the bag a few more times.

"We need to come up with a way to take your mind off of things for a little while," Justin said.

"I'm open to suggestions." Crystal turned and faced him. There was a gleam in his eye that made Crystal smile. He was up to something.

"Have you ever played War?" His voice had a seductive quality to it that made Crystal burst out in laughter.

"I never considered war something you could play," she said, biting back her laughter.

"It's a card game." Justin rolled his eyes as he talked, a bad habit he must have picked up from Flint. "I used to play it with my grandmother when I was growing up."

"What's a card game?"

"Seriously? You don't know what a card game is?"

"No, I don't." Crystal put her hands on her hips.

"That's unacceptable. We are going to remedy this immediately." Justin grabbed her hand and started to gently pull her out of the combat room.

"Just let me change," Crystal said.

"No time. This is an emergency." Justin led her through the corridors of the ship. His enthusiasm was contagious, and Crystal couldn't help but smirk at the sideways glances they got from the crewmembers they passed on their way to Justin's quarters. Normally, she wouldn't have been comfortable with the public display of affection, seeing it as unprofessional, but in that moment, it was exactly what she needed.

Justin finally released her hand once they were inside his quarters. He deposited her in one of the desk chairs and started searching the room. "I know I have a deck of cards around here somewhere."

Crystal watched in amusement as he rifled through the drawers under his bunk. The room Justin shared with Tyler was identical to the room she shared with Flint in all ways except one. The guys' room was much cleaner, even with Tyler's excess of computer equipment taking up most of the shelves in the room.

"Found it." Justin emerged from under the desk holding a small box high over his head. He sat down at the chair across from her. She watched in fascination as he pulled a stack of thin cardboard from the box and started to maneuver them with his fingers. "So, War is a simple game. First I'll deal."

"Deal?" Crystal raised an eyebrow at him. It was like he was speaking a different language.

"Pass out the cards." He quickly divided the deck in two, passing her every other card. "Now pick them up, but don't look at them."

She was trying hard to keep the smirk off her face, but it was a lost cause. He just looked so cute trying to explain the game to her.

"On the count of three, we both flip over the top card. Whoever has the highest card gets both. The first person to run out of cards loses." Justin picked up his cards and straightened them into a neat stack.

"That's it?" She tried to keep the skepticism out of her voice, but was pretty sure she failed.

"That's it." His face was serious. She sat up a little straighter. She didn't want him to think that she didn't appreciate his efforts to cheer her up.

"It seems pretty juvenile." Crystal picked up her cards and mirrored Justin's movement until she had a neat stack. The cards were worn and felt familiar in her hands, despite not knowing what they were less than an hour ago. It was almost like she was becoming part of

Justin's history when she held them.

"Just give it a chance, ok?" The smile on his face faltered, and a wave of guilt shot through her. He was only trying to help.

"Ok." She leaned across the table and planted a small kiss on his lips. The warmth and excitement in his face were back in full force by the time she settled back in her seat.

"On the count of three. One, two, three." Justin flipped his card over and laid it on the table between them. Crystal did the same. "Ten beats a three. The cards are yours." He pushed them toward her.

"So, I won?" Crystal asked as she gathered up her prize.

"You won the first round, but we're just getting started." Justin tapped the stack of cards in his hand on the metal table for emphasis.

A muffled beeping came from Justin's pocket. He set his cards down and pulled out his communicator. Crystal watched as his eyes darted over the screen. He quickly typed backed a response while shaking his head.

"What was that about?" Crystal hoped he wouldn't have to leave. She was just starting to relax.

"It was nothing. Just Desi checking up on you." Justin picked up his cards and tapped them on the table.

"Really? Desi took time out of leading a mission to check up on me?" Crystal felt her nose wrinkle in surprise. "That doesn't sound like her."

"Well there was a long string of obscenities there too. She's not a real big fan of Ben." Justin's face fell as soon as the words were out of his mouth. Crystal tried not to let her smile falter. She wouldn't let her father ruin this, too.

"Let's go again." Crystal flipped her card over.

Instead of number, it had a picture of a woman wearing a crown on it. She looked at Justin, confused.

"That's good. That's a queen. The only thing that can beat her are the king or ace card."

"I'm pretty sure she could take out any king you throw at her." Crystal tapped the card in front of her.

"I keep telling you Earth's a pretty messed up place." Justin flipped his next card over to reveal another queen.

"What do we do now?"

"Now we war." Justin cocked an eyebrow at her before placing three cards face down on the table. Crystal did the same. "The next card, we turn up. High card takes it all."

They both flipped over the card. Crystal had an ace. She couldn't help but do a little dance in her seat as she gathered up all the cards, making Justin laugh. She quickly got absorbed in the game. The jolt of excitement that shot through her every time she won a hand was addictive. She felt her pulse quicken as they got to Justin's last card. He flipped over a jack. It was good, but not good enough to beat the ace she had won the first war with. She jumped out of her seat. "I win, I win, I win!"

"Are you ready to collect your prize?" Justin rose to his feet, wrapped his arms around her waist, and pulled her tight against him.

"I do like prizes." His touch left her slightly breathless. She placed her arms around his neck and leaned in closer.

He was a fraction of an inch away from her lips when the intercom in his room came to life. "Ensign Anderson, report to the bridge."

Disappointment filled her as she pulled away from him. "You have to go."

Justin pulled her back. "They can wait a few minutes."

"No, we agreed when we started this," she said. "Work always come first." Crystal wished it didn't have to be that way, but she knew it was the only way she could make the relationship work.

Justin let out a long breath. "Raincheck?"

"Raincheck." Crystal tried to pull away again, but he still hadn't loosened his grip. He was searching her eyes while he held her in his arms. "I'll be fine," she promised. "Now go before they have to page you again."

"Right." He gave her a quick kiss before racing out of the room.

# Chapter 5

Desi leaned against the side of the school while she waited for Ben. The rest of her team milled around the center of the colony, waiting for her orders. She thought about sending some of them back to *Journey,* but she wanted to keep a strong presence until they found the person who planted the virus. She didn't think they would attack again as long as LAWON was here. What would be the point?

"I sent four guys to guard our docking port," Grady said as he walked over to her. "One guy could probably handle it, but I needed to keep them busy."

"Good. Why don't you send another team to go guard the server room? We don't want anyone tampering in there until Price has the chance to go through everything." Desi stepped away from the wall and looked up and down the street. It was taking Ben an awfully long time to wrap up his conversation with Shawn and exit the school. Desi had positioned a few men around the back of the school to make sure Ben didn't leave that way, though she supposed it was possible he had slipped out without anyone seeing him.

"Can't. We've been locked out of City Hall."

Desi turned to give Grady her full attention. "What do you mean locked out?"

"Locked out, as in someone physically locked all the doors in the entire building so we can't enter without breaking down a door." Grady cracked his knuckles as he glanced back at City Hall. "Which I'd be happy to do by the way, but I'm not sure that's the best way to go about making friends here."

"This is just getting ridiculous. Why are we even bothering to try to help these people when they clearly don't want it?" Desi waved her hands toward the residential section of the colony in frustration.

"Because if we don't and this virus takes down the colony, there will be food shortages across the planet," Price said, walking over while massaging his hands. Desi had never seen him do that before. How much tension was he suppressing? "The escape pods are back up."

"Well at least we've been able to accomplish something," Desi said in frustration.

"I could accomplish a lot more if I could get back in the server room." Price's facial expression didn't change as he spoke. Usually Desi had no problem telling how he was feeling from one look at his face. The fact that she couldn't concerned her. She should probably send him back to the ship, but she had to be careful how she went about it. Price's military career was still so new, even the impression of being pulled from a mission could damage his chances at moving up the ranks. She would have to trust that he would give her some clue if he couldn't handle it.

"That's going to be a problem," Grady said.

Just as Price was about to respond, the door behind

Desi opened, and Ben finally emerged from the school. "We need to talk." Desi moved so she was standing directly in front of him. Price and Grady fell in on either side of her.

"Yes, we do." Ben seemed unfazed by their ambush.

"Why won't your people give us access to the servers?" Desi folded her arms in front of her. She wouldn't be intimated by Ben, despite the good six inches he had over her.

"You can have access to it as soon as our programmers are finished securing our confidential technology."

"And what if one of your programmers planted the virus in the first place?" Desi could feel her anger boiling below the surface.

"I only sent people I trust," Ben said defensively.

Desi couldn't contain a sarcastic laugh from escaping her lips. "Right, and that's supposed to make us all feel better."

"Do you really think that's going to matter anyway?" Price spat out. "Your people couldn't even locate the virus, let alone stop it. Do you really think I won't be able to get through whatever pathetic defenses they put up?"

Desi turned to look at Price in shock. She had never heard him talk like that. If anything, he usually tried to downplay his genius with a computer.

"So, you are here to try to steal our farming technology for LAWON." Ben took a step closer to them. Was he really thinking of taking on all three of them? He wouldn't stand a chance. Desi's own foot moved forward before she'd even intended to move.

"Just calm down." Grady stepped between Ben and Desi. He glanced down at her hands. She hadn't realized she had curled them into fists. "Nobody wants to steal anything. All we want to do is find the person who tried to kill you so that we can get out of here and leave you alone with your plants." Grady stared Ben down until the colony leader finally took a step back.

"Before I give you access to anything, I'm going to want some reassurances," Ben said.

"Fine. I pinky swear we won't steal anything." Desi couldn't stop herself from rolling her eyes. She really needed to work on her composure. Though to be fair, it wasn't like he deserved any kind of common courtesy from her.

"Not from you," Ben protested. "I want to talk to someone with actual authority. I want to talk to your captain."

"I'm sure that can be arranged," she said through gritted teeth. It was taking every ounce of her willpower not to punch him in the jaw.

"Good," Ben said, either oblivious or unconcerned about Desi's temper, which only made her angrier. "If that goes well, I'll give you access to everything you'll need to do your investigation. I'll be waiting in my office in City Hall. I'll make sure they let you in when your captain arrives." Ben brushed past Desi.

"What a jerk," Desi said as she watched him walk across the street to City Hall. "Sorry Price."

"It's not like I actually know him. I'll be waiting with the rest of the team." Price didn't meet Desi's eye as he walked away. The last thing she wanted to do was make this harder for him.

Desi and Grady met Reed at the colony's docking port. Now that Price had gotten the systems back online, there was no reason to use the hard seal they had been forced to make in the west field. Wolf had sent a few members of her engineering team over to repair it with Reed, something Desi never would have thought to do. Desi was grateful that Wolf still had her back, even if she couldn't be there.

"What seems to be the issue?" Reed asked in a way of a greeting.

"We've been unable to begin investigating the virus," Grady said.

"We're getting a lot of resistance from the colony's leader." Desi led the way out of the docking bay and toward City Hall where she knew Ben would be waiting for them.

"I'm not surprised," Reed said. Desi watched his face carefully, but it remained unchanged. Maybe he didn't know about the connection between the colony's leader and certain members of *Journey*'s team?

"He's demanding to speak to you before allowing us to access to anything," Grady said.

"And in the meantime, the colony's computer programmers are working to secure all information about their farming techniques and hide who knows what else." Desi pulled open the door to City Hall. Part of her expected it to be locked, but it wasn't.

"We'll have to put a stop to that," Reed acknowledged, "though I'm confident Ensign Price will be able to get through anything they are trying to cover up. Where is Price?"

"He's standing by with the rest of the team. Would you like me to call him, sir?" Desi asked.

"No, not yet. Let's go talk to Mr. Martin first. I'm sure things will get a lot easier for you once I've had the chance to speak to him." A small smile formed on Reed's lips. Maybe he *did* know who Ben really was.

The receptionist greeted them coolly, showed them to a conference room, and left without a word. The building was so quiet Desi was pretty sure they were the only ones there. After everything the colonists had been through, she guessed no one else had felt like getting back to work. They didn't wait long before the door to the conference room opened and Ben walked in.

"It really is you." Reed rose to his feet and held his hand out to Ben. "Part of me didn't believe Crystal when she told me."

Ben took Reed's hand, though there was a hint of shock on his face. "Jonathan. I had forgotten that you were captain of *Journey*. If I had remembered…" Ben's voice trailed off.

"You wouldn't have demanded to speak to the Captain or given my officers such a hard time?" Reed raised an eyebrow as he clutched Ben's hand.

"Yes, well." Desi couldn't help but think that was a non-answer. Ben pulled his hand free of Reed's and took a seat at the table. "Should we get started?"

"Why don't start with what the problem is, so Lieutenant Flint and her team can get to work." Reed finally retook his seat at the table. Desi thought he had done a nice job asserting his authority. She only hoped it would be enough.

"That's the problem," Ben said. "I can't just turn over control of my colony to LAWON. My people would have my head if I did. I have to protect my people's interest."

"I bet they're pretty interested in living," Desi said. Reed shot her a look, but didn't say anything, so she figured she hadn't gone too far, yet.

"My people are extremely leery of LAWON having any kind of presence here," Ben continued. "We have to be extremely protective of our farming methods if we want to remain one of the top suppliers of food on the planet. We've seen LAWON acquire other farming colonies, and within a few years, none of the original citizens are left. They're forced out by LAWON's scientists, who think they can manage the farms better. I won't let that happen here. We've worked too hard to get where we are today." Ben sat up straight in his chair as he spoke. Even though Desi didn't really care about the politics surrounding underwater farming colonies, Ben's speech captivated her. It was almost like she was listening to Wolf explain the finer details of how *Journey* worked. Desi didn't really care about Wolf's lecture topics, either, but something always made her sit up and listen.

"We aren't here to try to convince you to join LAWON." Reed leaned a little closer as he talked. His tone had switched from authoritative to compassionate. "We responded to your distress call, and we want to see the job through to the end. I doubt you have the resources necessary to trace the virus's origin. We do. We aren't the bad guys, Jed."

"It's Ben now."

"Have you really given up everything from your old life?"

"I've been Ben Martin almost as long as I was Jedidiah Wolf."

Out of the corner of her eye Desi saw Grady giving her a look. She knew what he was thinking. If Ben had shed all of his old life, did that include his old loyalties as well? Desi knew he had served in the Kincaron military, which had become one of the biggest contributors to LAWON. If he wasn't on their side anymore, could he be on Teria's?

"Let's get back on topic," Desi interrupted. "Are you going to let us investigate, or should we leave and let you fend for yourself the next time the saboteur attacks?" Desi needed to be careful. She was talking in front of her Captain after all, but she couldn't sit back and let the meeting spiral out of control.

"Fine," Ben acknowledged. "I will allow you to lead the investigation, but I have a few conditions."

"What kind of conditions?" Grady asked.

Ben sat up straight and carefully folded his hands on the table in front of him. He was acting like he was in control of this meeting. Desi wished she could do something to shake his confidence but she didn't think Reed would look too kindly on that. "First, I want to be present for all aspects of the investigation, and I will intervene if I feel like you are trying to get any kind of confidential information out of anyone. My people expect me to protect our technology at all costs, and I intend to do that."

"Fine." Desi clenched her teeth in an attempt to contain the string of swear words waiting for a chance to escape. She had no idea what was so special about Stapleton's farming practices, and honestly, she didn't care. It did make her wonder what else Ben might be trying to keep them from discovering.

"Second, when all of this is over, I don't want to hear a word about joining LAWON. Not from your crew or any of the higher ups." Ben turned to Reed as he spoke.

"I will do everything in my power to make sure that doesn't happen," Reed said.

"Is there anything else?" Grady was tense, and Desi couldn't blame him. So far Ben's conditions seemed pretty straight forward. There had to be something else.

"Yes. You don't get to talk to anyone here until I get

the chance to speak to my daughter."

Grady jumped to his feet. "No way." Reed shot him a look and a few seconds later he retook his seat.

"This is blackmail." There was so much more Desi wanted to say but out of respect for Reed and a desire to keep her job she kept it to herself. She deserved a medal for her self-restraint.

Ben looked at Reed, clearly ignoring Desi and Grady. "She left before I had a chance to explain things to her. She deserves to know what happened."

Reed didn't speak for a few minutes. "Fine, but not tonight," he finally said with a sigh.

"But sir," Grady started.

"He's right." Reed turned to face them. "If Crystal is ever going to accept this, she needs to know the truth. And she needs to hear it from him."

"But we can't really force her to talk to him, can we?" Desi said.

"Of course not." Reed turned back to Ben. "Which is why I will allow you to come to *Journey* and give you the chance to talk to her. However, the final decision will be left up to Lieutenant Commander Wolf. If she decides she doesn't want to speak to you then that's it. You will grant us permission to conduct the investigation. Otherwise, I'll place a call to the Kincaron government and will see to it that you are arrested for desertion."

"I understand," Ben said shrinking back into his chair.

"Good. Lieutenant Flint, I want you to keep guards posted at every docking port in the colony." Reed rose to his feet. Desi and Grady followed suit. "There will be someone waiting in the launch bay to bring you to the ship at 0800. Don't be late, Jed. You only have one chance." Reed left the room without another word.

Crystal wasn't sure how long she had been in the computer lab. She shifted uncomfortably in her seat as she waited for the video to reload. Crystal had tried to watch it on her personal computer in her quarters, but she didn't have the programs needed to really be able to manipulate the video like she wanted. With Tyler still at Stapleton Farms, she knew she wouldn't be disturbed. As *Journey's* chief computer programmer, he technically controlled who had access to equipment in the lab.

The screens in front of her reset, and she was once again faced with the image of her mother standing on a platform above a tank of low oxygen liquid. She had watched her mother's execution so many times over the years that she was easily able to detach herself from any emotions that might threaten to rise to surface. Besides, it wasn't her mother she was interested in at the moment.

She had loaded the video on three separate monitors. The first she left alone so that it would play as originally aired. On the monitor in front of her, she zoomed in on the man standing next to her mother with a cloth bag over his head. Up until a few hours ago, she had assumed that man was her father. On the monitor to her right she focused the video on President Rank. She wanted to know if he gave off any indication that he knew the man he was about to execute was not Jedidiah Wolf as he claimed. The computer quickly enhanced the images and Crystal hit play.

The video played simultaneously on all three screens. Crystal watched the screens carefully, scanning from one to the other, but just like every other time she had tired, nothing stood out to her. She took a deep breath and reset the screens, this time hoping that slowing down the playback would give her some answers.

The door to the computer lab opened suddenly, causing Crystal to nearly fall out of her seat. No one had been scheduled to use the lab. She looked up to see Tyler standing in the doorway looking at her in shock.

"What are you doing back?" Her voice was harsher than she intended it to be.

"What are you doing in my lab? You're not authorized to be in here." Price closed the door and made his way over to her, carrying his laptop in one hand.

"I'm third in command of this ship. I'm authorized to be wherever I want to be." Crystal stood up and tried to block the monitors from view. It was useless of course.

"How many times have you watched that?" Tyler pointed to the screen behind her.

"I've lost count."

"Why are you doing this to yourself?"

"I want answers." Crystal stood a little straighter. If he was going to challenge her then she was prepared to go down swinging.

"You know where would have been a great place to get those answers? Back on Stapleton Farms. But you decided to play the victim and give up." Tyler turned away from her and set his computer down on the empty desk behind her. He pressed his palms against the table and took a few deep breaths.

"You don't understand what I'm going through," Crystal yelled.

"He's my father, too." Tyler turned to face her. She had never seen so much anger and pain in his eyes before. She should have backed down, but she couldn't. Her anger had finally found an outlet and she wasn't prepared to give that up.

"It's not the same. You hadn't even met him before

today. You can't possibly feel the betrayal I feel. He abandoned me and started a new life." Crystal pointed to herself as she talked.

"How is that any different from what he did to me?" Tyler yelled. Crystal didn't know what to say, and the unformed words made a lump in her throat. "Never thought of that, did you? If it wasn't for you and your mom, I might have had a chance to get to know my father. At least you had him for seven years. I never even got that much."

"Your mom was the other woman. He never would have stayed with her, even if he wasn't married." Crystal had absolutely no proof to back up what she was saying, but she couldn't let Tyler have the last word.

"You're nothing but a scared little girl," Tyler snapped. "No wonder you ran away today. I bet you didn't even give the rest of us a second thought. Just couldn't wait to have everyone bending over backward to make sure you're ok." Tyler gestured towards the rest of the ship. "Well, you're not fooling me." He turned his attention to one of the computers. Crystal had never seen him like this.

"I might not be on this mission anymore, but I'm still your commanding officer so I'd watch what I say if I were you." Crystal sat hard and turned back to the computer station she had been working on, angrily punching the keys until the images disappeared from all three monitors. "I don't have to take this from you. Enjoy the lab."

Crystal stormed out of the room, not even bothering to close the door behind her. She made it to the end of the hall before the weight of what she had said to Tyler came crashing down on her. She sat down on the top step of the staircase, unable to move any further. She thought about going back to apologize, but how could she face him after that? She thought it would feel good to get some anger out, but she felt worse now than she had before.

# Chapter 6

After her run in with Tyler, Crystal made a point of not being in her quarters when Flint returned from the colony that night. If calm, even tempered Tyler was angry at her for leaving the mission, she could only imagine how pissed Flint would be. Crystal wasn't ready to face her relentless questioning. Instead, she spent most of the night down in the engine room, monitoring the ship's battery units. She only returned to her quarters once she was certain Flint had gone to the mess hall for breakfast. Crystal should have at least an hour before she returned.

The downside of avoiding everyone was that Crystal had no idea what was going on with the mission. She might not want to be directly involved, but she hated being left out of the loop. Trying to solve the mystery behind the virus would have been a welcome distraction. Instead, she sat cross legged on her bunk holding a framed picture of her and her parents. She couldn't remember picking it up, but the metal was no longer cool to the touch.

She had spent countless hours over the years looking at this picture and dreaming about what life would have been like if her parents had survived the war. She traced her father's face with her finger. He looked happy as he held her up for the camera, his other arm draped around her mother's shoulder. It had been taken outside of Marco's Diner hours before they left for what would be their last mission. They had made plans for her eighth birthday that day. Her parents had promised they would be home, and the three of them would spend the whole day together. They had been killed before that could happen. Or her mother had, at least.

A knock at the door pulled Crystal's attention away from the picture. It was probably for the best. She wasn't sure she was ready to head down the path her thoughts were taking her. She put the frame back on the shelf next to her bunk. "Come in."

Justin swung the door open, balancing a tray of food in one hand. He walked in, shutting the door behind him. Part of her still felt like they were breaking some kind of rule whenever they were alone like this, but of course they weren't. As long as their relationship didn't interfere with their duties, the LAWON military didn't have any issues with it.

"When was the last time you had anything to eat?" Justin set the tray down on the corner of the bed before sitting down next to her. He gently cupped her chin and kissed her. Crystal felt butterflies in her stomach when he pulled away. She was always caught off guard by how much Justin's touch affected her, even after being together for a month.

"Before we got the distress call from Stapleton Farms." Crystal leaned in for another kiss, but Justin backed away.

"You need to eat something." Justin moved the tray of food between them, as though warding off her affections until after she ate.

Crystal picked up the cup of kiki and took a long sip of the warm purple liquid, holding it on her tongue to relish in its sweet berry flavor. She felt herself becoming more grounded with every sip she took. It almost didn't matter that she hadn't gotten any sleep the night before.

"I don't know how you drink that on an empty stomach," Justin said with a smile on his face.

"You get used to it."

"I think I'll just stick with coffee."

"Coffee is for the weak." Crystal reached for the second cup of kiki waiting for her on the tray, but Justin pulled it out of her reach. He held up a plate of buttered toast. Reluctantly, she took a piece. "How's the investigation going?" She asked between bites. She always seemed to forget her hunger until she started to eat. She finished the piece of toast and then grabbed another one. Justin looked a little too proud of himself. He had brought her toast, not saved a baby from a burning building.

"I don't know actually. Tyler wasn't talkative when he came back to our room last night. I think he's more affected by what happen than he's letting on." Justin passed her a plate of scrambled eggs.

"Yeah, I guess so." Crystal focused intently on her eggs to avoid the surge of guilt she felt at Tyler's name. She was partly to blame for his anger. She made a vow to apologize to him as soon as he would speak to her again.

Crystal set her empty plate down and leaned back against her pillows. Now that she had eaten, exhaustion threatened to overtake her, despite the kiki now flowing through her body. Justin got off the bed, picked up the tray of food and put it on the desk.

"Don't go," Crystal said, as she stretched out on the bed.

"I wasn't planning on it." Justin climbed in the bed behind her and draped his arm over her.

Crystal felt herself relaxing under the weight of his arm. Her eyes drifted to the picture of her and her parents at Marco's Diner. "He has a family. I saw them." Crystal's voice was soft, and she was glad that she was facing away from Justin so she wouldn't have to see the pity in his eyes.

"That couldn't have been easy." Justin gently stroked her hair.

"There was a little girl. Gina, I think. She looked about the same age I was when my father…" Crystal's voice trailed off. She was going to say when he died, as she had for the last eighteen years, but she couldn't. She wasn't sure what word to replace it with now that she knew the truth. "I don't understand what could have happened to keep him from coming home. At the very least he could have contacted us somehow, let us know that he was alive."

"I hate that he's putting you through this." Justin's voice was soft and comforting, almost like a lullaby.

"There's so much I want to ask him, but I can't bring myself to face him." Crystal's eyelids were starting to get heavy. She was safe in Justin's arms. "Why didn't he want me?"

Justin leaned down and kissed her forehead. "You need to get some sleep. Close your eyes." Crystal's body responded to his words as if he had her in a trance.

A knocking sound jerked her awake. Someone was at the door. It took her a second to realize that the heavy warmth behind her was Justin. She rubbed her eyes on the palms of her hands and looked at the clock on her desk. She had been asleep for maybe forty-five minutes. It was better than nothing. "Yes." Crystal slowly removed herself from Justin and sat up.

The door opened and Grady walked in. He grabbed her desk chair and pulled it over to her bunk. He sat down on it backwards so that his arms were resting on the back of the chair. "Hey," was all he said in way of a greeting. Crystal noticed that his gaze lingered on Justin for a faction of a second longer than was necessary, though she was grateful Grady didn't comment on his presence in her bed.

"Hey." Crystal sat up a little straighter and tried to smooth out the wrinkles in her uniform. She knew in the pit of her stomach that whatever Grady had come to tell her wasn't good.

He grabbed the second cup of kiki from the discarded food tray and handed it to her, as if that would make whatever he was about to tell her more bearable. "He's on board."

Crystal took a long sip. The kiki had gone cold, but she didn't care. She would need every drop of it if she was going to have the energy to get through what was coming. "And?"

"And, he won't allow us to conduct the investigation unless he has the chance to talk to you."

"So, they sent you here to convince me to talk to him." Crystal drained the cup of kiki, wishing it was something stronger.

"You don't have to talk to him if you don't want to. Captain Reed made it very clear that the final choice in the matter was yours. All I'm doing is giving you the opportunity. I'll gladly send him packing if you want," Grady said with a smile.

Crystal took a deep breath. She looked to Justin and was rewarded with a warm smile as he gently rubbed her back. She knew he would support her whatever she decided to do. "I think I want to talk to him. I need answers, and it's the only way to get them. I'm just not sure I'm ready to face him alone."

"You won't have to. He's waiting in the Ward Room with Reed and Flint," Grady said.

"Will you guys come with me?" Crystal looked from Justin to Grady. Of all the people on the ship, these were the two she trusted the most. If she was going to get through this, she would need a strong support team behind her.

"Of course." Grady gently patted her knee then rose to his feet.

"I'll be by your side the entire time." Justin took her hand and helped her off the bunk. She was so nervous that her knees almost buckled under her weight.

She looked from Grady to Justin again. They weren't enough. Someone was missing. "Tyler should be there too. Do you know where he is?"

"He was in our room when I left this morning, but I don't know if he's still there," Justin said.

Crystal grabbed her communicator off the desk where it had been charging and punched in Tyler's number. "Ensign Price." She wasn't sure if he was on duty so she figured it was better to keep in professional. Besides, after last night, she wasn't sure he would answer if he thought it was a personal call.

"Yes, Commander Wolf." The communicators had a way of flattening out everyone's voice, but Tyler's almost sounded robotic. His lack of emotion hit her in the gut. She should have known he wouldn't have forgiven her yet.

"I need you to report to the Ward Room." Crystal fought to keep her voice even.

"Crystal is this about Ben?" His voice was laced with annoyance, but it was better than no emotion at all.

She guessed it was safe to assume that he was alone. If he was dropping the formal tone, then she would too. "Yes. He wants to talk to us." She didn't like lying to him, but she knew it might be the only way to get him there.

"I'd rather not."

"Please, Ty." She took a deep breath. "I need you there." This time she wasn't lying.

"Fine." The line went dead. She looked at her communicator for a moment before she put it in her pocket.

"I guess we should go," Crystal said.

Grady pulled open the door and held it for her. Crystal hesitated. The photograph of her and her parents caught her eye again. She grabbed it off the shelf and headed out the door with her head held high. If she was going to do this, she was determined to be the one leading the conversation. She would do whatever it took to make Ben understand the pain he had caused her.

Tyler was waiting in the hall outside the Ward Room when Crystal arrived. He took one look at her flanked by Grady and Justin and shook his head. "It looks like you have more than enough back up, so I'll be going."

"Tyler, wait," Crystal called after him as he started to walk away. Tyler stopped but didn't turn to face her. Crystal turned to Grady and Justin. "Would you guys give us a minute?" They both nodded and made their way to the Ward Room. She had to fix this first.

Tyler looked at her now that they were alone. His face was hard. He stared her down with his arms crossed in front of his chest. "Are you going to tell me what this about?"

"Da— " she started, but stopped. She had no idea what to call this man. Dad was way too personal. She could call him Jed. It was what her mother and grandparents had called him, but that felt wrong. He stopped being Jedidiah Wolf the moment he decided not to come home. That only left her one option. She would use the name he had taken when he chose to abandon his family. "Ben is insisting on speaking to me before he allows us to investigate."

"And what, you think the more people you have there the easier it will be for you? That didn't seem to matter to you yesterday. Well no thanks, you're on your own." Tyler spit his words at her. Crystal missed her calm and caring brother.

"It's not like that." Crystal squeezed the bridge of her nose. She really should have tried to get some sleep last night.

"Then what's it like?"

"We're family, and you deserve an explanation just as much as I do. And you're right, I was weak and selfish and said horrible things to you last night. I should have found a way to set my feelings aside and see the mission through, but I took the coward's way out. It's something I'll regret for the rest of my life. I'm sorry I left without considering your feelings. I'm sorry I wasn't stronger. I'm sorry I said that you weren't hurting like I am. I'm sorry for all of it." Crystal leaned against the railing running along the corridor. She felt deflated. She was grateful the hallway was deserted and no one else had witnessed her shame.

Tyler walked over and leaned next to her. "No, I'm sorry. I never should have said those things to you. You had every right to do what you did. Walking away was the brave thing to do. None of this is your fault. I just feel so..."

"Angry, hurt, betrayed, abandoned," Crystal offered.

"Yeah, and he didn't even know I existed. I can't imagine how much harder this is for you."

"We are going to get through this together." Crystal took his hand and squeezed it. "Are you ready to go in there?"

"Nope."

"Me either." Crystal released his hand and opened the door. She didn't make eye contact with Ben as she entered. Grady was standing in the corner of the room. He grabbed her hand as she passed and gently squeezed it twice. She guessed it looked like a sweet supportive gesture, but it was a code the two of them had used during the counterterrorism days. It meant he was ready to move if the situation called for it. She glanced down at his hip to make sure he didn't have his sidearm on him. As tempting as it might be to unleash Grady on Ben, she really didn't need him causing a scene. She took a seat next to Justin and crossed her arms behind her, their signal to hold position.

Ben sat directly across from her at the oval table. Crystal's seat put the most distance between the two of them as possible. Reed and Flint sat at the center, facing the large screen on the wall opposite the door. Flint looked pretty frustrated about the whole situation. Crystal couldn't blame her. Grady moved to stand behind Crystal, leaning against the small counter that held a pitcher of water and several glasses. After a quick glance at Ben, Tyler took a seat next to her. She was glad they were presenting a united front.

"You wanted the chance to talk to me. Well, here I am. Start talking." Crystal sat back and folded her arms.

"I was hoping the two of us—" Ben started but stopped when his eyes landed on Tyler. "I mean, the three of us could speak in private."

"That's not going to happen. Anything you want to say to me, you are going to have to say in front of everyone in this room. If you can't do that, I'll leave." Crystal started to rise to her feet.

"Commander Wolf, please stay." Ben's eyes pleaded with her, even if his voice was calm. She must have gotten her ability to hide her emotions from him.

She sat back down and saw Reed giving her a sideways look. "Crystal is fine." Reed's slight nod and small smile made it clear he thought she had done the right thing. She hated to disappoint him.

"Thank you." Ben sounded relieved, a small break in his calm. "I was the one to choose your name. Did you know that?"

"No, I didn't." Crystal felt a crack forming in the wall she had put up.

"My precious gem, my Crishelie," Ben said, a faraway look in his eye.

"No pet names." No one had called Crystal that since her parents' funeral, when she had told her grandmother that it hurt too much to hear the name her father always used for her. If she allowed him to use it now, she feared she would revert back to that seven-year-old little girl who just wanted her daddy back. She had to be strong.

"I'm sorry. Now where should I start?" Ben said more to himself than anyone else.

"How about you start with this?" Crystal slid the picture across the table to him. She wasn't about to let him lead the conversation. She wanted the truth, not some rehearsed story that would paint him in the best possible light. Ben picked up the picture. The color started to drain from his face as he looked at it. Good, she had him right where she wanted him. "Do you remember when that was taken?"

"Of course I do. This was right before your mother and I left for our last mission together in Teria." Ben's voice was barely louder than a whisper.

"Do you remember what you said to me right before you left?" Crystal's voice cracked slightly as she spoke. She hoped no one noticed, but she felt Justin's hand gently squeeze her knee under the table. She closed her eyes a moment and released the breath she wasn't aware she had been holding. She looked at Ben with determination. With Justin by her side she had the strength to get through this.

Ben was quiet for a few minutes. When he finally looked up from the picture, there was something new in his expression. Was it shame? "We were making plans for your birthday," he said, not quite meeting Crystal's gaze. "We had missed being home for your seventh birthday by three weeks, and you wanted a guarantee we would be there for your next one."

"You made me a promise that day. A promise that you would be there for me. A promise you didn't keep." Crystal's voice was flat and controlled, but she guessed Ben could feel the heat beneath it. "I was angry when my eighth birthday finally came, and you and mom weren't there. As I got older, I understood that it wasn't your choice. I believed you would have been there if you could, but war isn't fair and we all had to make sacrifices. I accepted that, but I never celebrated my birthday again. It was too hard." She stretched her fingers out in front of her on the table, feeling the cool metal beneath them, grounding her. "Now here you are, and I realize that you did, in fact, have a choice. You could have been there every year, but you chose not to. You chose to break your promise." She felt as if a weight had been lifted. With every word she spoke, a tiny piece of her anger went with it.

"It's more complicated than that."

"Not to me." Crystal got up from the table and went to pour herself a glass of water. She wasn't really thirsty, she just couldn't look at Ben any longer. She could feel tears starting to form behind her eyes. She would not let him see her cry. She had to be stronger than that.

"How did you survive? Everyone saw your execution broadcast live," Tyler said. No one else had dared to speak while Crystal had her say, but now that she had said her peace, she was glad Tyler had joined the conversation. It was for the best.

"It wasn't me on that platform next to Kendra." Ben's voice had returned to normal. This must be an easier line of questioning for him; at least now they were discussing facts instead of broken promises and hurt feelings.

"I think we've worked that out for ourselves, thanks," Flint said. Crystal couldn't help but crack a smile, knowing Ben wouldn't see it while her back was turned. Flint could always be counted on to break the tension. It was enough to give Crystal the strength to reclaim her seat.

"Who was it?" Tyler asked.

"Ensign Elias Patterson. He was the third member of our team." Ben looked down at his hands as he talked.

"Third member? Every record showed that you and Kendra were a two-person team," Reed said.

"It was a covert mission deep in enemy territory,

Johnathan. I'm sure that isn't the only detail left out of the official reports."

"So who was he, what did he do?" Crystal asked.

"He worked behind the scenes, securing weapons, identification paperwork, places to stay. Whatever we needed to fit in, Eli could get it for us. We couldn't have completed any of our missions without him." Ben looked from Crystal to Reed as he talked.

"If he operated behind the scenes, how the hell he did end up on that platform instead of you?" Flint asked.

"Kendra and I were ordered to infiltrate Rank's inner circle. We had already made quite a bit of headway with several lower level government officials, but all intelligence pointed to Rank as the one pulling the strings. We were to gather intelligence on Teria's military plans and be in place in case the order came to take Rank out." There was a robotic quality to Ben's voice. Crystal wondered if it was hard for him to talk about her mother. She had always believed her parents were very deeply in love, even after the discovery of her father's affair that had resulted in Tyler. It was probably easier to talk about her if he distanced himself from what he was saying. It was what she had learned to do every time she had been asked to speak about her parents.

"So, what went wrong?" Tyler asked. He was leaning slightly over the table, as if he was hanging on Ben's every word. Crystal was glad he'd come; he needed this as much as she did.

"Rank was hosting a big party at his mansion that night," Ben explained. "I had a contact that could get us on the guest list. I was leaving the meeting when I was IDed by a low ranking Teria officer. He had spent part of his youth in Homestead Colony and remembered me from there."

"Who was it?" Crystal had a hard time believing anyone from their colony would betray Jed Wolf. Her family had always been an important figure in her colony, even before the execution. Most of the people living there had ties to military. They all looked out for one another. When the rest of the world was making a martyr of her parents and thrusting her into the spotlight as their orphan, Homestead Colony was the only place that none of it mattered. It was the only place she could get away from it all and just feel like a kid.

"You wouldn't have known him. His family only lived there for a few years when we were kids. I barely remembered him, but unfortunately he remembered me," Ben said.

"What did you do?" Justin asked. Crystal wasn't sure why—there was only one thing Ben could have done to protect his cover.

"I took him out before he had a chance to tell anyone who I was. I told Kendra and Eli what had happened, and we all agreed it was too risky for me to attend the party. I wanted to abort the mission, but Kendra thought this would be our only chance to get close to Rank. In the end, Eli agreed to take my place." Ben's voice trailed off.

"I assume Kendra and Eli got caught at the party?" Reed asked.

Ben nodded. "I hadn't been fast enough, and the officer that IDed me had already alerted the military. They were waiting for us at the party." Ben stared at his hands.

"That doesn't explain why you were the one reported killed in action," Reed said.

Ben looked at Reed pleadingly. "You know how sporadic communication was during the war. We tried to report the switch, but the network must have been down, and the message never went through. As far as the paperwork was concerned, I was the one undercover with Kendra. When they saw her face, it was only natural to assume I was the man standing next to her."

"What about after the bodies were returned? They must have run DNA tests or something," Flint said.

"All we got back were ashes," Crystal said slowly.

"Why didn't you say something?" Tyler asked. "You could have come forward."

Ben shook his head, but the shame was still there, hiding behind his expression. "It was too dangerous. The war wasn't over when Kendra and Eli were killed. I was alone in the capital of Teria. The only thing I could do was bide my time until the war ended."

Crystal was embarrassed to be related to him. She had grown up being told she was the daughter of heroes. Every decision she had made in her life had been in the hope of living up to her parents' legacy. Turns out she came from equal parts hero and coward. She could not imagine a situation where she would lay low and wait for the danger to pass. Except—that was exactly what she had done yesterday. The second she saw Ben, she had run away. She was no better than he was.

"What about after the war?" Flint asked the question Crystal was too afraid to put into words.

"I wanted to come back, but I wasn't sure if it would be safe for Crystal to have me around."

Crystal couldn't believe what she had heard. "You're blaming this one me?" She could feel Justin tensing beside her. If he tried to make a move against Ben, she wasn't sure she would be able to stop him. Or that she would want to.

"No of course not." Ben's words tumbled out of his mouth as he backpedaled. "It's complicated."

"Then explain it," Grady said through clenched teeth. He was feeling the anger she should be at the moment, but she was too astonished to be angry.

"Rank had been named President of Teria. He had more power and resources than he ever had during the war. I thought if he found out I was still alive, he would send someone after me, or you, to punish me," Ben said to Crystal. "I knew my parents would take good care of you, so I did what I thought was best for everyone. I assumed a new identity and tried to live out the rest of my life quietly."

Nothing Ben said was funny, but Crystal couldn't stop herself from laughing. "You haven't protected me from Rank," she said bitterly. "A month ago, he attempted to take me prisoner so he could torture me into building him a ship grander than *Journey*. And I did have a good life with Grandma and Grandpa, until they died three months apart when I was sixteen. You know what would have been really great to have then? A father."

"I thought about coming back when I found out they had died, but so much time had passed…"

Crystal rose to her feet. She was done listening to his excuses. "I've listened to you. Now cooperate with the investigation." She walked out without another word.

# Chapter 7

The door to the Ward Room had barely closed behind Wolf before Ben rose to his feet.

"Where do you think you're going?" Desi was anxious to get the investigation started so they could put this whole thing behind them.

"I need to go after her." Ben waved his arm at the closed door as he spoke. "I need to make sure she's ok."

"I don't think so." Grady moved so that he was blocking the door.

"You've had your say. Now sit back down so that we can get down to business." Reed didn't need any threat of physical force to assert his authority. Ben took one last look at Grady and sat with a sigh.

"So, can we conduct our investigation or what?" Desi pressed, with a lot less tact than Reed.

"Yes, fine, start your investigation." Ben threw his hands up and looked longingly at the door.

"Wonderful." Reed gestured to Ben. "I'll walk you back to the launch bay and see to it that you are returned to Stapleton Farms right away."

Ben rose to his feet in outrage. "Our agreement was that I would be involved in the investigation."

"And you will be, once we are ready to start questioning people." Reed held the door open for Ben, but he didn't move.

"I'll provide you with a list of people we would like to talk to. I'm sure you'll be happy to ensure they cooperate," Desi said. Reed clamped a hand on Ben's shoulder and started to lead him out of the room. They were almost out of the room when Desi said, "Ensign Price, why don't you go back to the colony with him and get started working on the servers. See if you can find anything useful."

"Yes, ma'am," Price said with a confused looked on his face. Desi tried to keep her expression even as Price left the room with Reed and Ben. Desi closed the door behind them.

"Why exactly did you send Price with that man?" Grady took a seat at the table next to Justin.

"Because I think we need to consider the possibility that Ben planted that virus, and Price shouldn't have to be here to hear that." Desi leaned forward over the table. She wasn't surprised to see a shocked look cross Justin's face. Grady, on the other hand, was nodding in agreement.

"You two can't honestly believe that Ben did this." Justin looked back and forth between them. "He's Crystal's father." Desi wasn't sure he was capable of thinking badly about anyone. When they were growing up and Desi would trash talk the kids that were bullying Justin, he would always come to their defense. Some problem at home or school that, in his mind, justified their being a jerk to him.

"Exactly." Grady leaned back in his chair, as if he had

just won the argument. Desi, on the other hand, knew it wouldn't be that simple with Justin.

"I don't follow," Justin said.

"It's common knowledge that Crystal is serving on *Journey*. He could have planted the virus and waited to activate it until he was sure we would be the only ones able to respond. Then he would be able to corner her," Grady theorized.

"You're saying that he risked the lives of everyone at the colony, including his wife and children, just to corner Crystal?" Justin's mouth opened in disbelief. "For what?"

"It's been eighteen years," Desi offered. "It's not like he could just call her up. Maybe this was the only way he could think of to reconnect with her."

"It seems like an awfully big risk." Justin slid his chair away from the table and folded his arms over his chest.

"Not if he had control over the virus the whole time. He probably could have brought the life support systems back online anytime he wanted to." Desi had zero proof to support her theory, but she didn't let that deter her.

"It would also explain why he doesn't seem concerned about finding the person who planted the virus before they could make another move." Grady sat up straighter. At least Grady agreed with her. Maybe she was on to something.

"He was too shocked at being face to face with Crystal again," Justin argued. "There's no way he set it up."

"The man is a trained spy. I'm pretty sure he could fake his emotions to cover his trail," said Desi.

"Then question him, but I think you are wasting your time." It was clear by the look on Justin's face that he was only humoring her.

"We have to be smart about this," Grady leaned

toward Desi. "If we are right, and Ben suspects we are on to him, he can revoke our permission and send us packing."

"What do you suggest we do?" Desi asked.

"You could question all the colony's leadership," Justin offered in an off-handed way. "That way he'll think it's routine."

Grady nodded. "It's a good place to start. And we'll need a list of people we want to talk to in case we are wrong. We're going to have to go after this from a couple of different angles."

Desi nodded. She had no idea how to pull together a list of suspects, but she didn't want to let on how out of her element she was on this. "Let's get to work."

Crystal had been wandering the ship aimlessly for the last two hours. There were plenty of things she should be working on, but she couldn't focus on any of them. She kept replaying everything Ben had told her. He had abandoned her in order to protect her. She desperately wanted to believe he was telling her the truth. That she would have been in danger had he returned home. It would validate, at least on some level, that he really was the self-sacrificing hero she had grown up believing him to be.

But no matter how she looked at it, she couldn't justify what he had done. She needed some space. A chance to clear her mind, to think about something else, before she drove herself crazy. She had already knocked on Justin's door before she fully realized where she was.

"It's open," a voice called through the door.

Crystal opened the door and did a quick survey of the room. "Is Tyler around?"

"No. Desi sent him to the colony to start working on tracking the virus," Justin said.

"Good." Crystal closed the door, making sure to secure the latch. Justin turned his chair away from the desk as she made her way over to him.

"Is there something I can do for you, Commander?" He gently grabbed her hips and guided her closer to him.

"I came to collect my winnings." She leaned down and kissed him.

"I think I can help with that." Justin pulled her down into his lap. One hand came to rest on the small of her back with his other tangled in her hair. His kiss was raw and full of passion. He stood up, never breaking contact, and carried her over to his bunk. He released her long enough to pull his shirt off before climbing on the bed with her.

Crystal allowed herself to get lost in Justin. The way his skin felt against hers, the way his kiss left her breathless and longing for more, the way his eyes seem to look straight through to her soul. Her hands explored his body, from the well-defined muscles of his arms and chest to the soft contours of his face. She could feel every negative emotion in her melting away. Nothing mattered other than Justin's arms wrapped around her.

Later, when they were both satisfied, Justin lay on his back, his elbow crooked so she could put her head on his shoulder. Crystal snuggled close to him, pulling the blankets tight around them. She wasn't ready to leave the comfort of his touch. He propped himself up on his side so that he could look down on her. Crystal gently caressed his cheek before leaning up and giving him a small kiss.

"How are you?" He slowly stroked her hair as he

studied her face.

"I'm doing pretty good at the moment," she said with a small laugh.

"I'm glad." He leaned down and kissed her again.

Crystal let her head sink back into the pillow. "We should play games more often," she said lazily. "I like what happens when I win." She couldn't remember the last time she felt this relaxed.

"I'll keep that in mind," Justin said with a wicked grin.

Crystal looked over at the desk that divided the room in two. His laptop was open, though she couldn't see what was on the screen. His tablet was sitting on top a stack of several old paper books off to the side and several pages of handwritten notes were strewn across the desk. "I interrupted you."

"You can interrupt me like that anytime you want. In fact, I encourage it."

Crystal halfheartedly flung her hand back to hit him on his chest. "What were you working on?"

"It's not important."

"It looks important," Crystal said taking in the mess on his desk.

"I was doing some research on Neophian immigration laws." Justin's voice was hesitant. Why didn't he want to tell her?

Crystal rolled over so that she was facing him. "Trying to find a way to bring your family here?"

"Yeah." He didn't quite meet her eye as he talked.

"I think that's great." She didn't want him to avoid talking about his family for fear that it would remind her of her own screwed up family. His situation was completely different than hers. He was separated from his family and trying to find a way to bring them to

Neophia for a better life. It was a welcomed change from what she had been dealing with. "How's it going?"

"The more I read, the more unlikely it seems. Between the extensive background checks, medical exams, and never-ending waiting lists, it's amazing anyone from Earth ever clears the list before they've grown too old to travel to Neophia."

Crystal knew the immigration laws for the planet were strict. The one thing everyone agreed on was that the planet's population needed to be controlled so that what happened to Earth wouldn't happen on Neophia. From what Crystal could remember from her Earth history classes in primary school, over population had been the main cause of most of Earth's wars. It was also what brought humans to Neophia in the first place three hundred years ago.

"From what I can piece together, a census is taken every five years to determine Neophia's population, and that's compared to the planet's sustainability index. If there's a gap, then every country is allotted a certain number of citizen credits for new immigrants. Of course, every credit allotted to Teria gets wasted, but that's how the law is written." Justin's muscles tensed as he talked. Crystal knew his deepest desire was to bring his family to Neophia and protect his three younger sisters from having to fight in the wars on Earth.

"There are other ways to get citizenship," she reminded him. "Have you tested your blood to see if you have any Aquinein or Sertex in your ancestry? Then you could claim birthright citizenship." Crystal traced the lines his muscles formed in his chest as she talked. She wanted so badly to fix this for him. To be of use again.

"That's the first thing I tried. Not a drop of Neophian blood in me."

"We'll figure this out together. Maybe there are some strings I could pull or something. You never know who's connected." Her family name usually carried some weight with people, though once the news of Ben broke, that might not be the case anymore. Crystal quickly dashed the thought of Ben from her mind. She wouldn't let it taint her time with Justin.

He sat up and looked at her with such intensity in his eyes. Crystal wondered if she had said something wrong. "You'd do that for me? For my family?"

"Of course. A family that wants to be together should have every chance to be."

Justin rolled her onto her back so that he was once again lying on top of her. "You're pretty amazing, you know that?" He leaned down and kissed her slowly.

"We're here to see Mr. Martin," Desi said to the receptionist in the lobby of City Hall. She and Grady had spent the past three hours putting together a list of people they wanted to talk to and coming up with a strategy for questioning them. Desi felt pretty good about it considering the only reference she had were the cop dramas her mother use to watch when Desi was little.

The receptionist didn't look up from her computer. Grady cleared his throat and moved closer to the desk. "He should be expecting us," Grady said, flashing her his most charming smile. It didn't seem to have much effect.

"You'll be in conference room C. First floor, end of the hall, turn right." The receptionist continued to stare at her computer the whole time.

Grady tapped the desk twice then walked away. Desi

stared at the receptionist for a few seconds longer while the women continued to pretend they weren't there. Finally, Desi walked away, shaking her head as she went.

"She was friendly," Desi said once she had caught up with Grady.

"My real concern is the lack of security," Grady responded. "Anyone could walk in here like they owned the place."

"Speaking of that, how about we make a little detour?" Desi nudged his arm and made a left at the end of the hall. Grady followed her amused. It didn't take her long to find her way back to the server room, even if it was much farther from the front of the building than she remembered. There was a bored security guard standing near the door, though he didn't do anything to stop Desi and Grady from walking right in.

"Can I help you?"

At first Desi couldn't locate where the voice was coming from. She scanned the room until her eyes came to rest on an irritated looking man sitting in the corner with his arms crossed. "I'm looking for Ensign Price," Desi said. At the sound of his name, Price emerged from the rows of servers. "Have you made any progress?" Desi asked.

"A little," Price said, running his hand through his hair. "The coding on the virus is extremely complex. I'm pretty sure it originated from the chip we removed from the life support system yesterday, but it's spread to the entire system at this point. I've deleted traces of the virus from the inventory, planting, and laboratory systems so far."

"Can you tell us anything about who planted it?" Grady asked with a hopeful tone. Desi couldn't help but wonder if maybe he wasn't completely sure of their plan either.

"No. I'm searching through the archived data files to see if I can pinpoint when the virus was first installed, but it's going to take some time." Price glanced back at the rows of servers. Desi noticed that bags had started to form under his eyes. He couldn't have gotten much sleep last night.

"Why don't you take a break? Head back to the ship and get a little rest," Desi said.

"Are you sure?"

"Yeah. You can pick it back up in a few hours. Hopefully we'll have some more to go off of after we talk to a few people." Desi smiled. Price just nodded and left the room. He must have been more worn down than she realized if he willingly left a room full of computers without protest.

"We should go find that conference room. Don't want to keep Ben waiting for too long," Desi said. She and Grady left the server room and went in search of conference room C, which they eventually found at the very end of the hallway. Desi was surprised to find the room empty when they entered. Did the receptionist even let Ben know that they had arrived? It had been at least twenty minutes since they left the lobby.

Grady popped his head back out the door to double check the room number. "This is the right room. What do you want to do?"

"Let's give him a few more minutes. If he doesn't show up, we'll go in search of his office." Desi took a seat at the small table, making sure she was facing the door.

But they didn't have to wait long before Ben walked in. "Sorry to keep you waiting." He looked awfully calm for someone whose colony had almost been killed by a saboteur the day before.

"I'm sure you are." Desi rolled her eyes. She was certain Ben had intentionally taken longer than necessary to show up. Too bad he didn't know they weren't just sitting around waiting for him to show. "We sent you the list of people we need to talk to. Did you see it?"

"I did, and I was able to arrange for two of them to meet with us in a few hours. The rest will have to wait until tomorrow." Ben hadn't taken a seat at the table. Instead he leaned on the back of one of the chairs as if he was a teacher about to lecture them. Desi wasn't thrilled with the current power dynamic. She needed to take charge of the conversation.

"That's not good enough. I don't think you are taking this situation seriously Mr. Martin." Desi carefully folded her hands in front of her on the table.

"I still have a colony to run, despite your investigation. I lost a day of harvest time on two of our dry fields yesterday, not to mention the planting of our largest submerged kelp field. Our harvest and planting scheduled is perfectly timed with the rapid growth nursery to the point that if we are off schedule by more than a few days, the survival rates of our seedlings drop dramatically. I can't pull people out of the fields and slow the whole process down further."

"Well since you don't seem to be out in the fields, how about we start with you?" Grady got to his feet and causally walked around the table until he had positioned himself between Ben and the door.

"Me? You honestly think I had something to do with planting the virus?" It was almost like Ben was laughing at them.

"It's a great cover to get to Crystal," Grady said.

"And you are awfully calm about the whole thing," Desi agreed. "Everyone here was minutes away from death yesterday, and rather than try to find the person responsible, you're concerned about picking vegetables." Desi rose to her feet. She was having a hard time keeping her anger under control.

"Do you know what would happen if we don't complete our harvest on time, Lieutenant Flint?" Ben stepped closer to her, his lip curling as he said her name. "The nation of Oceanica would go without any kind of grain for the next three months. The bread factories there would be forced to close, thousands of people would lose their jobs, and whole colonies wouldn't be able to afford to keep running. If we miss our planting window on any of the kelp fields, the ranchers in Kincaron won't have any food for their herds, and there will be meat shortages across the planet. Not to mention it would destroy the livelihood of every person here. So, I'm sorry if I can't stop everything while you investigate."

"That doesn't mean you didn't plant the virus." Desi stepped forward, further decreasing the gap between them.

"Why would I try to destroy something I spent years of my life building?" Ben turned to look from Desi to Grady, taking a small step back as he did. Desi was back in control.

"Who's to say you couldn't have stopped the virus and brought everything back online if we hadn't shown up? The virus has been on the colony's computer for a long time, maybe since the beginning. This could have been your plan all along," Grady said.

"Right of course, I spent fifteen years of my life developing underwater farming techniques and building this colony so one day I could trigger a computer virus to lure my daughter here to save me on the off chance she decided to join the military. Makes perfect sense." Ben ran his hands through his hair in frustration. Just like Price always did.

Desi didn't want to acknowledge the point. "It didn't have to be from the beginning. You could have been planning this for years. Crystal has a pretty substantial public presence. From what you told people about us yesterday, you knew she joined the military." Desi's resolve was starting to waver, but she pushed her unease aside. She wasn't ready to back down yet.

"Don't you think if I had wanted to connect with Crystal, I would have found an easier way to do it?" Ben snorted. "Like you said, she's not very hard to find. If it had been up to me, she would have lived the rest of her life thinking I had died." He paused, looking away from them, then said quietly, "I never wanted to hurt her like this."

For the first time Desi believed he was telling the truth. She glanced at Grady, unsure what to do now, but didn't find any help there. She had been so sure that Ben was behind this. "We'll need access to your personal computers just to make sure," she said trying to save face.

"Feel free to go through anything you want. I have nothing to hide." Ben moved toward the door, but Grady didn't move out of the way.

"About the other interviews you lined up," Desi said.

"I'll be back with the first one in an hour. Now if you'll excuse me, I have to get back to work." Ben pushed past Grady and out the door.

Grady closed the door and then took a seat at the table. "What do you think?"

"I don't think he did it." Desi sighed and sat down next to him.

"Me either."

"I still don't trust him, though." Desi looked at the closed door, as if the answer would be written there.

# Chapter 8

Justin had been on duty all afternoon, leaving Crystal alone with her thoughts. She considered heading to the bridge herself, but she wasn't sure she could face the rest of the crew. She was sure the story of Ben's request to talk with her had spread throughout the ship by now.

Instead she spent her time researching Ben. She was left with more questions than answers after their conversation that morning, and she hoped the internet could yield some answers. It seemed easier than facing him again. Unfortunately, the only thing she could find about Ben Martin was a handful of patents for farming technology. Despite being the colony's leader, he wasn't the public face of Stapleton Farms. That honor went to his wife, Andrea, and someone named Ian McFarland. There was even less about Jedidiah Wolf—at least nothing she hadn't already read a thousand time over the years. She found next to nothing about Elias Patterson.

Crystal knocked gently on the door to Tyler's quarters. She knew Justin was still on duty for a few more hours and was hoping for a chance to talk to Tyler alone. As she waited, her mind wandered to the back copies she'd found of Stapleton Farm's local newsletter. It hadn't given her any answers about Ben, but it was full of pictures and stories about the colony and his new family. She had spent more time than was probably heathy going through them.

Crystal knocked again, shaking her head to clear the "what ifs" from her mind. She needed answers, not more questions. That was why she had come here, though it was taking Tyler longer than she expected to answer. She had checked the duty list and saw he was supposed to be off right now, but maybe he was still at Stapleton Farms. Crystal had just turned away when the door suddenly opened.

"Justin's not here." Tyler looked distracted. Maybe she had woken him up.

"I came to talk to you actually. Can I come in?" Crystal asked. Tyler stepped aside. Crystal glanced over at his desk where his laptop was only halfway closed.

"What's up?" Tyler positioned himself between Crystal and the computer.

"I had some questions, and I thought maybe you could help me." She had to be careful; what she wanted to ask him to do wasn't entirely legal.

"I'll help if I can," Tyler said. "You know that."

"I've been trying to find some information about Elias Patterson, but there isn't much out there. I've only been able to dig up his enlistment profile and a dishonorable discharge for desertion," Crystal said.

"And you wanted me to see if I could find you more information?"

She blew out a breath. "Yeah. I mean, I know it's against the rules to look at people's files, but I thought maybe in this case it might be worth making an exception." That was as clear as Crystal could make the request without flat out saying what she wanted him to do. Tyler was smart; she was sure he would pick up on what she needed.

"You could always petition LAWON to see his file," Tyler offered, shrugging his shoulders. He really couldn't be that obtuse could he?

Crystal shifted her weight from one foot to the other. She couldn't understand why he was making this so difficult. He was going to her make her say it. "That could take months, and I was hoping to get some answers today."

"Are you ordering me to hack LAWON's network and pull his records?" Tyler raised an eyebrow at her.

"I'm not ordering anything," she said carefully. "I'm asking my brother for help."

"Come take a look at this," he said with a wide grin. He sat down at the desk and opened his computer the rest of the way. Crystal pulled Justin's chair over so she could get a better look at his screen. Elias's file was already open.

"You're a jerk." She punched his shoulder.

Tyler winced, even though she hadn't hit him that hard. "You're still my commanding officer. I had to make sure you weren't going to bust me." He looked a little too proud of pulling one over on her.

"What have you found?" She inched her chair closer to the screen.

"Not much actually. It's weird, like his whole service record was erased." Tyler began sorting through the several tabs he had open. "I found that he attended the Academy. He finished in the middle of his class. He was in the same year as your mom actually."

"Really? Maybe that's why he decided to go undercover with her. Maybe they had been friends?" Crystal wished she remembered more of her mother's stories. Maybe she had mentioned Elias at one point.

"Could be." Tyler turned back to the computer. "It looks like he served on a carrier at the start of the war before transferring to special ops, and then nothing until the desertion claim the last month of the war."

"Why desertion do you think?" Crystal asked.

"It makes sense, I guess. He wasn't supposed to be in the line of fire, working behind the scenes, and he was well connected. It would have been easy for him to disappear. No one knew he had taken Ben's place." Tyler pushed away from the desk.

Crystal's head spun as she tried to process it. "What about his family? Someone must have asked what happened to him."

"Let me see." Tyler leaned forward and went to work on the computer. Crystal tried to follow what he was doing, but the windows changed so fast that she was barely able to see what was on each window before he moved onto the next. "Ok here. He had a wife and parents that filed a petition after the war to have his dishonorable discharge changed." Tyler pulled up a picture of an older couple and a young woman. She was pushing a double stroller.

"Are those his kids?" If they were babies when he died, Crystal wondered if Elias had ever met them.

"I guess so," Tyler said.

"If he had a dishonorable discharge, they wouldn't have received any benefits from the military." She thought back to all the checks she had received over the years for her parents' sacrifice. They all went directly into a savings account she never touched.

"I guess not."

Crystal got up and started to pace around the small room. The anger she had been able to set aside was building again. Ben's cowardliness hadn't just affected her, it had affected Elias's family as well. The twins in that picture had grown up without a father because of him. His wife would have had to support them all on her own, without the assistance from the government that was due to her. The injustice of it burned in Crystal's stomach. Half the money in her savings account belonged to that family.

Crystal made the mistake of glancing at the family's picture again. She couldn't stop her mind from wandering to the image of a different family. A family with a little girl clinging to her mother's leg in fear while sirens echoed around them. A teenage boy arguing with his dad to stay behind and help. And a father putting his family first. "He replaced us Ty." She sat down on Justin's bed. She was suddenly too tired to give into her anger.

"What are you talking about?" He turned away from the computer to face her.

"Ben," she said absently. "He replaced us. He has this perfect little family. I saw them during the evacuations. It was clear that they loved each other. I wonder what that must be like." Crystal twisted the top of Justin's blanket through her fingers, longing for the peace and comfort she had found beneath them earlier that day.

"He didn't replace us. You can't think like that."

"Why not? It's true. If he had come back the three of us could have been a family." Crystal looked at the picture of Justin's family he had tapped to the wall above his bed with longing.

"No, we wouldn't have." Tyler slumped down in his

chair. "Ben didn't even know about me."

"No, but if he had lived, don't you think your mom would have told you about him sooner?" Crystal arched an eyebrow at him. "When did you start asking who your father was?"

"I don't know. I was young. Probably about the time I started primary school." Tyler didn't quite meet her eye as he spoke.

"So maybe if Susan had known he was alive, she would have told Ben about you—or at the very least told you his name before you turned sixteen. Maybe Ben would have even gone back to her with my mom gone. We could have all been a family. Instead he found a new wife and had new kids, without even giving us a second thought." Crystal's eyes lingered on the neat stack of books on Justin's side of the desk. A reminder that some families would go to great lengths to be together.

Tyler got up and stood directly in front of her so that she had no choice but to look him straight in the eyes. "I doubt very much that he forgot about you. You heard what he said this morning; he thought he was protecting you by staying away. I'm sure he still loved you even though he wasn't with you."

Crystal met his gaze without looking down. "Are you? Because I'm not."

Desi flung open the door to her quarters. It had been a frustrating day, and while she had tried her best to control her emotions, she was sure that she had failed. She was surprised to see Wolf sitting at the desk in their room, working, as if the last two days had never happened. Desi froze in the doorway, unsure if she should go in or back away quietly to give Wolf some space.

"I didn't expect you back this soon," Wolf said, looking up from her computer. "How did the interrogation go?" Desi was surprised by how normal she sounded, even if her tone was a little flatter than normal.

"Not great." Desi plopped down on her bunk and stared at the ceiling. "Ben had only arranged for us to talk to two people today."

"Do you think either of them did it?" Wolf asked.

"No." Desi turned to her side so that she was looking at Wolf, who was awfully interested for someone who had removed herself from the mission. Part of Desi wanted to ask Wolf to come back, but she didn't think that was fair. Besides, Desi wasn't one to cry for help at the first hiccup. "The first one was a computer programmer who had only been at the colony for a month. We're fairly certain the virus has been on the system longer than that, so there is no way she could have planted it."

"And the other one?" Wolf asked.

"A security guard with more muscles than brains. I'd be shocked if he even knew how to turn on a computer."

Wolf cracked a smile. It was the first time Desi had seen her do that since they arrived at Stapleton Farms. She was glad to see that Ben hadn't broken Wolf completely. It had taken Desi and Wolf so long to become friends; she would hate to have that wrecked now.

"I'm sure tomorrow will go better. Do you have any serious suspects?" Wolf asked.

Desi couldn't meet Wolf's eye. "We had one, but it didn't pan out." Desi prayed that would be enough to satisfied Wolf.

"Really? Not one of the two you told me about?"

"No." Desi really didn't want to tell Wolf that they had cornered Ben, but she didn't see away around it. Wolf would know in an instant if Desi was lying and even if she didn't, Desi was sure Ben would rat her out the first chance he got. It was better that Wolf heard about it from her. "Grady and I thought Ben might have the most motive to try to lure *Journey* here. To lure you here."

"Oh." Wolf looked down at the computer that was open in front of her.

Guilt flooded Desi's body. "But after talking to him, we don't think he did it." The words tumbled out of her mouth so fast she wasn't entirely sure they made sense.

"That's good, I guess." Wolf still didn't look at Desi.

"I'm sorry." Desi said sitting up.

"No. It was a good hunch. I would have followed it too." Wolf tore her eyes away from the computer and looked at her. Desi wished she could know what Wolf was thinking but the other woman was so good at masking her emotions. "What's he like?" Wolf asked softly.

"He's..." Desi wasn't sure what to say. Surely, she couldn't tell Wolf that she thought Ben was a spineless coward who couldn't be trusted and that Wolf was better off without him. Desi searched her mind for something positive to tell Wolf about Ben that wouldn't be a flat-out lie. "He cares a lot about the colony. I think he just wants a quiet life in the shadows."

"Do you think he regrets how things are now?"

"I do," Desi said without hesitation. "But you can't fix the past."

"Can't fix the past," Wolf repeated slowly to herself as she looked down at her computer again. Desi wished she knew what Wolf had been working on when she walked in. "Do you know where Ben is now?" Wolf asked with a renewed energy.

"He was in his office when we left. He's probably still there. He seems to work almost as hard as you do." Desi regretted the comparison as soon as she said it, but Wolf didn't seem to be paying attention to her anymore.

"I've got to go take care of something." Wolf snatched her computer from the desk and left the room before Desi could say anything.

Crystal walked through the center of Stapleton Farms with determination. Given what she had heard about the colony's feelings toward LAWON, she expected to receive some comments, but no one really paid any attention to her. Which was good, as she had to get herself in the right mind set for what she was about to do. Flint's comment about not being able to fix the past struck something inside her. Sure, she couldn't go back in time and change what happened, but she could do something to fix some of the damage Ben had caused.

The lobby of City Hall was completely deserted when Crystal arrived. She knew it was late in the evening, but she still expected to find someone there that could point in her the right direction. What if she had been wrong about Ben and he had already gone home to his family? She knew she wouldn't be able to face him there. She almost turned around and went back to the ship, but she was drawn to the doors leading to the rest of the building. They opened without any resistance and she slipped inside. Even if she couldn't find Ben, it was a good chance to survey the building's security and report back to Flint any weaknesses the saboteur might have exploited.

She did a quick walk through of the first floor, without running into anyone, before heading upstairs. She knew that was where she would find Ben's office. Every room on the floor was dark expect for one. Crystal took a deep breath and started toward it. She hesitated when she reached it. It still wasn't too late to leave without Ben ever knowing she was here. She raised her hand to knock, embarrassed by her momentary weakness, but stopped short of making contact as voices reached her ear. Crystal moved closer to the crack in the door so she could hear better.

"No, they didn't find anything today," Ben said.

"Are you sure you should be allowing LAWON to investigate our people?" The second voice was accompanied by some soft static in the background. Whoever Ben was talking to wasn't at the colony. Crystal knew she should walk away; she didn't like spying on a private call, but something about that second voice made the hairs on her arms stand on end.

"We can't do this by ourselves Ian. Like it or not we need their help. I can't risk a repeat of what happened yesterday." Ben sounded tired.

"And you're sure you can trust them not to take any of our tech back to LAWON?"

"I trust them. Though, if I'm being honest, I do wish you were here to help me keep an eye on them."

"Remind me which ship responded?" The more the second man talked, the more Crystal was sure she had heard his voice somewhere before. She was certain she would be able to place it eventually.

"*Journey*, so at least we have the best LAWON can offer," Ben said.

"If you say so."

"I know you're critical of LAWON, but they aren't all bad. How are things with your family? Can we expect you back soon?"

"I need to be here at least a few more days."

Crystal moved closer to the door. She needed to hear that voice on the phone better if she wanted to place it. She reached her hand out, hoping to ease the door open a little more without Ben noticing, when a sharp voice rang out behind her.

"Can I help you with something?"

She spun around to find an older woman marching toward her. "I wanted to have a word with Mr. Martin," Crystal said quickly. She couldn't help feeling like a child that had been caught snooping.

"Do you have an appointment?" The woman had closed the gap between them quickly. She was now standing directly in front of Ben's door with her hands on her hips.

"No, but I'm sure he won't mind." Crystal straightened herself out. She was a military officer, she didn't need to accept being scolded by this woman, even if she had been ease dropping on a private conversation.

"Mr. Martin is extremely busy, and if you want to talk to him, you'll need to make an appointment."

The door to Ben's office opened suddenly. He surveyed the scene quickly before his face broke out in a huge smile. Crystal felt a moment's gratitude before she remembered what she had come here to do.

"It's fine, Margot. Why don't you go home for the night?" Ben opened the door wider. Reluctantly, the woman left, and Crystal allowed herself to be ushered into Ben's office.

"This is a pleasant surprise." Ben leaned against the front of his desk.

Crystal stood awkwardly in the middle of his office, her body filled with nervous energy. Why did she think she could do this alone? "I want you to make an official record of what happened to Elias Patterson." The words spilled from her mouth. She didn't think she could handle wading through formalities before getting to her point.

"Oh, Crystal." Ben ran his hand through his hair and started to pace in front of his desk. "I'm sorry but I don't think I can."

It wasn't the response that she expected. "Why not?"

"Do you know what could happen to me if I make a statement and the Kincaron military decides to press charges? I can't put my family through that."

"Aren't I part of your family?"

Ben looked at her with a pained expression. "Of course you are."

"Then why won't you do this for me?" Crystal hadn't moved from her spot in the middle of the office.

"You don't know what you're asking me to do." Ben sat down on one of the sofas in his office and put his head in his hands.

Crystal couldn't help but feel sorry for him. His whole world was crumbling before him. She decided to try a softer approach. She went over and sat down next to him, pulling out her computer as she went. She set the computer up on the table in front of them and pulled up the picture of Elias's family Tyler had found. "Do you know what happened to Elias after the war?"

"I assume he was labeled missing in action, presumed dead." Ben didn't look up from the ground.

Crystal fought every instinct in her and put a hand on Ben's shoulder. She felt him tense at her touch but she didn't move it. She knew the next thing she had to tell him was going to hit him hard, and she wanted to try to comfort him. "He was given a dishonorable discharge for desertion."

Ben raised his head to look at her. "That can't be true."

"It is. That's his family." Crystal nodded to the computer. "They never received any compensation from the government. I know you are worried about your family, but what about his? What about his sons? Did he even get a chance to meet them?" Crystal knew it was a low blow, but she was determined to convince Ben to make a statement about what happened. She had to make this right.

"He was there when they were born," Ben said, staring at the photo. "That's why your mother and I came home that last time. I know you don't remember, but it wasn't a planned leave. We nearly gave your grandmother a heart attack when your mom and I showed up in the middle of the night." A small smile formed on Ben's lips.

"Don't we owe it to them to try to make it right?" She pulled her hand away. The physical contact was to much for her to handle.

Ben sighed. "It's not that simple. I can't change what I've done. I wish I could, I really do, but I can't."

"You told me once that if I see something that I don't think is right, and no one is doing anything about it, then it's up to me to do whatever I can to fix it."

Because he was still leaning down, his elbows on his knees, he looked up at her, something like amazement, or gratitude, on his face. "How do you remember that? You couldn't have been more than five when I told you."

"I remember most of what you told me." Crystal glanced around the office. She needed to give herself some distance.

"You always were too smart for your own good." Ben reached out and tucked a loose strand of hair behind her ear. His fingers lingered on her cheek for a moment before he pulled his hand away.

"I've tried to live my life by those lessons you taught me. I wanted you and mom to be proud of me, of who I've become." Crystal closed her eyes for a second to push the tears back down.

"I am proud of you." She couldn't see his expression, but she thought he might have been as choked up as she was.

"Then don't make me live the rest of my life with this hanging over me," she whispered. "You can't change the past, but at least we can fix some of the damage."

Ben reached up and stroked her cheek again. "All right. I'll make the statement."

Crystal felt as if a burden had been lifted from her heart. "Thank you."

# Chapter 9

Crystal had gotten a decent night's sleep for a change. She felt so emotionally drained by the time she left Ben's office the night before that she barely remembered coming back to the ship, let alone getting into bed. She hadn't even heard Flint leave their quarters, and Crystal was sure Flint hadn't gone out of her way to be quiet. She knew Flint and Grady were in for a long, frustrating day as they questioned people. Part of Crystal envied them. She needed to find something productive to do with her time or she would go crazy.

Her gaze wandered to the pile of blue prints pushed to the corner of the desk. She had been working on collecting data on the ship's bio-skin when they got the distress call. The LAWON scientists she worked with to develop it were hounding her for updated growth rates. Their samples in the lab were starting to show signs of deterioration that wasn't happening on *Journey,* and they were frantic to understand why. Crystal tried to tell them that the simulated ocean they had set up in the lab didn't have right nutritional balance to support long term growth, but they didn't listen. Apparently, she wasn't qualified to provide insight on a product she developed. She had been putting off taking manual growth readings, claiming it wasn't practical to gather data while the ship was moving—honestly, she was enjoying making them wait.

She grabbed her gear and headed toward the gym. The small pool there had the main access port that would allow her to swim off the ship. She made a quick pit stop in the locker room to change into her wetsuit. She was always amazed by how light the suit's material was. It was specifically designed to allow water to flow through it freely so that her Aquinein skin cells could easily pull oxygen out of the water, but it was strong enough to protect her from the force of an underwater explosion.

The gym was busier than normal. She suspected a lot of the crew had been given some extra down time during the Stapleton Farms investigation, and there were only so many places to hang out on the ship. Thankfully, the pool was empty. Crystal walked over to the video terminal next to the pool and called up the bridge. There were strict protocols to follow to exit the ship. "Bridge," Dewite said once his face filled the screen.

"Commander, I'm requesting permission to perform an external survey of the ship's hull." These calls were all logged, so Crystal made sure to keep her request professional.

"Is anyone going with you?" Dewite's face was masked with concern she knew had nothing to do with request. It was why she had been avoiding the bridge the last few days. She couldn't handle the looks of pity she was sure she would receive.

"No, sir." Crystal made sure that her face remained

emotionless.

"How long do you estimate the job will take?"

"No more than five hours." It was well within her range of submersion time.

"Check in at thirty-minute intervals," Dewite said.

"Understood." Crystal ended the call.

She entered the pool slowly. It didn't take long before she started to feel the skin on her legs come to life. She stopped once the water was up to her waist and turned on her wrist computer. Dewite had already sent her the code that would open the hatch and allow her access to the open water. She dove to the bottom of the pool. For a moment, her lungs protested as they fought with her Aquinein skin cells for control. She closed her eyes and concentrated until she felt her skin start to pull oxygen from the water. She swam over to the hatch, keyed in the access code, and left the ship.

She swam in large loops as she allowed the cool ocean water to cleanse her soul. She didn't spend nearly enough time in the water. She always seemed to forget how being submerged, surrounded by it, seemed to heal her. Her mind refocused, and all the anger and sadness that had built up inside of her washed away.

After a few minutes she swam back to the ship. Gathering the growth data the lab wanted would be time consuming and tedious. It took her almost two hours to get all the samples from the port side of the ship. As she moved to the starboard side, Stapleton Farms came into view. The colony had a picturesque quality to it, with its shimmering glass dome surrounded by vast expanses of kelp and other underwater crops. There were two people working in the field closet to her. She was surprised to see one of them wearing a suit that matched her own.

Curiosity got the better of her and she swam closer to

the colony. She watched as they chased each other through the multicolored kelp. It didn't take her long to realize who they were. Crystal had first bonded with Tyler in the ocean; it only made sense he would try the same thing with their new found brother. Crystal wondered if Leo knew he was related to the man swimming with him or if he thought Tyler was just being nice. Tyler hadn't mentioned that he had met Leo, though Crystal wouldn't be surprised if Tyler had sought Leo out. She hesitated. She didn't want to impose. It did look like they were having a lot more fun than she was though. She could always come back out later to finish collecting the samples she needed. She put her tools back in her pocket and swam over to them before her resolve wavered.

She cut across Tyler's path at top speed, forcing him to stop suddenly. Crystal turned around in time to see his shocked look give way to a huge smile. He motioned to Leo to follow him as he took off after her. The three of them wove through the fields in an elaborate game of tag. Crystal couldn't hide her joy, a sentiment she saw echoed on the faces of Tyler and Leo. Their worlds had been ripped apart the last few days, but right now, that didn't matter. All that mattered was the three of them and the water.

Her happiness was short-lived as she came out of one of the fields to see someone working on the colony's life support system. Most maintenance was done on these systems remotely, and if manual work was needed, standard practice was to have at least two people working on the system at a time to reduce any down time. Crystal put her arm out to stop Leo and Tyler as she watched the man remove the door to the control panel. Her eyes locked with Tyler's as she motioned toward the life support system. It took him a second before he turned back to her and nodded.

The computer on Crystal's wrist started to vibrate. She needed to check in with *Journey*. The timing was perfect. She quickly typed out a message to send back to the ship. **Unknown tampering with colony life support. Price and I will detain. Have colony stand by.** She looked at Tyler, who was motioning to Leo to stay out of sight, and signaled for him to come at the saboteur from the left, while she came at him from the right. With a determined look, Tyler took off.

Crystal was proficient at underwater combat, but it was her least favorite fighting style. Speed and precision were her strengths during a fight, both of which were hindered by water resistance. She sized up her opponent as she made her approach. He had at least fifty pounds of muscle on her, but at least he was distracted.

She spun him around by his shoulder and landed a weak punch to his right eye. It barely caused his head to turn. Anger flashed across his face. She had gotten his attention. He lunged toward her, but she was able to swim over him, pulling his head lamp down so that it was covering his eyes. He recovered quickly. He grabbed her ankle and flung her toward the colony. She had barely recovered her equilibrium when he rushed at her and pinned her against the colony's metal frame.

She struggled to free herself, but it was useless. He pulled his arm back to deliver a punch Crystal was sure would knock her out. She braced herself for the impact, but his fist never got the chance to connect. Tyler had managed to overpower him, yanking him away from Crystal.

Tyler attempted to trap the man in between a cross bar, but the two of them were locked in defensive holds.

Crystal removed the dive knife from her ankle and swam over. She came up behind the saboteur, making sure Tyler was aware of what she was about to do. He backed off a little, giving her just enough space to snake her arm around the man's neck. She carefully pressed the blade against his throat.

His body instantly went slack. Crystal motioned toward the man's hands. Tyler nodded and swam off. She applied a little more pressure to the blade. It wouldn't leave a mark, but she hoped it would discourage him from trying anything now that she was on her own. She really didn't want to hurt him.

Tyler returned a few minutes later with Leo. He pulled the man's hands behind his back and secured them with a zip tie. Crystal smirked when she saw the field identification label dangling between the man's hands. Now that Tyler had him under control, Crystal re-strapped her knife to her ankle.

She swam over to Tyler and showed him the message she had typed into her wrist computer. **Take him in. I want to make sure he didn't screw up life support. I'll meet you in the colony when I'm done.** Tyler grabbed the man by the arm and started to lead him to the colony. Leo followed faithfully in their wake.

Crystal watched them for a few minutes to make sure the prisoner didn't try anything, but he swam straight for the hatch. It wasn't behavior she expected from someone who had just been caught trying to compromise the colony.

Desi and Grady had been questioning people all day and were no closer to finding the person who planted the virus. Desi could have handled the failure if it wasn't for Ben. He became smugger after every interview. He was not shy about telling them he didn't think it was possible for the attack to be an inside job.

"There are two more people we need to talk to: Ian McFarland and Shawn Bergen." Desi scanned through the list on her tablet to make sure they hadn't missed anyone. If nothing came from these last two interviews, Desi wasn't sure what she would do. At what point could they throw their hands up in defeat and retreat?

"Ian isn't here. He had to attend to family emergency on the mainland two days before the incident." Ben leaned back casually in his chair. "I am surprised Shawn isn't here yet. He probably just lost track of time."

Desi was about to respond when her communicator went off. She turned her back to Ben to give herself the illusion of privacy before answering it. "This is Flint."

"I've received word from Commander Wolf that someone is tampering with the colony's external life support system." Dewite's voice filled the tiny conference room. Ben jumped out of his chair. He looked as if he wanted to say something, but Desi shot him a warning look. She didn't need his input on this. Her only concern was that Wolf had the situation under control and hadn't taken any unnecessary risks. "She is in the process of detaining them," Dewite continued.

"Does Wolf need backup?" Grady asked over Desi's shoulder. She realized he'd moved to her side while she was staring down Ben.

"Price is with her," Dewite answered.

"We will have a team standing by at the access port. Flint out." Desi turned to Ben. "What access port is closest to the external atmosphere generators?"

"There's a hatch on the south side of the colony near the kelp fields." A concentrated look of determination formed on Ben's face and for a second Desi could have sworn she was looking at Wolf.

"Lead the way." Grady opened the door and ushered Ben out of the room.

Desi pulled out her communicator as they raced through City Hall and out onto the street. "Squad A, report to access hatch, south side of the colony."

The room was empty when they arrived. Desi and Grady pulled out their weapons and trained them on the access hatch. Desi had no idea how long they would have to wait for something to happen. She was anxious for some excitement after their grueling day interrogations.

A beeping sound filled the room, and a second later the hatch swung open. Price pushed someone forward. The rest of Desi's team arrived. She nodded at two of them, who went to collect the prisoner from Price.

"Shawn?" Ben took a step closer, as if that would change the identity of the man before them.

"Guess we know why he was late," Desi said under her breath. "Take him to the jail. We'll be there shortly to question him." One of Desi's men tried to push him forward, but Shawn didn't move.

"You can't throw me in jail. I didn't do anything wrong." He struggled against his captors but it was useless.

"You'll have your chance to talk soon enough." Desi returned her gun to its holster.

"Ben, are you really going to let them do this?" Shawn yelled.

Ben didn't look him in the eye as he stepped aside to let Desi's men take Shawn away. It was only then that he noticed Leo standing in the background. Ben rushed over to him. "Leo, what are you doing here?"

The teenager shrugged. "Tyler was helping me tag the new kelp field when we saw Shawn."

"Where's Wolf?" Grady asked.

"She stayed back to check that the oxygen generator was functional. I'm going to go change." Price walked past them without saying another word. Desi didn't fault him. He was always detached after a fight. He was a good solider, but Desi knew his softer side always took a hit after something like this.

An hour later they assembled in the small police station in the rear section of City Hall. Desi would have let Shawn sweat it out a little longer, but Ben was anxious to confront him. He had already claimed one of the chairs at the table in the interrogation room when she and Price arrived. Desi claimed the chair next to him; this was supposed to be her investigation after all. Price retreated to the corner of the room, tablet in hand. The room was immaculate, and Desi couldn't help but wonder if it had ever actually been used.

Grady brought Shawn in. Desi noticed right away that his hands were no longer secured. She shot a look at Grady, but he clearly didn't think Shawn was much of a threat. Grady did position himself in directly behind Shawn's chair, though.

"You can't hold me like this," Shawn said.

"Yes, I can." Ben's voice was calm. "Why did you do it?"

"I didn't do anything."

"Was the virus meant to be some kind of retaliation for me beating you in the last election? Was this your way of showing that I wasn't a competent leader?"

Desi was irritated that Ben was taking charge of the questions when he was only supposed to be here to observe, but she let it go. There was certainly some history between the two of them that she knew nothing about. For once, she kept her mouth shut, but she was ready to jump in the second she saw an opening.

"I wouldn't need to risk the lives of everyone here to prove you aren't capable of running this colony." Shawn leaned toward Ben in a threatening manner. Grady placed a hand on Shawn's shoulder and guided him back into his chair.

"But you did want to take control of the colony? Why?" Desi asked.

Shawn smirked. "I don't have to tell you anything. I'm not a LAWON citizen. You can't do anything to me." Desi desperately wanted to smack that smirk off of his face.

"I've granted them temporary authority here. Don't make this any harder than it has to be. Just answer the question," Ben said. Shawn remained silent.

"We don't need him to talk." Price stepped out of the corner of the room. "Your real name is Shawn Persselli isn't it?"

Desi watched all the color drain from Shawn's face. "How did you...?"

Price cut him off. "Your grandfather owns Persselli Farm, which hasn't made a profit for the last five years. It looks like most of his buyers now get their crops from Stapleton Farms." Price casually scrolled through his tablet as he talked.

"So that's what this is all about? You were willing to kill eight hundred people in order to save your family's farm," Desi said.

"Yes, I came here with the intention of trying to save Persselli Farm," Shawn admitted, "but I didn't plant that virus." Shawn shifted his focus from Desi to Ben. "I wouldn't hurt anyone. My plan was to take over leadership of the colony so that I could have control over where we sold our crops. That way Persselli Farm could get my grandfather's buyers back."

"Then what were you doing with the atmosphere generators?" Ben demanded. "You're a field supervisor, you don't have the authority to be anywhere near them."

Shawn raised an eyebrow at Ben. "Just because I don't work with engineering here, doesn't mean I don't know how the equipment works. I maintained all the equipment on Persselli Farm before coming here."

Desi leaned forward in her seat. "Then answer the question."

"I was trying to isolate them from the rest of the colony's systems so that if the virus came back, it couldn't take them down again," Shawn said with a sigh.

"Why should we believe anything you say?" Ben spat out. "You lied about who you really are. You lied about why you came to Stapleton Farms. Why wouldn't you lie about this too?" Ben seemed to take Shawn's betrayal personally—and maybe it was. Ben was the one who would have been out of a job had Shawn beat him in the election. Desi couldn't help but wonder how close it had been to make Ben this defensive.

"He's telling the truth." Wolf was standing in the doorway. Desi had no idea how long she had been there. She had to have gone back to the ship to change, though Wolf's hair was still wet.

"There. Now let me go so I can go back out there and finish the job." Shawn started to stand, but Grady put his hand on the man's shoulder again and pushed him back into the chair.

"I already took care of it," Wolf said. "Once Price builds a few decent firewalls into your system, the risk of them going down again will be reduced to almost zero."

Wolf turned and looked at Ben. "I don't know what contractor you got to build this place, but they cut a lot of corners installing those generators."

"What makes you think you are qualified to work on our equipment?" Shawn looked at Wolf with daggers in his eyes. This man's hatred of LAWON ran deep.

Wolf walked toward Shawn. She leaned down so her face was only inches away from him. This wouldn't be good for him. Desi knew Wolf would let most things roll off her back, but no one dared insulted her mechanical knowledge. "Did you happen to see that submarine hovering outside your colony? It's the most technology advanced sub on the planet. And you know who designed and built it? I did. I also happen to be its chief engineer. I think I'm more than qualified to rewire a couple of atmosphere generators." Crystal stared at Shawn for a few seconds before straightening up. "It's your call, but I don't think he's your guy."

"Let him go," Desi said to Grady. Shawn jumped out of his chair and stormed out of the room.

"So what now?" Grady asked.

"I guess we're back to square one." Desi put her head in her hands. "Let's take an hour to regroup, then meet back in the Ward Room." Out of the corner of her eye, she saw Ben follow Wolf out of the room. Desi wished she had the energy to stop him.

# Chapter 10

Crystal made it to the City Hall lobby before she heard Ben calling her. For a second, she considered ignoring him. It would have been easy to keep walking and act like she never heard him. Too bad her feet betrayed her, and she hesitated long enough that it was evident she had heard him. She thought it would be easy to face him after confronting him in his office the night before, but she was wrong. At least then she had gone to see him with a set goal in mind. She could control the situation to ensure that she wouldn't get hurt. That wasn't the case this time.

The soft echo of footsteps on the marble floor grew louder as Ben approached. The steps weren't even though. He wasn't alone. Crystal turned to see Tyler walking toward her with Ben. This was an ambush.

"You left so fast I wasn't sure we would be able to catch you," Ben said with a cheerful smile. Crystal wasn't sure why he was so happy. They had yet to catch the person responsible for trying to destroy his colony, and Crystal had just cleared the only real lead they had.

If anything, he should be pissed, or extremely frustrated at the very least. Crystal was, and she wasn't even directly involved in the investigation anymore. The fact that Tyler was with Ben baffled her even more. She had no way of knowing if this encounter was meant to be professional or personal.

"What can I do for you Mr. Martin?"

Ben's smile faltered. "I understand that you can't call me Dad, but at least call me Ben."

Crystal took a deep breath. "Fine, Ben. What can I do for you?"

"I was hoping you'd join us for an early dinner."

"Us?" Crystal looked from Ben to Tyler and then back again. Tyler merely shrugged his shoulders.

"Every Wednesday I take Leo and Gina to the diner for dinner while Andrea works late in the lab."

Crystal crossed her arms over her chest. "I don't know if that's the best idea."

"Would you give us a minute?" Tyler said to Ben. He grabbed her arm and pulled her a few steps away.

Crystal tugged her arm out of his grasp. "What are you doing?"

"I was going to ask you the same thing."

"I don't know what you're talking about." Crystal scanned the lobby so she could avoid looking Tyler in the face.

"I get that you're still mad at him. Honestly I am, too. But I think it's time you started to give him a chance."

"I have. I went to see him last night." Crystal enjoyed the shocked look on Tyler's face a little more than she should have.

"You did?"

"Yes. So, I've made my peace with him. I've moved on."

"You did all that in one conversation?" Tyler prodded. "I'm not buying it. What did you talk about?"

Crystal sighed. "I had him make an official record of everything that happened." She knew this wasn't the answer Tyler was looking for.

"Crys, that's not making peace with him." Tyler's voice was gentle.

"It's good enough for me." Crystal tried to step around Tyler so she could make her getaway but he moved to block her path.

"Is it good enough for that seven-year-old girl who wanted nothing more than to have dinner with her dad one more time? You finally have the chance, and you're wasting it," Tyler said.

It was a low blow. "He's not the man I thought he was." She knew it was a feeble argument, but it was the best she had.

"No, he's not, but he's still our father. Nothing can change that." Tyler closed his eyes and squeezed the bridge of his nose. "I'm not asking you to forget everything he's done. Just give him a chance to make up for it."

Crystal glanced over Tyler's shoulder where Ben was waiting for them. The lobby had gotten busier while she and Tyler talked. She watched as Ben exchanged pleasantries with everyone as they left for the day. Did they have any idea who he really was? "He doesn't deserve it."

He grabbed her hand and turned her back to face him. "Then do it for you, not him. You'll regret it if you don't. Not right away, but eventually."

Crystal pressed the palms of her hands to her eyes. "Fine."

Tyler clapped his hand on her shoulder. "I'm proud of

you." Tyler walked back to Ben with Crystal following a step behind.

"Can I take this as a sign that you'll be joining us?" Ben asked hopefully.

"I have one question first," Crystal said.

"Anything."

"What do Leo and Gina know about us?" She waved her hand between herself and Tyler. Given that Leo and Tyler had been out swimming together a few hours ago, she assumed Ben had told them something, but that didn't mean he had told them everything.

"Everything," Ben said. "I told my family everything the night of the incident. Leo took it the hardest, but I think things will get easier once he has the chance to get to know you both. Gina's only eight so she doesn't really understand everything I've done, nor should she have to, but she knows who you both are and that I'm your father too." Ben put a hand in his pocket and looked around the lobby. Was he afraid of being overheard?

Crystal took a deep breath. At least she wouldn't have to pretend. "All right, let's go." She followed Ben and Tyler out of City Hall and down the street. The silence between them grew thicker with every step. Crystal searched her mind for something to say to break the tension, but it was blank. Thankfully it wasn't long before they saw Leo and Gina walking toward them.

At the sight of Ben, Gina started to run down the street. Ben took a couple of quick steps to meet her and scooped her up in his arms. Crystal felt her heart twist. She fought the urge to flee.

"I wasn't sure you were going to make it with everything going on," Leo said when he finally reached them. He looked at the three of them, confused.

Ben set Gina back on her feet. "Leo, you've met Tyler

and Crystal," he said to his son—her half-brother. If she was struggling to get her mind around it, she knew it must be hard for Leo, too.

"I don't think we've met officially yet." Crystal held her hand out to Leo.

Leo eagerly shook it. "What you did out there was amazing. I've never seen anyone move like that in the water before. You think you could teach me a few moves?"

"Sure, why not? Though it's easier to learn underwater combat once you've mastered it on land." Crystal felt herself relax. This was safe. It was no different than talking to any overly enthusiastic recruit. It didn't matter that they shared half of their DNA.

"I'm not really sure when you'd ever have the need to know how to fight, let alone underwater." Ben patted Leo on the back.

"It would give me an advantage when I apply to the LAWON Military Academy next year," Leo said.

"I don't know how many times I've told you, you're not going to the Academy." Ben stared at Leo. Crystal had a flashback of being on the other end of that look as child. She did not envy Leo.

"I thought now that everything was out in the open..." Leo's voice trailed off. Crystal shot Tyler a look. It was hard not to feel like they were intruding on a private family matter. She had to remind herself this was her family.

Ben took a deep breath. "We will discuss it tonight." When he turned back to Crystal there was a strained smile on his face. "We should head over to the diner."

Crystal just nodded. What could she say? She felt like the fight had been her fault. Her guilt was starting to take hold when she felt a hand slip into hers. She looked down in shock to see Gina standing next to her.

"I always wanted a big sister," Gina said with a huge smile. Crystal tried to return it, but she wasn't sure how to act. She looked to Tyler for help, but he just seemed amused by the whole situation. Gina didn't let go of Crystal's hand until they entered the diner. Crystal watched as the girl ran over to claim a large circular table in the middle of the restaurant. Crystal scanned the room. It was surprisingly similar to Marco's diner, where she would meet her parents between their missions. She closed her eyes and shook her head slightly. She could get through this.

Crystal wasn't sure what to do with herself. Tyler and Leo were talking animatedly across from her. It seemed they had spent a decent amount of time together over the three days *Journey* had been at Stapleton Farms. How had Crystal missed that information? Ben was helping Gina get settled in next to Crystal. "This place is nice," she said awkwardly. She couldn't stand the tension building up inside of her. She wondered if she was the only one feeling it.

"We're lucky to have it. We didn't have any kind of restaurant the first few years," Ben said.

"They have the best food here," Gina said. She leaned closer to Crystal, whispering, "It's better than Mom's, but don't tell her I said that."

"I won't," Crystal whispered back, a small smile finding its way to her face.

"Speaking of food, how about I go order us some?" Ben got up and went to the counter. Crystal felt more at ease the moment he left.

"How did you guys find each other? Did you grow up together?" Leo looked expectantly between Crystal and Tyler.

So, Ben *had* told them everything, right down to his affair with Tyler's mother. "No, we didn't grow up together," Crystal said.

"I met Crystal when I was sixteen." Tyler paused for a moment when Ben returned to the table. "I had convinced my mom to tell me who my father was before I left for university. Once I had a name, it was easy to track them down. I spent that summer with Crystal and my grandparents."

"It was a great summer." Crystal started to relax. This wasn't too bad. It almost felt normal.

"I'm glad you two had each other," Ben said.

"We did lose touch with each other for a while." Crystal looked down at her hands as if she had been caught sneaking candy before dinner. She wasn't sure where the guilt was coming from. It wasn't like she owed Ben anything.

"But now that we're both on *Journey,* we see each other more than any siblings would want." Tyler for the save. Crystal hoped he could see the appreciation in her eyes. "Not only that, she's my boss." Tyler turned to Leo. "How you feel about having to do everything Gina told you to do?" Gina giggled. Tyler had already won her over.

"Hey, I'm a fair and reasonable commanding officer. You should consider yourself lucky." Crystal thought back to the commander of the combat team she served under on the *Legacy.* He had made it perfectly clear that he didn't like her on day one and had taken every opportunity to remind her of how incompetent he thought she was. He had thought putting her up for LAWON's new anti-terrorism team would be the end of the career. Boy did that blow up in his face.

"If by reasonable you mean having me reprogram

every system on the ship to your exact specification because the standard programs aren't good enough, then sure." Tyler flashed her huge smile.

Crystal grabbed her napkin off the table, balled it up and then threw it at him. Everyone at the table laughed. Crystal glanced over at Ben. He looked so at ease with his arm draped across the back of Gina's chair. Is this how it would have been had she been given the chance to be part of their family? Ben caught Crystal looking at him. She gave him a weak smile.

"Hey Ben, your food's ready," someone behind the counter called.

"Coming!" Ben got up to go get the food.

"I'll help." Gina jumped out of her seat, took Ben's hand, and together they walked up to the counter.

Crystal picked up her drink and took a sip. She wasn't thirsty she just needed something to do. She looked to Tyler for help—he was always good at starting up a conversation—but he was lost in his own thoughts.

Crystal nearly jumped out of her chair when Gina reappeared next to her. "Dad told me to give these to you." She handed Crystal a basket of fries. Crystal felt like the wind had been knocked out of her. She turned in her seat to look at Ben, still holding the fries in her hand.

"They were always your favorite," Ben said with a small smile. Crystal's mom had always given her a hard time about not eating enough vegetables, to the point where she wouldn't let Marco give Crystal any fries at the diner until Crystal had eaten everything green on her plate. Her dad had made a game out of passing her fries under the table whenever her mom wasn't looking.

"I, um…" Crystal said, choking on her words. "We should be getting back to the ship." She set the fries down on the table and got to her feet. She shot Tyler a pleading looking that sent him scrambling to his feet.

"Crystal, I— " Ben called after her.

She turned around. "Thank you for the food." She made a beeline for the door. She could feel the tears starting to build behind her eyes. She wouldn't let the first time she cried in years be in front of Ben.

Desi paced in front of the screen in the Ward Room while Justin, Price, and Grady watched from the table. She had hoped a brilliant idea or a new lead would hit her during the two hours break she had given them, but of course it hadn't. "Anyone have any bright ideas on what we do now?"

"I might actually have something," Price said. Desi noticed he seemed a little distracted since he had returned to the ship with Wolf, so she was surprised he was the first one to speak.

"What is it?" Desi leaned across the table, as if that would make it easier for her to process Price's response.

"I've narrowed down the time frame of when the virus was first introduced to the system to two and a half years ago."

"Whoever planted that virus could be long gone by now." Grady pushed his chair away from the table. Desi was just glad he didn't try to flip it.

"It's possible, though I still think they had to be at the colony to activate it," Price explained. "What I haven't been able to nail down yet is if there was any kind of delay between activating it and when the colony's life support systems started to shut down." It wasn't like Price to struggle with anything even remotely related to computers. Desi wondered if everything happening with Ben was affecting him more than he was letting on. The other possibility was that whoever planted this thing was a better programmer than Price, and that wasn't something Desi wanted to think about.

"So, we're basically back to square one." Desi plopped down in a chair and put her face in her hands. It shouldn't be this hard. "There has to be something we're missing. I mean we are all intelligent people; we should be able to figure this out."

"Intelligent, sure, but that doesn't make us investigators," Grady said.

"Maybe it's time we got the colony's police force involved," Justin offered. "They might have a detective that could help us."

"There's no way they would be impartial. That's why we took over in the first place," Grady said. He got up and took over Desi's place in front of the screen. The longer this whole thing went on, the less time he spent in one position. Desi wondered if he would start running in place if they hadn't made any progress in the next few days.

"What I don't understand is why someone would plant a virus and then wait so long to activate it. What would be the point?" Justin asked.

"I only know what the code tells me and motive isn't in there." Price gestured at the tablet in front of him.

"If we knew what they were after then we wouldn't be where we are now." Desi turned to Grady. "You spent years working undercover gathering intel on terrorist. You must have received some kind of investigative training."

Grady smirked. "I'm pretty sure they gave us a book to read."

"And you never read it, did you?"

"Of course not," he rolled his eyes at her. "That's

what I had Wolf for. I gathered the pieces and she put it all together. That's what made us a great team." Grady waved his hand at the door as if that would make Wolf appear and all their problems would be solved.

Desi hated that it had come down to this. If she thought there was any other possibility she wouldn't say it, but she knew this couldn't go on forever. "We need Wolf, don't we?" Desi looked around the room waiting for someone to contradict her. No one did. "Anyone know where she is?"

"She was pretty shaken up after our almost-meal with Ben," Price said.

Justin moved as if to say something, but Grady beat him to it. "I'll get her. I know where she'll be."

Desi nodded. If anyone was going to be able to convince Crystal to rejoin the mission it would be her old partner.

Crystal sat on the floor outside of *Journey's* engine room. There was rarely anyone in this part of the ship. The engines were monitored remotely from the bridge, and visual inspections were only done in the beginning of a shift. Unless there was an issue with one of the engines, no one would be down here for another three hours. That would give her more than enough time to get her emotions under control.

The noise of the engines was doing a nice job covering up the sounds of her sobs. She rested her head on the crook of her arm as her tears flowed, soaking the sleeve of her uniform. She hadn't cried in so long that once she started, she wasn't able to stop. She had forgotten how cathartic crying could be. She felt herself getting lighter with every drop of water that rolled down her cheek.

"I thought I might find you here." Grady sat down next to her.

Crystal sat up straighter while using the back of her hand to wipe away her tears. "How did you find me?"

"Come on," he said, nudging her with his shoulder, "noisy, secluded, close to heavy machinery—where else would you be?"

"I'll have to come up with a better hiding spot next time." She tried to choke down her tears. It was bad enough that she was crying. She wouldn't do it in front of anyone else. Not even Grady.

"Why are you hiding anyway?"

"Isn't it obvious? I can't let anyone see me like this." There had to be a way to make the crying stop.

Grady pulled a pack of tissues out of his pocket and tossed them to her. Crystal gave him a sideways look. "Just in case," he said with a shrug of his shoulders. They sat in silence for a few minutes while Crystal attempted to regain her composure. "You know," Grady finally said, staring at the wall in front of them, "I've seen you covered in blood—yours and others—get the shit kicked out of you more times than I can count, and literally inches away from death, but I don't think I've ever seen you cry."

"The last time I cried, I was still at the Academy." Crystal wiped the last few tears from her cheeks.

"When your grandparents died?"

Crystal didn't answer. She wasn't sure why. It's not like he didn't know about her history with Ryan, but confessing that breaking off their relationship had broken her down so completely seemed like a bad idea. She didn't want anyone thinking she still had some lingering feelings for him.

"It doesn't make you weak you know. There's no

shame in crying." It was like Grady was inside her head. She shouldn't be surprised after everything they had been through over the years. There were times when she was sure Grady knew her better than she knew herself. He gently grabbed her chin and turned her face so that she had to look him straight in the eye. "You are the strongest person I know."

Crystal pulled away. "I don't feel very strong at the moment. Look at me. I'm just like him. A coward."

"Crystal."

"I ran away, just like he did. From the mission, my team, everything I believe in. I couldn't even make it through one meal with him." She absentmindedly played with the pack of tissues in her hand.

"You just need some time to regroup," Grady said. "There's nothing wrong with that. No one blames you." He chuckled. "I know this is a new experience for you, but everyone falls apart sometimes. It makes the rest of us mere mortals feel more comfortable in your presence."

Crystal let a small laugh escape.

"And I know once you get this out of your system, you're going to pick yourself up, dust yourself off, and get back to work," Grady said.

"How can you be so sure? I mean, look at where I come from. If Ben can walk away from everything without looking back, how do you know I won't do the same thing? He's part of me."

"Maybe," Grady admitted, "but he's not you."

She put her face in her hands. "I don't even know who I am anymore."

"Then let me remind you." He moved to take her hands so she couldn't hide while he looked at her, and she let him. "You're the commanding officer who would stay up all night going over attack plans while the rest of your team was out living it up. You are the person who would sacrifice everything to protect the people you care about without a second thought. You love the military and everything that comes with it. I mean, look around you. You designed and built this ship. None of this would be here without you."

Crystal sighed as Grady released her hands, but she didn't turn away. "I'm only those things because of who my parents are. They are the reason I joined the military in the first place."

"But they aren't the reason you stayed." Grady looked over at the other side of the engine room, almost embarrassed. "For what it's worth I don't think your father is a coward either."

"How can you say that? I thought I was going to have to wrestle your sidearm away from you to keep you from shooting Ben in the Ward Room the other day." Crystal couldn't help but smirk.

Grady held his hands up in defense. "Don't get me wrong, I hate the guy for what he's doing to you. Just say the word and I'll gladly take him out. But you can't deny everything he did during the war. He dedicated a large part of his life to the war effort, led countless missions in enemy territory, saved countless lives. There's still some hero in him even if he made the wrong decision in the end."

Crystal shook her head. "It doesn't cancel out everything he did after the war."

"No, but maybe it makes it a little easier to forgive him." Grady rose to his feet and held his hand out to her. "Now get up. We have a job to do."

Crystal kept her hands firmly in her lap. "I pulled myself off the mission remember."

"We've hit a wall with the investigation. We need your help."

"Desi sent you to get me, didn't she?" And here Crystal thought he had come to find her purely out of the goodness of his heart. Imagine, he had the nerve to call himself her best friend. Despite the ulterior motive, Crystal couldn't keep the smile off of her face.

"I listened first, didn't I?"

"All right, let's get to work." Crystal grabbed his hand and let Grady pull her to her feet. He was right after all; the military was where she belonged. She had always known it in her heart. She would set her feelings aside and get the job done. She was done hiding. Her team needed her; she wouldn't let them down again.

# Chapter 11

During the walk from the engine room to the Ward Room, Crystal had Grady get her up to speed on what they had found out so far. He ran down everything just like he used to when they worked counterterrorism together, quickly going over the highlights while including as much detail as possible, in case it meant something he hadn't picked up on. By the time they reached their destination, Crystal felt like she had been part of the investigation since the beginning.

She held her head high as she entered the Ward Room. She was a good soldier, and she would do her job. This was where she belonged. She smiled at the sight of Flint pacing in front of the room while Justin and Tyler worked computers at the table. That smile faltered when she realized Ben was sitting on the other side of the room. She glared at Grady—he should have warned her—but her anger dissipated as Grady held up both hands. He clearly hadn't known Ben would be here. Things must really be desperate for Ben to be here this late into the evening. He should be at home tucking Gina into bed.

Ben started to make his way over to her. "Crystal about what happened at the diner..."

Crystal held up a hand to stop him. "Forget about it. We're fine. Let's focus on what we have to do." She took a seat next to Justin. "Grady has gotten me up to speed on everything that you've uncovered so far. It's a good start."

"But we're no closer than we were three days ago." Desi plopped down in a chair at the front of the room.

"Give yourselves some credit. You've cleared the most likely suspects, and you've narrowed down the window of when the virus was planted. It's a great start." Crystal tried to sound encouraging. It was her fault that Flint was leading the investigation in the first place.

"When was it planted?" Ben leaned across the table, eager for this new piece of information. He had been involved in the investigation from the start, and yet Crystal still knew more than he did. She liked having the upper hand for a change.

"Two and a half years ago," Flint answered.

"That's not possible. We would have picked it up on our scans," Ben said.

Tyler drummed his fingers on the table, annoyed. "Your scans probably only look for system failures," he said, "and until three days ago, there were none. The virus has been running quietly in the background, copying and transmitting data. That is until someone triggered it to start attacking the life support systems." Tyler spoke as if he was explaining things to a child. Apparently, Tyler's acceptance of Ben didn't extend to the questioning of his computer skills.

"Sending data to where?" Justin asked.

"I haven't been able to pinpoint the final destination yet. The signals bounce all over the planet." Tyler waved a hand at his computer.

"So, what do we do now?" Flint turned to look at Crystal as if she would know the name of the saboteur off the top of her head.

Crystal just smiled. "You know what you need to do, you just don't want to admit it."

"We have to look at every single person at the colony again don't we?" Flint put her head down on the table in defeat. Tyler's fingers moved across his keyboard. A moment later, the screen at the front of the room filled with tiny pictures of every citizen of Stapleton Farms.

"I think we should be able to narrow it down a little." Crystal got up from the table and walked to the screen at the front of the room. "The program has been in place for two and half years, so it's safe to assume that anyone who has been at the colony less than that can be ruled out."

"No problem." The only sound in the room were the keys clicking on the keyboard. Pictures disappeared from the screen. "That leaves us with 632 people."

"It's a start." Grady shifted in his chair to find a more comfortable position.

"We can do better than that." Crystal turned to study the screen.

"The coding on this virus is some of the most complex I've ever seen. It had to have been written by a professional—unless you have some kind of computer genius living here." Tyler looked at Ben from over the top of his computer.

Ben looked around the room, as if he was confused why anyone was asking him questions. "There's a computer club at the school, but as far as I'm aware, they only learn basic programing."

"Let's take anyone under the age of sixteen off the board, except for the kids in the computer club and their teacher." Crystal watched as more faces disappeared.

"You really think it could be one of the kids in the club? I just told you they only know basic stuff," Ben said.

"Have you ever actually attended the meetings to know what is being discussed in there?" Grady didn't break eye contact with Ben as he spoke.

"Well, no."

"Then there's the possibility they could have skills you aren't aware of." Grady leaned back in his chair with a smug look on his face.

"Who else can we eliminate?" Crystal asked trying to keep everyone on track.

"Is there any kind of security in the area? You can't let just anyone into the server room, right?" Justin asked.

Once again, all eyes turned to Ben. Crystal didn't really need Ben to give an answer. She already knew their security was terrible. She had spent at least an hour roaming the building without anyone noticing before heading to Ben's office to get his statement recorded.

"Access to City Hall is technically restricted to colony officials," Ben said.

"Technically?" Flint raised an eyebrow at him. Crystal didn't like where this was going.

"Well, it's not uncommon for family members or significant others to drop by with lunch or something like that." Ben's words tumbled out of his mouth. Crystal just shook her head and turned away. She expected so much more from him.

Flint looked like she wanted to grab Ben by his collar and shake answers out of him. "All right, so people can get into the building, but there's additional security on the server room, right?" Was it just Flint being Flint, or had Ben driven her to the breaking point over the last few days? Either way, it was probably good they had brought Crystal back in. Maybe she could diffuse some of the aggravation built up between them.

"There's no security on the server room itself." Ben looked down at the table as he talked.

"You can't be serious!" Tyler nearly jumped out of his chair. "Everything in the colony runs off of the servers in that room."

"You have to understand, we're a small colony. A lot of us have been there since Stapleton Farms was built. We trust each other." Ben looked to Crystal for support, but she couldn't give him any. His training should have taught him that you can't trust anyone. It was careless not to do more to protect his people.

"How's that been working out for you?" Flint waved a hand at Ben.

Crystal chose to ignore Flint's comment. "Narrow the group down to anyone who works in City Hall, their relatives, and any close connections you can find." She tapped her lip, thinking. "See if you can access the visitor log for around the time the virus was planted and make sure any visitors are all on our list, too." Crystal sighed. It's wasn't a great solution, but it was the best she could do for now. She knew it was entirely possible for the person who planted the virus to have no connection to anyone at City Hall, but they had to start somewhere.

Tyler worked at his computer for a few minutes while they waited. Slowly, faces started to disappear from the screen. "That leaves us with 189 people." Tyler leaned back in chair and ran a hand through his hair.

"What do we do now?" Justin asked.

"We go through them one by one until we figure out who planted the virus." Crystal took a seat next to Flint. This was going to take a while.

Tyler brought up the citizens files one at a time. Crystal and Grady profiled them the best they could with the limited information they had. Ben gave them some background information on each, but none of it was really helpful. He was spending more time defending the person than giving them any actual information. Crystal guessed he was having a hard time accepting that one of his citizens had sabotaged the colony. She wondered how he liked the sense of betrayal he had to be feeling. Even if it paled in comparison to her own.

All the faces on the screen blurred together. Crystal was only half listening to what Ben was saying. She probably should suggest they take a break. She was about to say something when the picture on the screen changed.

Crystal looked carefully at the man's face. Something about him was so familiar. "Who is he?"

"That's Ian McFarland. He's basically my right-hand man. He helps me run all the day to day operations of the colony, as well as manages all our disruption contracts." Ben's voice sounded robotic at this point.

"How long has he been at the colony?" Crystal got to her feet walked to the screen so she could study the man's face.

"About three years, I think."

Something clicked in Crystal's brain. Three years was exactly how long Ryan had been out of the public eye before his appearance at Soupionia a month ago. If she was right, then they were in a lot more trouble than any of them had imagined. Was it possible that the blond, brown eyed man on the screen was him? Her gut screamed at her, even as her mind struggled to process it.

"What is it? What do you see?" Grady came and stood next to her.

The longer she looked at the picture, the more positive she was. She just had to make the rest of them see it. "Price, how good are you at photo manipulation?" She couldn't tear her eyes from the screen. The curve of the face, the shape of the eyes, even the small scar on his temple. It had to be him.

"Just tell me what you need."

"Make his hair brown and get rid of the pony tail." Crystal could feel everyone watching her as Tyler worked on the picture. Out of the corner of her eye she saw Grady's mouth open slightly. He knew where she was going with this. "Give him a military haircut and lose the facial hair."

"Done," Price said.

The picture morphed again. There was no second guessing now; the picture was clear as day. Crystal glanced around the room and was surprised to see the looks of confusion. Grady was the only who seemed to recognize the man in the picture. He had his hand covering his mouth in shock. Crystal didn't understand how the others didn't see it.

"Remove the glasses and turn his eyes green," she said.

"How green?"

"A hundred percent Sertex green." If they didn't see it now, there was no hope for them.

Flint planted her hands on the table and pushed herself out of her chair. "You've got to be kidding me." It was about time.

"I think we found the person who planted the virus." Crystal sat down again. This mission just kept getting better and better.

"Who do you think that is?" Ben got up and moved closer to the screen.

"Ryan Young. He's a general in the Teria military. He reports directly to President Rank." Grady looked at Crystal with wide eyes. She simply shrugged her shoulders. What else could she do? At least now she understood how LAWON's intelligence hadn't been able to provide any information on Ryan for the last three years. Who in their right mind would have thought he was working undercover at a farming colony?

"That's not possible," Ben protested. "You could make anyone look like that with enough computer manipulation. Ian would never do anything to harm this colony. Sometimes I think he's more invested in its success than I am." Ben's eyes darted between them.

"Of course he is. He can't go handing Rank a failing colony after all," Flint said.

"There's a simple way to solve this, let me talk to him. Have you questioned him?" Crystal turned to Flint.

"We tried but he's not here."

"What do you mean?"

"He was called away for a family emergency a few days ago," Ben said.

"That's convenient. I guess you're just going to have to take my word for it." Crystal stared Ben down. She knew her word was more than enough for others in the room, but she had a feeling it wouldn't be enough for him.

"I'm sorry Crystal, but I can't condemn him without proof, and a photograph you manipulated isn't proof."

"Then we'll search his house." Flint stood up. "Go

grab what you need and meet in the launch bay in five minutes."

Ben clearly wasn't happy about it, but he took them to Ryan's house. He kept muttering about invasion of privacy, but everyone ignored him. Crystal was glad to be part of the team again. The last few days had rattled her confidence. She needed to prove to herself that she could still do this. Taking Ryan down would be the perfect way to accomplish that.

"Ian's apartment is the last one on the left." Ben pointed down the hallway.

"Why is the door open?" Crystal exchanged a look with Flint. They pulled out their guns at the same time.

Crystal and Flint positioned themselves on either side of the door. She waited for Flint's nod before kicking the door open the rest of the way. They trained their guns on opposite sides of the room. It took a moment for Crystal to register what she was seeing. Leo was standing in the corner of the room with his hands up. A watering can lay on the ground, its contents spilling all over his shoes.

"All clear," Flint called, putting her weapon away.

"Leo what are you doing here? We could have shot you." Crystal's voice was harsher than she intended. How was he to know they were going to burst in with weapons drawn?

"Ian asked me to water his plants while he was gone. Dad, what's going on?" Leo looked past Crystal. She could hear the tremble in his voice as he spoke.

Crystal returned her gun to its holster. "Ian's not who you think he is."

"We don't know that." Ben moved between Crystal and Leo.

"I do." Crystal turned and walked to the other side of the room. She didn't have the energy to go through this with Ben again. He wanted proof, and she was certain she would find it.

Ben chased after her. "I'd appreciate it if you didn't say things like that to Leo. He looks up to Ian."

"Trust me, the sooner he finds out who Ian really is the better. If you don't want him involved, send him home," Crystal said with a shrug of her shoulders.

"Everyone spread out and start searching," Flint ordered. "Look for anything that proves Ian McFarland is or isn't who he says he is." They all split up. Crystal saw Ben ushering Leo out of the apartment as she made her way to the bedroom. Justin picked up the watering can, something Crystal never would have thought to do.

It was strange being in a place Ryan called home. She could feel his presence all around her, from the way he folded back the top blanket on his bed to how he arranged his clothes in his closet. Of course, none of that would prove that Ian was really Ryan. She quickly searched through the drawers, but wasn't surprised when she came up empty handed. She headed to the attached bathroom. In the back of the cupboard under the sink she found a box of hair nets and bobby pins. It was a start, but not enough to prove anything.

She went back to the bedroom. She had to think like Ryan. He wouldn't leave anything incriminating out where anyone might stumble upon it. In fact, there was a very real possibility he didn't have anything personal in the apartment that would link him to his actual identity. She dashed the thought from her mind. She couldn't go there yet. Ryan had always had a sentimental side. He wouldn't be able to go three years without at least some kind of token reminder of who he really was.

Crystal sat down on the bed and heard a soft thud as the mattress pushed against the wall. The sound had a solid quality to it, not what you would expect to hear from a mattress. Crystal jumped up and moved to the head of the bed. A small black box was wedged between the bed and the wall.

She pushed the bed out of the way so that she could easily retrieve the box. She dumped the contents out without a second thought. Her heart plunged into her stomach. With a shaking hand she spread the items out. Every one of them was related to her. A keychain she had given him a few months after they started dating, a placemat from Marco's diner with a submarine design she had scribbled on the back, tickets to every show they had seen together, even the boutonnieres from every formal they had gone to at the Academy. She hesitated before picking up a folded piece of paper. She carefully opened it to see it was a picture of the two of them. The same picture she had hidden behind a framed picture of her and Reed back in her quarters.

Why had Ryan kept all of this? It didn't make any sense. He had made it very clear that he had moved on. That his feeling for her were gone. He had chosen a life that would never have allowed the two of them to be together. And yet, he had brought a box full of mementos of their relationship with him on an undercover mission. She threw the items back into the box. It didn't matter why he had it. It was the proof she needed, and that was all she cared about.

She walked back to the living room and thrust the box at Ben. "How's this for proof?" She turned away as everyone crowded around to see what she had given Ben.

"I don't understand." Ben looked from the picture in

his hand to Crystal.

She turned back to face him. "I gave Ryan everything in that box. He is who I said he was."

"When is he supposed to be back?" Flint asked.

"I don't know. He said he was still taking care of things when I spoke to him this morning." Ben put the photo back in the box.

"Did you happen to mentioned that we were here?" Grady asked.

"Yes."

"He isn't going to come back until he is certain we're gone," Crystal said.

"How can you be sure he will come back?" Justin asked. Crystal didn't want to see his expression. She couldn't help but feel like she had hurt him by finding that box. Justin was fully aware of her past with Ryan, but she didn't need to remind him of it. She didn't want to be reminded of it, either.

"He has to," she said. She had to focus on the mission. "There's a reason Rank has had him here for the last three year. He won't stop until he gets it."

"So what do we do?" Tyler asked.

"We lay a trap," Flint said.

# Chapter 12

Desi had been up most of the night trying to come up with a plan that would convince Young to return to the colony. What she had come up with seemed weak if she thought about it too hard. Still, she had never been one to overanalyze things, so bright and early she took a small team to Stapleton Farms and sent *Journey* away. The only thing she was really sure of was that Young wouldn't dare return to the colony with *Journey* still in the area.

Desi headed directly to Ben's office, taking only Wolf with her. If anyone would know how to trick Young into returning to Stapleton Farms it would be her. Desi hesitated outside the office. If Wolf hadn't been there, she would have barged in, but she was sure Wolf wouldn't approve. So instead she knocked, a little more aggressively than was entirely necessary. Desi could feel Wolf's eyes on her, but thankfully Ben opened the door before Wolf had a chance to scold her. It was the first time Desi had been happy to see him.

Wolf led the way into the office and took a seat on one

of the couches. Desi noticed that Wolf seemed to know her way around. Were Wolf and Ben on better terms than Desi realized? She knew they had spoken a few times, but Desi wasn't aware that there had been any kind of reconciliation. Then again, it could just be Wolf's uncanny ability to keep all emotions buried deep inside.

"I've sent *Journey* away." Desi took a seat next to Wolf. "In a few hours she'll be on the other side of the ocean. Hopefully it will be far enough to make Young think we've really left. Now we just need to come up with a good cover story to get him back here."

"I thought I'd tell him I sent you away because you accused me of planting the virus. Doesn't seem too far-fetched, does it?" Ben looked pointedly at Desi.

"I guess that could work." Desi shifted uncomfortably in her seat.

"How much detail have you given him about the investigation?" Wolf asked.

"It's been mostly high-level stuff. A basic run down at the end of the day," said Ben.

"Have you given him names?"

"I might have mentioned Flint and Grady, but no one else."

Wolf was silent for a moment. Desi assumed she was running through every possible situation in her mind to determine how they should move forward. Was it really a big deal if Ben had told Young their names? He knew *Journey* was here; wasn't that enough even without giving Young names?

"We have to assume that Young knows who you really are," Wolf turned to face Ben. Desi noticed the muscles in her shoulders tensed as she did. "He'll want to know if you've met me and if I uncovered your true identity. I'm surprised he hasn't tried to bring it up, honestly."

"I assumed that might be the case given the two of you have a history, but there's no way I could have met you, because you were never here." Ben looked a little too proud of himself for Desi's liking.

"What do you mean?" she demanded. "Young's never going to buy that Wolf stayed on the ship the whole time." Desi rolled her eyes.

"This has been playing on every news station on the planet all morning." Ben picked up a remote and pointed it at the screen in front of them.

A breaking news alert came on the screen, replaced a moment later by a newscaster with a very serious face. "A creditable source from within the LAWON military hospital claims that Lieutenant Commander Crystal Wolf, daughter of war heroes Kendra and Jedidiah Wolf, was hospitalized ten days ago after being evacuated from her ship. Contacts at the hospital are reporting that her condition is critical. We are going to take you now to the hospital where the Dr. Dean Garza, the Chief of Medicine is about to make a statement."

The imagine on the screen changed, and now they were looking at a shot of a man in a lab coat standing at a podium. Desi was more annoyed by the second. The plan was brilliant, and she hated that Ben had been the one to come up with it—and that he'd put it into action without consulting them. She glanced over to Wolf, whose stone-faced façade was cracking to reveal the hint of a smile.

"Ladies and gentleman," Dr. Garza started. "I cannot go into details on Commander Wolf's case, but I can confirm that she is being treated here. While she is not out of the woods yet, I am hopeful that she will make a full recovery in time."

"Why was she evacuated from the ship?" one of the reporters in the crowd called.

"The medical team aboard *Journey* is not equipped to handle the long-term treatment Commander Wolf requires," the Chief of Medicine said calmly. "The decision was made with the best interest of Commander Wolf and the rest of the crew on the ship in mind."

"How is LAWON addressing the security leak that made this information public?" another reporter asked.

"We are investigating the leak and will take appropriate action when we find the person responsible." Desi was impressed that he never sounded like he was reading off a script, never gave any hint that he was lying. "However at this time we do not believe there is any security risk to the hospital or the patients." Ben clicked the remote again and the screen faded to black.

"How did you manage to pull that off?" Wolf asked.

"I served with Dean during the war. I had Tyler call him to cash in a few favors he owed me." Ben looked awfully proud of himself.

"Do you think Young will buy it?" Desi turned to Wolf. She wanted so badly to find fault in Ben's plan. Anything to wipe that smug look off of his face and restore her sense of authority over the situation.

Wolf didn't say anything. Desi could almost see the gears turning in her head. "I suppose it's possible that Teria could have spies at the hospital, but it seems unlikely. I'd say there's a good chance Young will buy the story."

"I guess the only thing to do now is call him." Desi rose to her feet and put her hands on her hips. "You're sure you know what you need to say?"

"I think I just proved that I can tell a believable story."

Ben got up so that he was once again at eye level with her.

"I forgot you're an expert liar." Desi felt her blood starting to boil. She needed to get the upper hand back. Ben had gotten far too cocky now that Wolf was back on the mission. Like he was showing off for her.

"Would you two knock it off so we can get this over with?" Wolf got up and walked over to the other side of the room. Maybe she wasn't handling things as well as Desi thought. She had never seen Wolf snap at anyone like that before.

"Make the call," Desi said.

Ben went and sat at his desk. Wolf and Desi stood on the other side so that Young wouldn't be able to see them on the video monitor. It was a shame they wouldn't be able to see what was happening on the screen. Desi still didn't trust Ben completely and would have liked to see both sides of the conversation.

Ben hit a button on the screen and it started to hum. Go figure he'd have one of the most dangerous people on the planet on speed dial. It felt like it took forever before the call finally connected.

"Ben, is everything alright? I didn't expect to hear from you until tonight." The fake panic in Young's voice made Desi want to throw up. She desperately wanted to call him out, but knew the success of the mission depended on her keeping her mouth shut, which she had never been all that good at. She looked over at Wolf. Her face had turned to stone. Desi knew hearing Young's voice had to affect her, but nothing escaped to the surface. She would have to get Wolf to teach her how to do that.

"No, not really." Ben's looked directly at the camera. One stray glance toward Desi or Wolf and they would be done for. She hoped Ben was as good as he claimed to be.

"What happened?" Young asked in that same, worried tone. "Was there another attack on the colony's systems?"

"No, nothing like that," Ben assured him. The anger in his expression was so real, Desi almost believed it herself. "But those stupid LAWON officers tried to frame me for the whole thing. You were right—they were only after the colony. They didn't care about helping us. I kicked them out this morning," Ben said. Desi balled her hands into fists, her real anger matching the lie of the jackass before her.

"I tried to warn you. I'm just glad you got them out of there before things really got out of hand." Desi could picture the smug look on Young's face.

"You were right," Ben said with an utterly believable sigh, looking down at his lap. "I don't know what I was thinking allowing them access to our systems. There's no telling what information they could have stolen from us. I was just so overwhelmed by everything that happened that I let them get in my head." He looked back up, directly at the camera. "That's why I need you to come home. I know you're in the middle of dealing with some family issues, but I need someone I can trust to help me get things back in control." Ben spoke with such conviction, it made Desi even more nervous about trusting him. She glanced over at Wolf to see if she shared any of her concern, but Wolf's face remained unchanged.

"I have a few things I really need to wrap up here first, but I can start heading back tomorrow morning," Young said.

"Thank you, Ian, I don't know what I'd do without

you."

"We'll figure this out together, don't worry." The line went dead.

Crystal left Ben's office the second the call with Ryan ended. She hadn't expected to be affected by the call, but the way he spoke to Ben, as if they were old friends, had been too much for her. She guessed in a way they were. Ryan certainly knew Ben better than she did, and that fact sliced through her heart.

Ben had set the LAWON team up in a temporary housing unit normally reserved for seasonal help. Crystal figured it would be the best place to hide out until she got her emotions back in check. She had been pacing the small bedroom for five minutes before she noticed Grady leaning against the door frame. "Get changed. The school has a pretty decent gym. I convinced them to let us use it. Someone is setting mats out for us as we speak."

"You want to spar? Now?" Crystal stopped pacing and looked at him with her mouth slightly opened.

"Yeah."

"You hate sparring, especially with me." Crystal had lost track of the number of times she had begged Grady to practice hand-to-hand combat with her during their time working counterterrorism. Everyone on that team was a decent fighter, but they all held back slightly when sparring with her. Grady was the only one she could count on to consistently put up a good fight.

"Yeah, well, my commanding officer is a real hard ass about mandatory PT and she's really been on edge lately. I don't want her to think I've been slacking and finally snap."

Crystal cocked a smile. "Sounds like your commanding officer really knows what she's talking about."

"Meet me outside in five minutes?" He raised his eyebrows and she nodded. Crystal quickly changed, excitement building in her as she did. When she got outside Grady was stretching.

"Ready?" He stopped stretching as soon as he saw here.

"Here?" She glanced around her. Hadn't he said something about mats? He flashed her a wicked grin and took off toward the center of town. It didn't take Crystal long to catch up with him. He maintained a steady pace that was just fast enough to force her to focus on her breathing. They did a quick loop through the town center before leading her to a side door at the school.

"I thought you said they were letting us use the gym?" Crystal bounced on the balls of her feet. She wasn't about to let her muscles go cold and give Grady an advantage once they hit the mats.

"Don't worry, I have connections." Grady knocked on the metal door.

"Of course you do." She rolled her eyes and started to stretch out her arms and legs. She nearly tripped when Leo opened the door a few seconds later. She had fully expected Grady to have charmed some young teacher into letting them into the gym. "This is your connection?"

"We've chatted a few times while I've been here," Grady explained. "I did promise to let him watch though."

Crystal shook her head at the sheepish look Leo gave her and entered the gym. There was a blue square of wrestling mats laid out in the middle of floor. Crystal headed for it and finished stretching while she waited for Grady to join her.

"I hope that's enough. I didn't know how much space you needed." Leo shifted from one foot to the other as he talked.

"It's perfect, thank you." She gave him a warm smile. She really hadn't done much to get to know him, and she felt bad for that. She made a vow to try harder to spend some time with him before they left.

Grady was milling around over by the stands. "What's the hold up, old man?" she called.

"That evil smile on your face is giving me second thoughts."

"Come on. It'll be fun!" Crystal threw a few punches into the air. "This was your idea after all."

Grady sighed and joined her on the mat. He didn't hesitate, throwing the first punch the second his feet were planted. Crystal was caught off guard, but not enough to let the hit get through. She was too slow to grab his arm, so instead she lunged at his mid-section. He grabbed her and threw her to the ground. She didn't stay down long. He jumped over her attempt to sweep his legs, but wasn't prepared for the punches she threw at his stomach. Another few moves and she took him down.

They went round after round, only giving each other a few seconds to catch their breath in-between. Grady was on point today. He was taking her down faster and more often than normal. Crystal wasn't sure if he had actually gotten that much better, or if her mind was still distracted. She tried to focus all her attention on what she was doing. After a half hour of intense sparring, Grady called for a rest.

Crystal grabbed one of the water bottles Leo had set

out for them. The kid had gone all out. She took a long sip before turning toward the bleachers. Leo was on the edge of his seat, even now when they were taking a break. She waved him over as she caught her breath.

"That was incredible," he said once he reached them.

"You want to learn a couple of moves?" Crystal took one last swig from the water bottle before putting it back on the floor.

"I'm not sure dad would like you teaching me how to fight," Leo said, with only a hint of complaint in his voice. Good kid. "You heard him yesterday. He doesn't want me to have anything to do with the military."

"He's not here though, is he?" Crystal pointed out, enticing. Apparently she was now the kind of big sister who would lead a kid brother astray. What would Tyler say about that? "Come on. Everyone should know how to defend themselves, military or not." Crystal put her hand on his shoulder and led him to the center of the mat where Grady was waiting. "Let's start with a few basic punches." Crystal nodded to Grady, who held up his hands as targets while Crystal coached Leo on the proper way to throw a punch. Once he had the basics down, she moved on to a couple of combinations. He picked it up fast.

They were just about to try a couple of kicks when Grady's watch buzzed. "Sorry, I have to get back. Flint has me on watch duty for the next few hours."

"Excuses, excuses. You just want to get out of here before I put you back on the mat," Crystal teased.

"Don't let her fool you, I could take her." Grady tapped Leo on the shoulder and took off running.

"Coward," she called after him. Crystal tried not to read into the fact that Flint hadn't put her on the rotation to guard the colony's launch bay. It was probably just on the off-chance Ryan decided to come back early; Flint wouldn't want Crystal to be recognized.

Crystal took Grady's place so Leo could keep working on his punches. "So, how are you doing with everything?"

Leo punched her hands a few more times before walking over to sit on the bleachers again. "It's a lot to process." He grabbed a bottle of water and looked at his shoes while he talked.

Crystal sat down next to him. "You're telling me. Honestly, I think you're handling it better than I am."

"I can't believe he's been lying to me my whole life!" he said, that steel she'd seen on the first day, when he tried to refuse to leave his father's side, underlying the words. "And my mom. She's trying to be understanding and everything, but she doesn't even know the man she married. She told Gina and me that it doesn't change anything, that they both love us and that's all that really matters."

"You don't agree?" Crystal envied his openness. Maybe if she could talk about her feelings, she wouldn't feel like one wrong comment could break her completely.

"I don't really know what I think," Leo said, his hands squeezing the water bottle. "He's just going on like nothing has changed. Like he hasn't been pretending to be someone he's not his whole life. What kind of person does that?"

Crystal picked up a bottle of water, too, and drank deeply while she figured out what to say. "Leo, he's still your dad," she said finally. "He's still the same man you've known your entire life, just now you know that he used to go by a different name. That doesn't change the type of person he is. He made some bad choices, got himself in too deep. But that doesn't mean he's a bad person." Crystal was surprised at how easy is was for her to defend Ben, and even more surprised that, on some level, she was starting to believe what she was saying.

"I feel like I stole him from you." Leo finally looked up from the floor. The tears forming in his eyes were a kick to her gut.

"None of this is your fault." As uncomfortable as it made her, Crystal looked him directly in the eyes. He needed to know that she didn't blame him for any of this. "You didn't keep him from coming back for me. He made that choice on his own. It wasn't like he was around that much anyway. Neither was my mom for that matter. They were always gone on some mission or another, trying to make the planet a better place."

"Is that why you joined the military? Did you want to be like them?" Leo wiped his eyes on the back of his hand. He didn't seem embarrassed by his tears at all.

"Partly," Crystal confessed. "I was desperate to find a place where I could belong, a family. The military gave that to me."

"I know Dad wants me to stay here and help him manage the farms, but it's not something I'm passionate about, you know? Being in the military, fighting to keep people safe—that sounds a lot more exciting than planning out harvest cycles."

Crystal laughed a moment in agreement. She couldn't really picture staying home to plan harvest cycles, either. But she didn't want him to be a starry-eyed recruit. "Don't get me wrong, Leo, I love the military, but it's not an easy life. You have to sacrifice a lot. It changes who you are as a person, and not always for the better. And sure, there are moments that are exciting, when you successfully complete a mission and get to play the hero, but those moments aren't as common as you'd think."

They sat in silence. Crystal tried to imagine what her life would have been like if she had grown up on Stapleton Farms. She would have loved her stepmother and siblings. She had always wanted to be part of a big family. Her childhood had been a lonely one. She could almost see herself tinkering with farming equipment as she helped her father run the colony. Would she have been drawn to the military if she had grown up here? She had always felt the urge to follow in her parents' footsteps, but would that desire to serve her country still be there if he had come back for her?

"I should be getting home." Leo rose to his feet. "I don't want my mom to worry."

"Sure thing." Crystal got up and followed him out of the gym, grabbing the empty water bottles while he snagged the ones they hadn't used.

"Thanks for today," he said as he locked the door. "I really enjoyed it."

"It was fun." Crystal dumped the bottles in the recycling bin just outside and leaned against the wall. Leo was a good kid. "Maybe we can do it again before I leave."

"Yeah, ok." Leo turned and started to walk toward his house. After a few steps he turned back to her. "You should come by the house for dinner tonight. I know my mom won't mind. She always makes enough food to feed ten people. Bring Tyler with you."

Crystal hesitated. "I don't know Leo. I'm not sure that's the best idea."

"Just think about it, ok?"

"I will." Crystal watched Leo walk away, then turned to head toward the temporary housing unit to be with the rest of her team.

# Chapter 13

Crystal rubbed a towel over her hair to remove as much excess water as possible before pulling it back in a messy ponytail. She was still trying to decide if she wanted to take Leo up on the dinner invitation. She had enjoyed spending time with him that afternoon, but it felt too soon for a family dinner, especially considering how the first attempt had gone.

She deposited the damp towel on the closet doorknob and headed out of the room. She ran into Justin immediately. Her stomach filled with butterflies at the sight of him. She was always amazed he still had that effect on her after all the time they've spent together over the last month. "I was coming to find you." She gave him a soft kiss.

He leaned down to kiss her back but didn't embrace her like he normally did. "Grady just took over for me in the launch bay, so I'm all yours for the night."

"Good." Crystal went to wrap her arms around him, but he stepped back. She couldn't help but think she had done something wrong. Was he upset by the things she had found in Ryan's apartment? Did Justin think she still had feelings for Ryan? It was only then that she noticed he was holding something behind him. "What's that?"

"This?" Justin pulled a picnic basket from behind his back. "I thought we could go find a quiet place and have dinner together.

"I'd love that." Crystal kissed him again. A picnic with Justin sounded so much better than having dinner with Ben. She had only promised Leo that she would think about it, which she had—she had no reason to feel guilty.

Justin took her hand and led her outside. They walked in silence, enjoying the artificial sunset as the colony transitioned from day to night. Justin pulled out a blanket once they reached one of the stripes of grass between the fields.

"This place reminds me of where I grew up." Crystal grabbed one side of the blanket and helped him spread it out.

"Tell me about it." Justin sat down and started to take several containers of food out of the basket, arranging them as neatly as he kept his room.

Crystal grabbed a handful of berries and popped one into her mouth. The sour juices burst on her tongue, causing her lips to pucker slightly. "Homestead is a bubble colony like this." Crystal looked up at the glass dome above them. "We didn't have any farms or anything. It's actually only about a third of the size of this place." She ate another berry, enjoying the sour taste. She'd loved eating these as a kid. She would see how many she could eat at once before the sour flavor got too intense. Her record was sixteen. "We have a nice little downtown area with a handful of shops and restaurants. There are a couple of small apartment complexes, but for the most part everyone has small single-family homes. There's a nice park that my grandparents would take me to."

"Sounds like it was a good place to grow up." Justin grabbed a sandwich out of the container closest to him.

"It was. I was safe there. It's really close to the Academy, so most of the families that live there have some connection to the military. They didn't make a big deal out of the execution like the rest of the country did. Everyone there tried to keep things as normal as possible. I think they all realized it could have easily been their family in the spotlight instead of mine." Crystal stretched out on the blanket and put her head in Justin's lap. "What was it like growing up on Earth?"

"My childhood was pretty boring." Justin gently stroked her hair as he talked. "My parents tried to keep what was happening in the wars from us, but we all knew what was going on. It wasn't like you could escape it. I guess they were trying to let us be kids for as long as possible. They taught us to always try to find the good, even in the toughest situations."

"So, they're the ones to blame for your unwavering optimism," she said with a small laugh.

"I guess so." Justin leaned back and gazed up at the top of the dome. "They would have liked to live somewhere like this. We didn't live in the nicest of areas, but it was the best they could afford. Especially with the extra taxes they had to pay for four kids. This is the kind of place to raise a family."

The guilt Crystal had managed to push aside came surging back at the word family. "Leo invited me over for dinner tonight." Her voice had a faraway quality to it that made her feel like a child again.

Justin sat up straight and looked down at her. "Why

didn't you tell me sooner?"

"I didn't think I wanted to go." Crystal sat up. This wasn't a conversation you had while lying in someone's lap.

"And now?" Justin studied her face carefully. Part of her hoped he would say something, be able to tell her what she was feeling since she seemed incapable of figuring it out for herself.

"I don't know, but it doesn't matter," she said in a rush. "I'm sure it's too late now anyway. Forget I mentioned it." Crystal reached for a sandwich but Justin snatched the container away before she could get it.

"Get up." He jumped to his feet and offered her his hand. She wasn't sure what she had said to cause his sudden change in mood. He started to pack up the food the moment she was on her feet.

"What are you doing?"

"We're going to Ben's house."

Crystal's stomach flopped inside her. This was really going to happen. Did she want it to? What would it be like to be inside her father's house? Would it feel the same as her childhood home? "I'm sure they're done with dinner by now."

"That's not the point," Justin insisted. "Part of you wants to go or you wouldn't have mentioned it. You need to give yourself the chance to get to know your father if you want to. What kind of boyfriend would I be if I let you waste the opportunity?"

"It was Leo that invited me. What if Ben doesn't want me there?" Crystal waved her hand through the air, as if that would make her argument more valid.

Justin took her hands in his and squeezed them gently. "Crystal, Ben's been doing everything he can think of the last few days to try to connect with you. He isn't going to turn you away."

"You're going to come with me, right?"

"Of course."

"Should I tell Tyler?" She looked back toward the building where they were being housed. For all she knew Tyler could already be at Ben's house.

"If you want to. Though he was starting to dig into the virus's code when I left so there's a good chance he won't answer." Justin smirked. Crystal wondered how many one-sided conversation Justin had had with Tyler over the last month sharing a room on *Journey.*

Crystal decided not to bother Tyler. She couldn't keep using him as a shield with Ben. She took a deep breath and nodded. "Ok. I can do this." She grabbed the blanket, balled it up, and shoved it back in the basket. She held out her hand. Justin's hand filled hers instantly. Together they made their way to Ben's house.

Desi carried a box of pizza through the halls of the temporary housing unit. The diner had dropped off a stack of them, each with different toppings. Most of the team had descended on the table like locusts. Desi had reached into the mess blindly and liberated a box. There was a member of her team who hadn't been enticed to the common room by the smells of fresh baked dough and melted cheese. She found Price in one of the bedrooms upstairs, completely absorbed in a computer screen.

She didn't bother to knock. The door was open, and he was too focused to hear her anyway. "You need to eat." She dropped the box down on the desk next to him. She'd been excited to see the pizza show up. She got excited anytime she saw food she recognized. That excitement faded the instant she opened the box to find one of her favorite foods from home covered in a variety of colorful vegetables she couldn't identify. She grabbed a piece and proceeded to pull off the offending toppings.

"That's not going to kill you." Price turned toward the bed where she was sitting.

"We'll never know for sure." Desi removed the last of the unidentified vegetables, tossed it into the open box, and took a bite. It wasn't half bad. "How's that going?" She asked with a mouth full of pizza as she nodded toward the computer.

"I'm getting a better idea of the data Teria was after." Price took a slice of pizza and ate it without a second glance. The show off.

"And?" Desi finished her slice and then pulled two bottles of water from her pockets. She tossed one to Price.

"And they aren't going after any of the personal information about the residents, which I guess is a good thing. Nothing about the colony's income sources either. They only seem to be interested in the actual farming techniques. Ghost copies were sent to Teria of all the farming procedures and blueprints for the submerged crop fields, all the science behind the modification of the plants, planting schedules, field rotations, even fertilizer formulations."

"That doesn't really seem like Rank's normal MO. I figured he would want a population run down first to see what the Sertex make up is." Desi grabbed a second slice of pizza and started to dissect it. The wheels in her head were turning. She had spent some time with Wolf trying to understand the politics on Neophia. The biggest thing she had taken away was that Rank didn't do anything unless he had a good reason. He was smart and calculating. So far, he had been focused on reclaiming land he had lost during the war. Why was Stapleton Farms different?

"That's probably why it took me so long to figure it out. I never imagined Rank would be so interested in farming."

Desi was silent for a moment. Why was Rank so interested in farming? Food wasn't in short supply, like it was on Earth. Desi was always amazed by how fast the rationing started when a new war was waged. It always seemed like food was one of the first resources to be cut from trade. "Do you know where Teria gets their food?"

"I can find out." Price turned back to the computer. "It looks like Teria only produces about fifteen percent of the nation's required food supply. The rest has to be imported."

"Do they get any from here?" Desi put her half-eaten slice of pizza back on the box and moved closer so she could see over Price's shoulder.

"Doesn't look like it."

"Have any of the other territories they've taken over been potential food sources?"

"No. In the last year, Teria has taken over several residential colonies, a few underwater mining operations, a handful of uninhabited islands, one of which has an abandoned research facility on it, and two unaffiliated island nations." Price spun around in his chair to look at Desi.

There had to something all these places had in common. Rank was too smart to just go around picking places off at random. Desi's gut screamed at her. This was all starting to feel a little too familiar. As much as Rank claimed that humans were destroying Neophia, he was sure thinking like them. "Could you pull up a map that shows all of Teria's land and colonies?"

"Sure. What exactly are we looking for?"

"I'm not sure yet, but I'll know it when I see it."

Price shook his head slightly then turned back to the computer. "I've highlighted all of Teria's territories in purple."

Desi moved off the bed to have a closer look. She could really use the wall screen in the Ward Room right about now. She leaned on the desk as she studied the map. She ignored the colonies closet to Teria's main landmass. It was the outliners that interested her. They were too far from Teria's capitol to be easily controlled, so Rank would need to devote a lot of manpower to keep them in line. There had to be a reason he wanted them. "Can you highlight the countries that are members of LAWON?"

"No problem." Price hit a few buttons on the keyboard and all of the LAWON land turned red.

There was a purple dot within a hundred miles of every major LAWON country. Rank was setting himself up to be within striking distance of all of them. "Do you know if LAWON intelligence has any theories on Rank's long-term plans?" Desi couldn't be the only one to see what he was trying to do.

"Rank's always been extremely vocal about his displeasure about not receiving more underwater colonies after the war. In fact, Teria lost most of their rights to the colonies they originally had authority over. Most people believe he is trying to reclaim what he thinks he is owed." Price turned around to look at her again. "I take it you have another theory."

"I think he's preparing for war." Desi stood up and put her hands on her hips. It felt good to figure something out for a change. This whole investigation had started to make her question her abilities as an officer. But this time she knew she was right.

"No way. Neither side wants to go to war again. We almost destroyed ourselves the last time."

"I know that's what everyone says, though I'm not buying it. Look at the evidence. Rank is taking over land and posting troops close to every LAWON stronghold. If he wanted, he could coordinate simultaneous attacks all over the planet and no one would see it coming."

"Then why hasn't he done it yet? It's not like Rank is known for his patience." Price folded his arms across his chest and leaned back in his chair. Desi wasn't sure if he was thinking about what she had said, or if he was silently judging her.

"Because he's not ready yet," she answered, thinking rationing and food shortages and her own hungry childhood. "He'd want to make sure his country could support itself once the fighting starts. It's what we do on Earth. If we aren't actually fighting another country, then we're building bases at strategic locations, securing resources, or positioning ships off the shores of countries we think poses the biggest threat. I can't tell you how many missions I was on where the goal was to secure food, water, oil, or precious metals. That way, we would be ready when the trade stopped. Rank's doing the same thing." Desi tried to spell it out as simply as she could. It was second nature on Earth; they had lived with wars their whole lives. But it was different here. They hadn't grown up where war was an everyday thing.

Price looked like he was considering what she said, at least. "Where does Stapleton Farms come in?"

"You said Teria imports all but fifteen percent of their own food requirements. How long do you think that will last them if other countries stop selling to them? Rank would need to secure a sustainable food source for Teria before he can declare war. Otherwise his people will starve to death." Desi paced as she talked ticking off her points on her fingers.

"Rank's never really cared much for the welfare of his people, except those with pure Sertex blood. And I'm sure he would divert all of the food to them," Price countered.

"Yeah, but Teria doesn't even produce enough food to support that portion of the population. At least not for any substantial period of time. That's why he needs Stapleton Farms and their farming techniques. Not to mention the added bonus of wrecking LAWON's economy by taking away a major supplier." She had thought Ben had been full of himself when he explained the colony's importance to the planet, but she was happy to use it now that it helped support her argument.

Price sat in silence with his hand covering his mouth. Desi could tell he was deep in thought trying to find some hole in her argument. The longer she waited for him to respond the more confident she grew. She was right. But as soon as she felt good about figuring it out, the pit of her stomach dropped out. Neophia was on the brink of becoming just like Earth. No matter how much she wanted to be right, she didn't want that.

"We need to tell someone," Price finally said. There was fear in his eyes. At least Desi knew he believed her.

"I'm sure they've already pieced it together for themselves."

"No. They're all so scared of another war breaking out that they won't be able to see what's happening. The peace agreement signed at the end of the Great War stated that every nation on the planet would agree to never engage in open warfare again. Rank signed it himself. Everyone thinks that agreement holds firm. They won't even consider war a possibility." Price was on the edge of his seat. Desi had never seen him this intense without a computer in front of him.

"What can I do?" Desi asked. It's not like I can call up Admiral Craft and say, 'Hey, just thought you should you know I think Teria might be preparing for a war.'" Desi picked up her discarded slice of pizza and sat down on the bed. She knew in her gut that she was right, but she also knew that no one would listen to her. She wasn't important enough.

"Then we'll talk to Reed when he gets back. He'll know what to do with the information." Price's voice rang with determination. The only thing Desi could do was nod. She would talk to Reed when *Journey* returned for them, though, if she was honest, she wasn't sure it would do any good.

Crystal stood in front of Ben's house. She had been fine until they had reached the red door with the sign declaring it the home of the Martin Family. She felt her confidence waver the longer they stood on the doorstep. She had gotten used to dealing with Ben in professional setting, but this was different. This was personal. She wasn't sure she was ready for that.

"We can still leave if you want to. No one would even know we were here." Justin gently squeezed her hand.

Crystal took a deep breath. If she backed out now, she knew she would never forgive herself. She had to be stronger than that. "No, I can do this. I want to do this. I think." She remained immobile.

"Do you want me to knock?"

Crystal nodded. It seemed like it took a lifetime before

the door opened. Crystal hadn't realized she was holding her breath. She felt a little light headed by the time Ben finally answered the door.

"Crystal, what are you doing here? Is everything alright?" The concern in Ben's voice was real and caught Crystal off guard.

"Leo invited me over. I hope it's ok that we stopped by." Crystal squeezed Justin's hand harder. "We can always leave if you're busy. I wouldn't want to intrude."

"Don't be silly. You're always welcome here." Ben's face softened instantly. Unfortunately, it didn't do anything to ease the knot that had formed in Crystal stomach. She didn't understand why this was so hard. After all the time she had spent with Ben over the last few days, she should be more comfortable around him.

"You remember Ensign Anderson." That felt wrong. It wasn't like they were on duty. "I mean Justin."

Ben glanced down at their joined hands. "I do." He held out his hand and Justin shook it awkwardly, never letting go of Crystal. "Please come in." Ben stepped aside.

Crystal looked around the living room. It was cozy, filled with worn furniture loaded with pillows. Two discarded dolls lay in the middle of the floor. Family pictures covered every inch of the small table in the entry way. She wanted to search through them to see if she could spot her face among them, but she knew it wouldn't be there. So instead Crystal averted her eyes. This was going to be hard enough without the constant reminders of what her life could have been.

"Who was at the door?" A woman walked out of the kitchen wiping her hands on a dish cloth. She stopped in her tracks at the sight of Crystal and Justin, but quickly recovered.

"This is my wife, Andrea." Ben led them over to her. "This is Justin and Crystal, my daughter." Crystal felt a shiver run through her at the word daughter. Crystal watched Andrea closely, but the woman didn't flinch. She had either come to terms with Ben's past or she was doing a very good job at hiding it.

"It's nice to meet you both. I can't thank you enough for everything your team has done for us the last few days." Andrea draped the dish rag over her shoulder and offered her hand to both of them. "I wouldn't have believed that anyone in the colony could do something like that to us, but I guess it goes to show that sometimes you don't know people as well as you thought." Her eyes slid to Ben as she talked. Crystal liked her instantly.

"It's nice to meet you, too," Justin said cheerfully. "What is it that you do here?" Justin was so natural with everyone. If Crystal had come by herself, she was sure she would have just stood there awkwardly until someone finally brought up a new topic. But not Justin. He had mastered the art of conversation.

"I'm a botanist. I run the labs here and developed the techniques we use to combine plant DNA strains from Neophia with those from Earth. That way, we can alter their growth rates and adapt them to grow here." Andrea's whole body seemed to change when she talked about her work. It was clear this was a passion for her. Crystal wondered if she transformed in the same way whenever she talked about ship design.

"Mom!" Gina called from the kitchen.

"Coming!" Andrea glanced behind her. The transition from scientist to mom was instantaneous. "We were just getting ready to have some dessert. You should join us. It's Ben's birthday."

"Oh, I didn't realize." Crystal turned toward Ben.

How could she not know it was her father's birthday?

"Don't worry about it," Ben said quickly. "We were never home for it when you were little. Besides, having you here is the best birthday surprise I could ask for." Ben led them into the small dining room right off the family room. "Leo!" Ben called down the hallway. "Come help me get a couple of extra chairs."

"Why, who's here?" Leo emerged from one of the bedrooms. "You came," he said with a large smile once he saw Crystal.

"How could I pass it up?" The smile on her face felt natural for the first time since she had entered the house.

Crystal and Justin stood off to the side while the family moved things around to make room at the table for them. It was strange to think that her last family dinner had been with the Crafts, and it was Ryan by her side instead. She had been so comfortable there, it felt almost like home. Now she wasn't even sure where to sit.

Gina ran from the kitchen directly to Crystal. "You can sit next to me." Gina grabbed her hand and pulled her over to the table. Crystal felt a quick tug on her other arm. She hadn't realized she was still gripping Justin's hand. She saw him flexing his fingers once they were free. She had probably cut off his circulation. She mouthed sorry as she sat down at the table, but he threw her a careless grin that eased some of the tension that had built up inside her. She knew she could do anything with Justin by her side.

Andrea set a cake down in front of Ben, who smiled awkwardly before blowing out the candles. There was a tension in the room that, for once, wasn't her fault. Andrea quickly snatched up the cake and brought it back into the kitchen to slice. Crystal couldn't help but wonder how much of this was just a show to assure Gina and Leo that everything was fine between their parents, even though Crystal was picking up that it wasn't. Andrea returned with the sliced cake and started to pass them out to everyone.

They chatted while they ate their cake. Crystal tried her best to participate, but Justin ended up carrying most of the conversation. After everyone had finished, Justin insisted on helping clean up. Crystal watched him from the kitchen doorway while she sipped a cup of kiki. She wasn't sure she deserved him.

A current shot through her body. Ben had gently grabbed her elbow to get her attention. "Will you come with me for a second?"

Crystal followed him into a small study at the end of the hall. "There's something I need to give you." He pulled a metal lock box from the top shelf of the closet and brought it to the desk. He gave her a cautious smile before opening it. It was full of pictures of her. Crystal put her mug down on the desk and started to pulled them out one at a time. They weren't only from her childhood. There were moments from her whole life in that box. Crystal turned to look at him. She could feel tears starting to form, and was surprised that she wasn't ashamed of them.

"I've thought about you every day," Ben said. "I've followed everything you've done with your career. I know it doesn't mean much, but you have to know how proud I am of who you've become. Even if I wish you would have chosen a different life for yourself. Something outside of the military."

"Did you really hate being in the military that much? Is that why you won't let Leo apply to the Academy?" It was the safest question Crystal could think to ask.

"I know the toll a life in the military can take on a person. How it can make you feel like there's no way out. How it can steal everything from you. How it can make you do things you never would have considered possible. How it can turn you into a version of yourself you don't recognize. I don't want that for him. Or for you." Ben ran his hand through his hair. Crystal smirked a little despite the tears collecting in her eye; there was no denying he was Tyler's father.

"It doesn't have to be that way." Crystal tried to reassure him. "I love my life."

"You are still so new in your career. The longer you're in it, the more it changes you. Just look what being in the military made me do to you." Ben turned around. Crystal wondered if he was trying to hide tears of his own. Did she get her need to hide her emotions from him?

"You know I want to forgive you." Crystal reached out and touched his arm. She wanted to look him in the eye. She needed him to know that she was telling the truth. "I've wanted you back in my life for so long. It's what I've always dreamed of. I just don't know how to get there."

"I know, and I'm so sorry I've put you through this. The last thing I wanted to do was cause you pain, but that's all I've done. Even now. I saw it in your face as we were sitting at the table. I know it's all my fault."

Crystal let her rational side go and threw herself into Ben's arm. She was too tired to be angry. She wanted to hug her father, so that's what she would do. Ben held her tightly, their heartbeats syncing. The longer he held her, the more Crystal felt her defenses crumble. The tears finally escaped and started to roll down her face. Ben didn't say a word. He simply held her closer as she cried.

When her tears finally slowed, she felt him kiss the top of her head. Just as he had done when she was child.

"My sweet, strong girl, you don't know how many times I've dreamed of getting to hold you again. I love you Crystal, more than you can ever know." Ben gently stroked her hair.

Crystal pulled away slowly and looked at the box on the desk. "Is that what you wanted to show me, the pictures?"

"No." Ben turned back toward the desk and started to riffle through the box. Crystal noticed that he wiped his own eyes a few times as he searched. He pulled out two computer chips. He handed her one and put the other back in the box. "Your mother recorded this before her last mission. She recorded a message for you before every mission in case something happened. I'm sorry it took me so long to deliver it to you."

Crystal held the chip as if it would disintegrate under the pressure of her fingertips. Ben didn't need to explain why he hadn't sent it to her. It was another thing Crystal should be angry about, but she wasn't. She was tired of being angry. She couldn't change the past. The only thing that mattered now was that she had her mother's message. "Thank you."

"Dad!" Gina's voice echoed through the walls.

"I should go see what she needs." Ben left the room. Crystal was about to follow, when she noticed the second computer chip. She picked it up and put both in her pocket.

# Chapter 14

Desi gathered her team in the docking bay early the next morning. They didn't know exactly when Young would be coming back and she needed to make sure they were ready to apprehend him as soon as he arrived. They couldn't give him the chance to figure out what was really going on. He knew the colony better than they did, and Desi would bet her life he had several escape plans ready to be put into action if the need arose.

"I'm showing a ship coming in on the radar," Price's voice reported in her ear. He had taken over the colony's control room so that he could coordinate the attack. Desi didn't trust anyone at the colony and had told Ben to kick everyone out. From all the arguing Desi had heard from the hallway, they didn't seem real happy about it.

"Are you sure its him?" Desi asked.

"Would you like me to ask? I'm sure an unknown voice coming from the colony wouldn't be suspicious at all."

"Point taken. Keep me posted." Desi made eye contact with Wolf, who was waiting next to the launch bay doors, and held up ten fingers. Wolf nodded. She had asked Desi that morning if she could be the one to apprehend Young. Desi couldn't say no, even though she really wanted to be the one to take him down herself. The honor belonged to Wolf.

The next ten minutes passed slower than any in Desi's life. Ben was getting antsy standing alone in the center of the room. If he blew this for them, Desi might actually shoot him. Finally, Price's voice came through again. "The shuttle is making its final approach."

A second later they heard the soft clang of the ship's docking port making contact with the colony before the launch bay door opened with a hiss. The distorted version of Young stepped out of the shuttle. The disguise was impressive. If Desi hadn't known it was actually him, she would have second guessed their plan. She was sure Wolf was the only person on the planet that could have spotted him for who he truly was.

"Ben." Young embraced Ben in a hug that made Desi want to throw up in her mouth.

"I'm glad to have you back," Ben said with a relief that sounded genuine. "I'm not sure who I can trust anymore. I didn't want to believe it was an inside job, but the more I look into things, the harder it gets to deny." The doors to the shuttle finally shut. Young wouldn't be getting out that way.

"Do you have any leads?" Young asked.

"I have a pretty good idea who did it," Wolf said into Young's ear as she pressed her gun into the back of his head. Her timing was perfect.

Young held his hands up and twisted his neck to look at her over his shoulder. "I see you've made a miraculous recovery."

The rest of the team emerged from their hiding places,

weapons drawn, but Young didn't seem to notice. His sole focus was Wolf. Somehow Desi had forgotten how intense the hatred between Young and Wolf really was. It filled the entire launch bay as they faced off.

Young attempted to elbow her in the ribs. She was able to dodge it and hit him across the face with her gun. The strike grazed Young's eye and sent his wig flying across the room. It caused him to stumble, but not enough to take him down. He recovered quickly and ran at Wolf's mid-section, throwing her to the ground.

Ben made a move to intervene, but Desi stopped him. "She needs to do this."

"I don't understand why no one is stopping this!" Ben looked between Desi and Grady.

"She can handle him." Grady's eyes were fixed on the fight. His gun traced Young's movements as he fought with Wolf.

Wolf wasn't on her back for long. She was quickly able to overpower Young. She threw him to the ground with a force Desi was sure would leave a dent in the metal floor. What was even more impressive was that Wolf had managed to hang onto her gun through the whole fight. She put her foot on Young's chest and pointed her weapon at his head. Desi was afraid to ask what the gun was set at. She didn't think Wolf would kill him, but given everything she had been through the last few days, Desi wouldn't put it past her. Years of pent up anger could be hard to control.

"Happy to see me?" Wolf snarled.

"Thrilled," Young said through gritted teeth.

"You should have known better than to come back here. You're getting sloppy."

"I didn't think you'd have the guts to face me after our last encounter. I'm glad to see you recovered though.

It will be fun to break you again."

"Get him out of my sight." Wolf removed her foot from him. She kept her gun trained on him as two members of the team pulled Young to his feet and cuffed him.

"Take him to a holding cell in the police station at City Hall," Ben said.

Desi hated that there was no better place to hold him until *Journey* returned. She nodded and her team moved out. Forming a box around Young, with Grady bringing up the rear, they took him directly to the cell, ignoring the gasps of the people they passed on their way. "Cortez and Alister, I want you to stand guard. No one talks to him without my permission." Desi nodded towards Young as she watched her people secure the cell door.

"That won't be necessary. We have a security team here that can handle it," Ben said.

"Not a chance. You don't know who Young has on his side." She made sure her people were in place before leaving the room, with Ben trailing after her. "I'll inform *Journey* that it's safe for them to return, and we can transfer Young to the ship and take him back to LAWON Headquarters for trial."

"He broke our laws. He should be tried here," Ben said. "My people deserve that much."

Desi slowly turned back around. She could feel her anger building again. Why couldn't he just step aside and let them deal with this? She took a deep breath and fought to keep her emotions in control. "You agreed to let us run this investigation."

"And you did. You caught the person who planted the virus. We thank you, but your services are no longer required."

"Do you really think you're set up to handle him?" Grady stepped between Desi and Ben. He must have noticed how her hands had involuntarily formed into fists. "Once Rank hears Young's been captured, he'll assemble a team to destroy this colony the second we are out of range."

"I appreciate your concern, but as I have repeatedly reminded you, we aren't a member of LAWON. You don't have any authority here. I'm not sure what it will take for that to sink in." The veins in Ben's neck were starting to pop out.

Desi was sure he was holding back the urge to scream at them, but she didn't care. She folded her arms, unable to get her hands to unclench. She couldn't believe they were back to this same argument again. "It's your funeral."

"Besides, I'm not sure I can trust your team around him. There seems to be a lot more history between him and Crystal than anyone let on. If I had known that, I wouldn't have allowed her to be involved in the mission this morning. She nearly killed him." Ben waved his hand back at the cell. Desi thought he was a little too concerned with Young's well-being—or was it that he didn't want to believe his daughter was capable of something like that?

"What makes you think you have any right to tell Commander Wolf what to do?" Desi said.

"And as for history, you'd think as her father you would know that Crystal and Young dated for six years before he left LAWON and defected to Teria." Grady turned and walked out of City Hall. He was as much on edge as she was. She followed him out. They could both use a few minutes to calm down before they started the interrogation.

Apprehending Ryan had felt good, but it didn't give Crystal the satisfaction she had been looking for. It didn't make up for abandoning her team. Or for the fact that he had to have realized who Ben really was and hadn't found a way to tell her. She knew they were on opposite sides now, but there had to be enough decency in him to give her a hint that her father was still alive. He could have easily sent her an anonymous message, or at the very least mentioned it while they were together at Soupionia last month. She had told him about his mother, and he had his chance to say goodbye. Why hadn't he shown her the same courtesy?

"Let's go for a walk," Justin said. Crystal hadn't realized that he had stayed behind in the launch bay with her while the rest of the team escorted Ryan back to City Hall.

"Yeah, sure."

Justin took her hand. They walked in silence, from the launch bay, through the town, until they found themselves in a deserted playground. She leaned against the monkey bars and put her hands in her pockets. Her fingers brushed against the computer chips she had gotten from Ben the night before. She had been carrying them around with her ever since. They were too important to leave unattended. She pulled them out.

"What are those?" Justin moved closer to look at the chips in her hand.

"Messages. At least this one is." She put the chip with *Patterson* written across it back in her pocket.

"What kind of message?"

"It's from my mother apparently. Ben gave it to me last night." Crystal carefully maneuvered the chip between her fingers as if that would reveal its contents to her.

"Have you watched it yet?" Justin stood in front of her so that she couldn't avoid looking at him. She could feel him searching her face for some clue as to what she was feeling. Too bad she wasn't entirely sure of that herself.

"No." She leaned her head back against the metal bars and looked up at the dome of the colony as if the answers she was looking for could be found up there.

"Don't you want to know what the message is?"

"Part of me does."

"And the other part?"

"I'm afraid. What if what's on that chip changes everything again? I don't know if I can handle finding out both of my parents are liars." Crystal clutched the chip in her hand.

"I'm sure it's nothing like that."

"And I was sure my father was dead." Crystal stepped past him and went to sit on one of the swings.

Justin moved behind her and started to gently push her. "You know you're going to drive yourself crazy until you watch it."

"I don't know if I have the strength to put the chip in and press play."

"Do you want me to do it?"

Crystal looked down at the chip in her hand. Justin was right; she wouldn't be able to move on until she saw her mother's message. Even if it confirmed Crystal's worst fears. "Ok."

Justin sat down on the swing next to her. Crystal appreciated how careful he was as he took the chip from her hand. He pulled a tablet from his pocket and inserted the chip. "Are you ready?" Crystal nodded. She couldn't bring herself to say anything for fear she might change her mind. Justin pressed play.

Her mother's face filled the screen. She looked much younger than Crystal remembered. She was only thirty-five when she was killed, ten years older than Crystal was now. "My darling Crystal," she said with a smile that reached deep into Crystal's soul. "I'm so sorry I'm not there with you right now. I wish there was a way for me to help you through this. It nearly broke me every time I had to leave you, but I knew you would be safe and happy with your grandparents. I hope you know that every day I spent away from you, I was fighting to make the world a better place for you to grow up in. One where you wouldn't have to live in fear, or hide your human side to be accepted. A world where Aquineins, Sertex, and humans can live together in peace. Nothing less than that could have pulled me away from you so often. I know you can't understand this now, but everything I did, I did for you."

A tear formed in the corner of Kendra's eye but it didn't fall. Did she realized this was the last message she would ever record for her daughter? "You are so strong, my sweet girl. You can do anything you want in life. Find the one thing that makes you come alive and devote your life to it. I wish so much that I could see you grow up to become the smart, successful women I know you will be. Just know that I am always by your side, no matter what."

Another face appeared in the background. It was her father. "Kendra it's time. We have to go."

Her mother turned to look at him. Crystal noticed the waves in her hair. She didn't remember them. "Give me a minute I'm almost done."

Her father nodded, blew a little kiss at the camera,

and then was gone from the frame. Her mother turned back around. A smile on her face. "Crystal, I hope you find love in your life, like I found with you and your father. You are my greatest accomplishment. You are the reason I fight every day, and the reason I have the strength to make the final sacrifice. I do it all knowing that I'm paving the way for you to grow up in a better world. I love you." The screen went black.

Crystal stared at the screen as if it would somehow bring her mother back. She was everything Crystal remembered her being and so much more. Crystal felt lighter after watching it. Freer. She didn't even realize she was crying until she felt Justin's hand brushing a tear off her cheek. He wrapped his arms around her and held her. The metal chains of the swings pressed into her arms, but she didn't care. She was at peace.

"We should head back." Crystal took a deep breath and stood up. "I should be there when they question Young."

"I'm sure Desi will wait for you if you need more time."

"I'm fine, really. Besides the less time Flint and Grady have to spend with Ben the better off everyone will be. Come on." She held her head a little higher as she walked to City Hall. She was the daughter of a hero after all.

Desi stormed into City Hall nearly ripping the door off its hinges as she flung it open. She had been in the middle of giving Commander Dewite an update on their capture of Young when she was interrupted by a call from Cortez, one of the soldiers she had placed at the jail to keep an eye on things. It seemed Ben had been trying to gain access to the prisoner on his own.

She surveyed the scene quickly. Cortez blocking the door leading to the cell, Ben trying to force his way through, and Grady in the middle trying to keep an all-out fist fight from breaking out. Personally, Desi's money was on Cortez; she was small but scrappy. "What the hell is going on here?" Desi tried to put on the same air of authority Wolf always seemed to have when she entered the room.

"You need to tell your team to stand down Lieutenant." Ben whipped around to face her.

"Once you tell me what you're doing here," Desi said, nodding to Cortez, who returned to the cell without another word. Desi noticed that Grady positioned himself so that he was blocking the door.

"What does it look like I'm doing? I'm going to start the interrogation." Ben waved his hand at the door leading to Young's cell.

"Not by yourself. We need to wait for Commander Wolf to get here before anyone talks to him. She knows him better than anyone. If he's going to slip up and give us anything useful, it will be while he's talking to her." Desi tried to keep her voice even as she talked.

"I think you forget that I've know this man for three years. He's eaten dinner in my house, been to my kids' birthday parties. I think I'll be just fine." Ben spit his words at Desi, and she felt the last shreds of her professionalism slipping away.

"You don't know him," she accused. "You were fooled by him for three years."

"Young is the master of manipulation," Grady said, adding his strength to her statement. "Commander Wolf is the only one who knows his tricks and won't fall for it."

"This is my colony. It's my call. I'm going to talk to him now. If you really want to help, bring him to the interrogation room for me." Ben patted Grady on the shoulder and walked away. Desi reached out and grabbed Grady's arm to keep him from punching Ben in the face right there.

"What do you want me to do?" Grady glared after Ben.

"What can we do? Bring him Young. Five minutes alone with the guy and Ben will be begging us to take over." Desi followed after Ben. If he was going to insist on questioning Young, then at least she would be there to hear every word. She headed to the small observation room attached to the interrogation room. Given the pile of multicolored party napkins on the table, she doubted the room had ever been used for its intended purpose.

She could see Ben sitting at the table on the other side of the one-way mirror. His back was to her, but she was sure he was wearing a smug look of success. How Desi wished she could knock it off his face. She really hated losing. She checked the speaker at least six times to make sure it was working while she waited.

Grady led Young into the room with his hands cuffed in front of him. He pushed Young into a chair and stood behind him. His hand came to rest on his gun.

"Thank you, Lieutenant Grady. I've got it from here." Ben's voice crackled through the speaker.

"I've been ordered to stay and secure the prisoner." Grady's jaw was clenched as he spoke. Desi was impressed how calm he seemed.

"That won't be necessary."

Grady stared down Ben. Desi was about to intervene when Grady finally relented and left. He joined Desi in the viewing room muttering obscenities under his breath.

"It's nice to see you Ben—or should I say Jedidiah." Young's cocky smile made Desi's veins boil with rage. "I'm assuming all secrets are out in the open now. How did Crystal take it when she found out you've been alive all this time? Was it a loving reunion?"

"I'm not going to fall for your games Ian." Ben's voice was calm, though Desi noticed the muscles in his shoulders had tensed. They had tried to warn him.

"It's General Young actually, though since we're friends feel free to call me Ryan. It's what Crystal calls me after all." Young leaned back casually in his chair. He didn't seem bothered by the handcuffs at all. In fact, he looked like he was enjoying himself.

"What made you do it? There are children here." Ben's focus was admirable. Desi only hoped he would be able to keep it up. Grady was leaning on the table, closely watching the scene unfolding in the other room. She could feel the anger radiating from him.

"I was given a job to do and I did it. What makes you think I'm going to tell you why?"

"You were part of this community. You had dinner at my house countless times. My children look up to you, and you tried to kill them." Ben was trying to appeal to Young's emotions; too bad Desi was pretty sure he didn't have any.

"Relax Ben, Leo and Gina are fine. They were saved by their older siblings, since you know you have more than three children. I wonder if there are any more out there that we don't know about. I'm sure Crystal would love to find out you kept something else from her. She loves secrets. Is she in there watching all of this with the rest of your saviors from *Journey*?" Young waved to the one-way mirror and blew a kiss. Desi wanted to jump through the glass and strangle him. Grady got up and started pacing in front of the glass, muttering under his breath. Maybe it was a good thing Ben had made him leave.

"Leave my daughter out of this." Ben pounded his fist on the table. Young was getting to him.

Young leaned forward and put his cuffed hands on the table. "But why? They must have told you that Crystal and I have a history. I know her more intimately than anyone on the planet. Don't you want to know what you missed all those years you were hiding? How she coped when she didn't have any friends at the Academy because she was better than everyone in her class, but still worked harder than anyone there? She had to live up to your reputation. She was terrified to disappoint you. It wasn't easy being the daughter of the nation's greatest heroes."

Desi was transfixed by Young's words. Wolf never talked about her relationship with him, and Desi couldn't help to be curious. Grady stopped pacing. He stood frozen next to the glass. Desi was pretty sure that wasn't a good sign. Her eyes bounced between him and Young.

"For the last time, leave Crystal out of this. This is between me and you," Ben said through gritted teeth. Desi knew she should go in there and save Ben, but part of her felt he deserved what he was getting. If he had let her handle things, none of this would be happening.

"Is it too painful to hear? How you could have been there for all of it, but chose not to?" Young inched closer to Ben. Desi took a few steps closer to the door so that she could intervene if Young made a move. Until then, she was happy to let him tear into Ben a little longer. "Like when your parents died, and I was the only one there to help her plan their funerals. It was my hand she was clutching through the services. I was the one that held her after everyone left. I was the one that wiped away her tears, when it should have been you." Young pointed to himself with each new declaration, the sound of the handcuffs banging together filled the room. "Or how every Peace Day, I would take her to the most secluded place I could find so she wouldn't have to face the hordes of reporters that followed her. Everyone wanted an interview from the Wolfs' orphaned daughter. It would guarantee them a spike in their ratings. No one cared that it was one of the hardest days of the year for her. You could have been there for all of that Ben, but you were too weak to face her. You chose to abandon her to a life of loneliness and pain. You chose to put yourself over the wellbeing of your child." Young spit in Ben's face.

Desi was shocked by the anger Young was showing. This had to be about more than getting caught. It felt way too personal. Was it possible that he still had feelings for Wolf? He seemed almost as hurt by Ben's betrayal as Wolf had been.

Ben calmly pulled a tissue from his pocked and wiped the spit off his face. "If you care about her as much as you seem to, why didn't you go to her when you first realized who I was? You've obviously known for some time." Ben's voice caught in the back of his throat.

"Crystal and I crossed the line between love and hate years ago. In most instances, I wouldn't hesitate to cause her pain. I'll probably be the one that ends up killing her one day, but I could never hurt her the way you have. Telling her about your betrayal would have destroyed her, and even I'm not that cruel."

Desi had been so transfixed by Young that she didn't

notice Grady's anger building until it was too late. He balled his fist and slammed it against the mirror causing it to wobble in its frame. It was the distraction Young had been waiting for. Desi watched in horror as he slipped out of the handcuffs, slammed Ben's face into the table and raced from the room.

He had made it out of the holding area and was running toward the lobby before Desi and Grady caught up with him. It was the middle of the day, and City Hall was filled with people. "Everyone get down!" she yelled.

Young made it to the lobby. If he thought the crowd would prevent Desi from shooting him, he was wrong. She reached for her gun, but Gray was faster. He fired a single shot directly into the center of Young's back. It was the first time anyone had ever beaten her in drawing her weapon.

Desi made her way across the lobby to Young's unmoving body, ignoring the screams of the bystanders, all crouched down on the ground, waiting for whatever happened next. She hoped that in his rage Grady hadn't over charged his weapon and killed him. She wouldn't be upset if Young died, but it wasn't worth the paperwork.

# Chapter 15

The short walk back to City Hall was peaceful. Justin didn't bring up the message from her mother and neither did Crystal. She wasn't sure she even had the words to describe what she was feeling yet. But with her hand intertwined with Justin's, the only thing she could put into words was a sense of calm. She savored it while she could. She would be facing Ryan soon and would need to put up a wall in order to deflect whatever mind games he would use to try to manipulate her.

She wasn't prepared for the scene that met her when they entered City Hall. The lobby was in complete chaos. People were lying on the floor; some of them were screaming. Grady was at the other side of the room, gun still in his hand. Crystal traced his line of sight until she saw Flint crouching down next to Ryan. He wasn't moving.

Crystal released Justin's hand, took a deep breath, and made her way over to them. It was time to be their commander. "What is going on here?" She put all of her authority into those words. The more she took in the scene, the angrier she got. How could they have let things get this out of control? Grady and Flint were supposed to be two of the best officers on *Journey*.

"He escaped, but I took care of it." Grady shrugged his shoulders and returned his gun to his holster. Crystal couldn't believe his nonchalant attitude. This wasn't like him.

"You didn't kill him, did you?" The last things they needed to deal with was a dead Teria general. It could be the trigger Rank needed to take down LAWON.

"Would you really be that heartbroken if I did?" Where was this coming from? While she had heard Grady talk back to other officers, he had never done it to her.

"That's not the point. Our orders are to deliver him to LAWON alive." Crystal voice was louder than she intended it to be.

"Relax, he's fine." Flint joined them. Crystal turned to see two members of their team carrying Ryan's unconscious body back toward the jail.

"Was anyone else hurt?" Justin asked.

"Not really," Flint said after the slightest hesitation. Crystal looked at her questioningly but got no more in response. She wasn't thrilled with Flint's caviler stance on the whole situation. The fact the Ryan was able to get away from them at all was alarming, but to have to take him down in a room full of civilians took it to a whole new level. As the lead on this mission, Crystal expected better from Flint.

"Oh really, no one was hurt?" Ben entered the lobby and slowly made his way over to them. His right eye was blackened and blood was pouring out of his freshly broken nose.

"What happened to you?" Crystal didn't even bother

to keep the anger out of her voice. This whole situation was out of hand.

"It's nothing." Ben waved her away with the hand that wasn't holding a bloody napkin to his face. She did a quick assessment and determined that it looked much worse than it probably was. He would be fine, though his nose might bend in a slightly different direction from now on.

"Young slammed his head into the interrogation table. It was impressive, you should have seen it." There was a manic quality to Grady's voice that Crystal hadn't heard in a long time. She would need to defuse the situation soon before he snapped. She looked him over. He wasn't lashing out physically yet, which was a good sign. She still had time.

"You started the interrogation without me? Who thought that was a good idea?" Crystal looked between Desi and Grady. They had all agreed that no one should talk to Ryan without her. They both pointed to Ben.

"I thought I could handle him," Ben said.

Grady took a step toward him. "And how did that work out for you?"

Crystal moved so she was in between Grady and Ben. She looked Grady straight in the eyes. He was close to the edge. She needed to pull him back a little so she could finish dealing with this mess before she could bring him back completely. "Jim," she said softly, "this isn't going to help anything." Their eyes locked, and for a moment she was afraid he wouldn't back down, that she had waited too long, but finally he turned away.

Crystal turned back to Ben. "Did you at least get anything useful out of him?"

"No." Anger twitched in Ben's jaw. What had Ryan said to him? She assumed he had used their past to get under Ben's skin. Clearly, it had worked.

"You should have waited for me." Crystal shook her head. How was she going to get things back on track now?

"I tried to tell him that, but see, he's in charge here and wants to take care of it himself," Flint piped in. Crystal took it as a bad sign that she hadn't said much up until now. The only time Flint kept her mouth shut was when she was angry.

"That's over. I will be overseeing the interrogation from here on, and when *Journey* arrives, I'll have Young transferred to the brig. It's a lot more secure than anything you have here." Crystal wouldn't risk Ryan getting away a second time.

"I can't let you take him Crystal, I'm sorry." Ben said.

"You can't honestly want to keep him here. You don't have the facilities or manpower in place to contain him. You also don't have the authority to tell me what to do. I'm the senior ranking officer here." For the first time she didn't see her father standing before her, nor did she feel like a child in his presence. He was just an obstacle standing in the way of her completing her mission.

"Yes, you are, but it's my right to keep him here. I'm the leader of this colony and we don't fall under LAWON's authority. You're not going to take him. We will hold a trail and the citizens here will determine the correct punishment." Ben took a step closer to her. He was trying to switch back the dynamic between them. She wouldn't let that happen.

Crystal felt Grady's muscles tense behind her. Ben was threatening her, and Grady would do anything to protect her, especially in his current state. She needed to stop him before he did something he would regret. She whipped around to face him. "You are dismissed

Lieutenant Grady." He looked at her without really seeing her. She had only seen him this far gone a few times, and it never ended well. She hoped she hadn't waited too long.

"You're pulling rank on me?" His eye focused on her.

"Yes I am."

"You can't do this." Grady clenched his hands so hard Crystal was concerned the force would tear the skin over his knuckles.

"You are confined to your quarters until further notice." Grady waited one beat, then turned and swore. Crystal watched as he stormed out of the building. She let out a breath. One crisis averted, for the moment anyway. She turned to Flint. "When is *Journey* scheduled to arrive?"

"Not for another four hours."

"Fine," Crystal said with a curt nod. "Since I can't question Young now, we will wait for Captain Reed to determine where we go from here." Crystal turned to Ben. "And if you try to get near him before then, I'll tell my team to shoot you and lock you up right next to him."

"You can't do that," Ben yelled.

"Try me." She turned away from Ben in time to see Flint stifle a laugh. "Lieutenant Flint, I'd like a word in private." Crystal walked out of City Hall without another word.

Desi followed Wolf out of City Hall. She knew that Wolf was pissed. Desi tried to hide the embarrassment threatening to take hold. She couldn't help but feel like she was being called down to the principals' office—something she experienced frequently throughout her education. She knew she should have handled the situation with Ben differently. She didn't need Wolf to tell her that. This was her mission after all. If anyone had the right to be pissed, it was her. She had everything under control when Wolf walked in and took over.

"I don't need a lecture," Desi said, having talked herself out of all sense of embarrassment.

"Too bad, you're getting one anyway," Wolf growled. "The way you and Grady are acting is completely unprofessional, and you're putting the whole mission at jeopardy." Wolf put her hands on her hips, but kept her voice low. Desi guessed she didn't want anyone passing by to overhear their conversation.

"You weren't there to witness Ben's epic arrogance. Am I not supposed to enjoy it when it all blows up in his face?"

"No, you're not." Wolf tried to keep a straight face, but Desi could have sworn she saw a hint of a smirk on the corner of her lips. "Look, I don't want to take command away from you, but I will if you can't handle it. You need to find a way to work with Ben that doesn't end up with him having his nose broken. As the face of this mission and of LAWON, you have to remain in control, no matter what."

"You're only trying to protect him because he's your father." Desi crossed her arms in front of her chest.

"Believe it or not, I'm trying to protect you. LAWON has a bad reputation here and you're only feeding into it. What if you push Ben too far and he decides he no longer wants to do business with LAWON? Who do you think the brass up at headquarters are going to blame when our afflicated nations can't buy food to feed their people?" Wolf waved her hand toward Desi.

"Politics don't matter to me."

"Well they should. The LAWON board oversees the military branch, and if they want to destroy your career, they will. And then there's the Young situation. We need to be able to take him back with us, but we won't be able to do that if you piss Ben off to the point that he kicks us out of the colony. We both know he can't handle Young on his own. Everyone here would be dead within hours of us leaving. You don't want that hanging over your head." Wolf squeezed the bridge between her nose and took a deep breath. "You need to see the bigger picture here."

Desi thought back to her conversation with Price last night. If she was right, and she was fairly certain she was, then Stapleton Farms falling into Teria's hands could lead to an all-out war. "Isn't there some way we can force Ben to hand over Young?"

Wolf was quiet for moment. She shifted her weight from one foot to the other. "There is, but as far as I'm aware, it's never been done before."

"That doesn't mean we can't do it now."

"That decision falls well above our pay grade."

"So, you want me to roll over and play nice." Desi rolled her eyes.

"I'm not asking for a miracle," Wolf said with a smirk. "I just want you to stop antagonizing Ben."

"I'll try." Desi dropped her arms to her side. Wolf did have a point. Desi wouldn't be able to accomplish anything if she kept fighting with Ben, and the one thing that had been drilled into her head on Earth was that she had to complete the mission, no matter the cost. It was just too bad that this time, the cost was her pride.

"Thank you. Now I need to go try to defuse Grady before he snaps completely." Wolf shook her head and started jogging toward the temporary housing. Part of

Desi wanted to go with her, though she knew that wasn't what was needed of her now. She took a deep breath and headed back into City Hall with smile plastered on her face that made her cheeks hurt.

Crystal approached Grady's room with caution. The last time he had allowed his anger to take hold like this was the night she got shot while leading the raid on the Church of Devine Clarity's headquarters. She hadn't been there to talk him down that night. He ended up getting himself thrown in jail after starting a fight with three guys at the Drunken Sailor. Needless to say, he was no longer welcome there. She knew that he had never gotten over the fact that the bullet that nearly killed her had been meant for him. Something pretty bad must have happened during the interrogation to push him this close to the edge.

She knocked on his door, but didn't get a response. That wasn't a good sign. He wouldn't disobey a direct order unless he had already lost control. She pounded on the door. "Jim, it's me. Open up."

The door flew open. "You didn't have to send me to my room. You're not my mother."

Crystal surveyed the room. The floor was littered with clothes, the desk chair was on its side, and the mattress was only halfway on the bed. His gun was back in his hand, three green lights illuminated on its side. He had never de-energized it after he shot Ryan. "Yeah I did." She put her hands up. She didn't want to come across as threatening.

"I was just doing my job." Grady paced in front of the door, clenching and unclenching his free hand with every step.

"You shot a man in a room full of civilians. What would have happened if you hit one of them by accident?" Crystal followed his weapon with her eyes. Every muscle in her body was on high alert. She made sure to keep her right hand by her side in case she needed to draw her gun.

"I didn't. I hit my mark. I always hit my mark." The words flew out of his mouth like daggers.

"That's not the point."

"You're only mad because you still having feelings for that piece of shit. You turn into a love-sick school girl incapable of thinking rationally whenever you're around him. It's pathetic." Grady waved the gun in her direction as he paced. He was liked a caged animal ready to break free. Crystal concentrated on the hand holding the weapon. His finger was hovering over the trigger.

"We both know that's not true." Crystal's hand shook. Grady knew her better than anyone, so of course he would know exactly what to say to hurt her the most. She knew he didn't mean it, but that didn't take sting away.

"You're just a child. Why anyone thought it was such a great idea to give you command is beyond me. Do you know the things people say about you behind your back?" Grady took a few steps closer to her.

Crystal's hand came to rest on the butt of her gun. "That's enough." She prayed that he would see her. She wasn't sure she would be able to shoot him if it came down to it. Grady didn't move. It was like he was looking straight through her. "Jim, please don't make me do this." Her voice cracked as she spoke.

Grady squeezed his eyes shut. The clouded look was gone when he reopened them again. His eyes traveled to Crystal's side where her hand lay on her gun. "Shit." He released the grip on his gun and it fell to the floor.

"Are you back with me?" Crystal slowly took her hand off her gun and held it up. Grady nodded and leaned back against the wall as he took slow even breaths. Crystal felt her whole body relax.

"Did I hurt you?" The regret in Grady's eyes broke her heart.

"No." She causally picked up his gun, powered it down, and stuck it in her waistband behind her back. Just in case.

"Good." Grady moved about the room slowly, muttering to himself. He picked up the mattress and put it back on the frame before sitting down. "About what I said before—you have to know I didn't mean any of it."

"I know and it doesn't matter." Crystal didn't dare move yet. She needed to give him space to pull himself back together.

He leaned forward and cradled his head in his hands. "You should have heard the stuff he said about you." Grady didn't look at her as he talked.

"I have a pretty good idea. I'm sure he brought up stuff from my past to try to get under Ben's skin." She tried to act normal, though her body was still on high alert. She knew Grady needed to talk through it, but there was a fine line between moving forward and falling off the edge again.

"He brought up your grandparents, peace day, things like that."

"Is that what pushed you over the edge?" Crystal moved closer to the bed.

"No."

"Then what did it?" Crystal sat down next to him and placed a hand on his back. He finally sat up and looked at her. There were tears in the corner of his eyes. "Jim, what did Young say?"

"That he would kill you."

"He was just trying to get a reaction. That's what he does. He'll say anything if he thinks it will help him manipulate the other person. He probably thought I was there and wanted to try to scare me."

"I know that, but the he way he said it. Like it would mean nothing to him." Grady clenched his fists.

"It's just words." Crystal gently turned his face toward hers. She kept her hand on his cheek to help keep him grounded. "Look at me. I'm sitting right here. He's locked up; he's not going to get to me." Grady nodded. Crystal removed her hand. "Besides we both know I can take him. I'd never give him the chance to kill me," she said with a wicked smile she hoped would lighten the mood. It didn't.

"It sent me back there. It was like I was back in the Church's headquarters, you limp in my arms with a bullet in your side that was meant for me." Grady put his hand on her side where the bullet had entered.

Crystal grabbed his hand off of her side and put it on her heart instead. Grady's eyes widened, but he didn't pull away as her heart beat against his palm. "I'm fine. The Church couldn't take me out, and neither will Young."

"You're my best friend Crystal, if anything were to happen to you..."

"Nothing is going to happen to me. I'm a lot tougher than I look."

Grady removed his hand from her heart. "I can still take you," he said with one of his killer smiles.

"No way." Crystal gently shoved him.

Grady was about to retaliate when their communicators buzzed. Crystal pulled hers out of her pocket and answered it "This is Commander Wolf."

"Commander, *Journey* has returned. Please report to Stapleton Farms City Hall," Tyler said.

"Thank you." Crystal put her communicator away. "I guess we should head back. Are you sure you're all right?"

"I'll be good as long as no one tries to kill you. Come on kid." Grady got to his feet, and tussled her hair. Crystal carefully stepped around the debris still scattered around the room and followed Grady out.

# Chapter 16

Desi met Reed in the launch bay at Stapleton Farms. She had sent another update after Young's attempted escape. It was hard to tell how Reed felt about the whole situation over the video screen, but there was no denying it now that she was in the same room as him. Reed was pissed.

"Take me to him." Reed didn't even break stride. Desi hurried to catch up. Ben was waiting for them in a conference room at City Hall with the rest of their team. Reed threw the door open and locked in on Ben. "Would you like to explain to me exactly what the problem is? I expected Young to be waiting in the launch bay when we arrived."

Desi slid past Reed and took a seat at the table next to Wolf and Grady. It was the best spot to watch the fireworks. Ben might not respect her, but Reed did, and Desi couldn't wait to see him take Ben down.

Ben slowly rose to his feet and stood behind his chair. "I'm sorry Johnathan, but I'm not going to let you take him. He broke our laws and should pay the price for that here. If I let you take him, I'm basically telling my people that I can't protect him."

"You can't protect them." Desi shoved her hand into her pockets to keep herself from slamming her fist onto the table. She had promised Wolf that she would try to stop antagonizing Ben, even when he was making himself such an easy target.

"The second we are out of range, he will break out of his cell and destroy this place," Wolf said, her voice tired. "At the end of the day, he still needs to answer to President Rank, and if Rank wants this colony, Young will do whatever he can to get it for him." Wolf wore a weary expression Desi had hadn't seen on her before. Even with no sleep and an extreme amount of stress, Wolf always presented herself as if nothing ever fazed her. But now all Desi could see were the cracks in her armor starting to show. How much had it taken to bring Grady back from the edge?

"Young's already escaped once under your watch," Grady pointed out. "What makes you think you can keep him locked up this time?" Grady waved toward Ben's now bandaged face. Desi watched him closely. There was no sign of his previous anger.

Ben turned away from Reed and sat back down. "I'll put my best security team on him. I trust my people, even if you don't. They will make sure he stays in that cell until we've determined the appropriate punishment."

Desi knew the colony didn't have any long-term prison facility on site. If they were going to handle things entirely themselves, there was only one answer: the death penalty. Desi wasn't sure how she felt about that. It wasn't as if Young didn't deserve it, but it was still extreme. The death penalty had been outlawed on Earth years ago, but when she asked Price about it, she found out it was still a common practice here. And yet, Neophia was supposed to be the more peaceful planet.

"Your security team is made up of farmers. You have one full time security guard with no military background." Price set his tablet down on the table.

"Before Young defected to Teria, he attended LAWON's military Academy." Wolf propped her elbow on the table and rested her head in it. "He graduated second in our class. Your people won't know how to handle him."

"This shouldn't be up for discussion. Young in a big international player. That alone should be enough of a reason to transfer custody to us." Desi leaned across the table. This was her fight after all, and it looked like Wolf was drained completely. This was Desi's chance to prove to everyone that she was more than just a combat solider. She would play the political game if that's what they wanted.

"How can I even be sure LAWON will prosecute him? How many times has Teria broken the peace treaty, and LAWON looked the other way? How many times has Young been in your custody, only to be released with an apology hours later?" Ben shot his words at Reed. As much as Desi hated to admit it, he wasn't wrong. It was something she had struggled to accept the first time they had caught Young on Soupionia, only to send him right back to Teria.

Reed finally took a seat at the table. "I've spoken with Admiral Craft and he has assured me that LAWON is prepared to go to trial this time."

"So it's settled. I'll go get Young ready for transfer." Desi looked to Reed for confirmation.

"Nothing is settled." Ben slammed his fist onto the

table. "He isn't going anywhere, and you don't have the authority to take him. Young will pay for what he did to us. I'm not foolish enough to believe that LAWON won't negotiate with Teria once they have Young in custody, despite your assurances."

"Be reasonable, Jed," Reed caught himself and took a deep breath. "I mean Ben. You don't have the resources to handle a prisoner of this magnitude."

"That's not your call to make." Ben's stubbornness was astounding. Desi couldn't help but wonder if there was some other reason Ben was so desperate to remain in control of Young. Did he want to approach Teria with a deal for his release? It seemed unlikely given everything that Rank had put him through. Maybe that was it. Maybe being able to kill Young in the name of justice was Ben's way of extracting revenge on Rank for the death of his wife? It always amazed Desi how personal everything was on Neophia.

"You know I can force your hand." Reed's words were carefully measured. Next to Desi, Wolf sucked in her breath. Was this what she had mentioned earlier?

"You wouldn't." Ben's shock was apparent in his face.

"I would," Reed said.

"Wouldn't do what?" Desi asked.

"There's a provision in the Peace Treaty that was signed at the end of the war," Wolf explained. "It allows for LAWON to take control of the governance of a nonmember nation when their actions threaten the safety of the planet. It was put in as an added layer of protection to keep Teria from jeopardizing the portal that connects Earth and Neophia. The intention was that it would never have to be used." Wolf didn't look away from Reed as she spoke. Desi could only imagine the different scenarios running through her head. Desi looked over at Reed to see if she could gain any insight, but his face was void of any emotions. Desi really hoped Reed wasn't bluffing.

"Do you really want to be the first one to enact it? Can you really make the case that by not turning Young over to you, Stapleton Farms is threatening the safety of the planet?" Ben looked at Reed with a triumphant smirk.

Desi felt the rage boiling under the surface. "I can." Every head in the room turned toward her. She looked to Price for support and saw him nod. She needed to do this. "I believe that Teria is preparing to start a war, and acquiring Stapleton Farms is essential to that plan. If you don't turn Young over to us and he takes control of this colony, as we all know he will, you will be thrusting Neophia into a war where Teria will have the upper hand."

A laugh escaped Ben's lips. "You can't be serious."

It would only take Desi a second to jump across the table and give Ben the black eye he so desperately deserved. Desi was a fraction of an inch out of her chair when she felt Wolf's hand on her forearm. Desi eased herself back into her chair. "I am and I can prove it," she said through gritted teeth.

"Flint, get a team together and start preparing your argument. I'll call Craft and have him convene the Board to make the determination." Reed stood up, and the rest of *Journey's* team followed suit. Out of the corner of her eye, Desi saw Wolf exchanging a look with Grady and Price. They all looked worried.

"Wait." Ben's exhaustion was apparent in his voice. "Before you go ruin your careers, let me discuss this with the staff here. I'm not saying we will hand him over, but at least let me see what they have to say before I make my final decision."

"You have four hours. If you haven't changed your mind by then, I will go to the LAWON Board for approval to take control of Stapleton Farms." Reed left the room without another word. Desi looked back at Ben as she filed out. His eyes were fixed on Wolf. In that moment, Desi understood the only reason they were getting this chance was because of Wolf. She might be able to forgive him for the lies and abandonment, but she would never forgive him if he ruined her career, and he knew it.

Crystal was glad to be back on *Journey*, though the Ward Room was starting to feel like her second home. Flint had left a few people behind to guard Young while they waited for Ben's decision. Crystal wasn't sure if they were there to keep Young from breaking out again, or to stop Ben from moving him before LAWON had a chance to intervene. Crystal didn't know what to think of Ben's reluctance to hand him over, but that wasn't what was important now. The only thing on her mind was Flint's declaration that Teria was preparing for war.

At first, Crystal thought Flint had lost it. There was no way Teria would want another war. They had lost more than anyone during the Great War. Their resources were depleted quickly, their army wasn't as well trained, and their allies jumped ship halfway through. The war had nearly destroyed the planet, which was why every nation on Neophia agreed to the Peace Treaty. Rank was a lot of things, but he wasn't stupid.

But as she listened to Flint go over her theory, Crystal couldn't help but see the truth in it. It was like Rank was playing a game of chess, while LAWON hadn't even bothered to sit down at the table. How could they have missed it? Fear crept deep into Crystal's soul. This was what she had been preparing for her whole life, but now that she was faced with the very real possibility of a war, she wasn't sure she was ready for it.

Crystal was so lost in thought, she hadn't realized Flint had stopped talking, and everyone in the room was looking at her. She knew they wanted her to confirm what Flint had told them, but she wasn't ready to do that yet. Not until she'd felt out the details a little further. "It's a good theory."

"But," Reed probed her.

"But do we really think Rank would want to start another war? It would make Teria the most hated country on the planet."

"Aren't they already?" Flint wasn't wrong.

"They're unpopular, at least among LAWON nations," Crystal conceded, "but that's just a fraction of the planet. There are plenty of others who have no problem doing business with Teria. There are some that even support his anti-human agenda. If he started a war, he would alienate those countries as well. It might even be enough to get them to join LAWON. So why risk it?"

"It's only a risk if he loses." Flint cocked an eyebrow at her.

"Which is where our theory comes in," Tyler said. "Rank is doing everything he can to make sure he doesn't repeat the same mistakes. Teria didn't have the resources to sustain a prolonged war. This time he will." Tyler pointed while he talked. Crystal wondered if it was because he didn't have a computer in front of him to keep his hands occupied.

"What kind of resources are we talking about?" Grady leaned forward. Crystal noticed the wrinkles around his eyes. He was nervous. He was born a year after the Great

War started. His entire childhood was clouded by it. The idea of going through it again had to be weighing heavily on him.

Justin took a deep breath. Flint's declaration hadn't shocked him like it had the rest of the crew. It seemed like a new war was started every few months on Earth. This was normal to him, and Crystal knew he hated it. "He would need to take care of his citizens first, since trade would be the first thing to go once war started," Justin explained. "Teria would need its own sustainable sources for food, water, energy, and materials."

"Stapleton Farms is the food source. They produce more than enough to support the entire population of Teria," Crystal said.

"Yeah, but he doesn't have control of them yet," Grady countered.

"But he does have all the information on how to replicate it." Tyler leaned back in his chair. Crystal knew how he felt. This was a lot to process.

"That could take years. Do we really think Rank would wait that long?" Grady asked.

"He's had Young here for three years before making a play for the colony. If you ask me, Rank's in this for the long game," Justin said.

"I'm guessing that's his back up plan if he can't get control of Stapleton Farms," said Tyler.

"Which is why we need to take custody of Young; otherwise we are basically handing Rank the colony." Flint tapped the table as she talked.

"That's only one piece of the puzzle though. It might not be enough to convince the Board to seize Stapleton Farms," Reed said. Crystal took it as a bad sign that he hadn't interjected until now. It meant that he believed Flint's theory, and Crystal desperately wanted her to be wrong.

"Teria has always been self-sustaining for clean water, so they're all set there. What about energy?" Grady looked to Crystal.

Crystal pulled out her tablet and started scrolling through the information LAWON had compiled on Teria's movements. She had never been removed from the intelligence networks when she stopped working counterterrorism. "Rank recently took over the island community of Echon. There is a company there that produces solar panels, batteries, wind turbines. Since then, Echon has decreased exports by seventy five percent. Almost everything they produce is being sent to mainland Teria. He's set for energy."

"Isn't it possible that Rank is just trying to isolate Teria from the rest of the planet so that he doesn't have to answer for his anti-human policies?" Grady asked. Crystal knew where he was coming from. Any answer would be better than war.

"It's possible, but if that was the case, why would he be targeting land within striking distance of every LAWON country?" Flint nodded to Tyler and a second later a map of Neophia filled the front screen. Crystal couldn't believe what she was seeing. How had they all missed it? She got up and moved closer to the screen. This couldn't be happening.

"Teria's military is better trained and better equipped than they were the last time," Tyler said. "If they can secure a source of food for their people, there would be nothing standing in their way from launching the first strike whenever or where ever they wanted."

"Flint and Price, I want you to pull all of this together and get ready to present it to the Board. I want you to be ready to go the second Ben's time is up if he hasn't agreed to hand over Young," Reed said.

"Yes sir," they said in unison. Reed left the room. Crystal turned and looked at the map again. The only thing standing between them and war was Ben's stubbornness. Would she go from being the daughter of heroes to the daughter of the man that destroyed the planet?

# Chapter 17

Crystal settled herself into her chair on *Journey's* bridge. The second she sat down, she felt herself starting to relax. This was her safe space. She could almost forget that she had spent the last hour helping Flint and Tyler put together their arguments for the Board. They were still at it when she had to report to the bridge to relieve Dewite. He had been holding command of the bridge for the last ten hours and deserved a break.

She clicked on the screens at her station and started a full diagnostic scan. She tried to run one at least every other day, but with everything going on, she had been neglecting her bridge duties. In fact, the last one she ran had been before they got the distress call from Stapleton Farms. It wasn't that big a deal—she knew her engineering team would keep *Journey* running at optimum levels even without her extra oversight. She watched the scan run for a few minutes before getting up and checking in with the rest of the crew on the bridge.

"Commander Wolf," Stiner called from her station. "I'm getting an alert from the diagnostic scan." There was a hint of concern in Stiner's voice. Crystal was sure she was the only one to pick up on it. Stiner knew the ship almost as well as Crystal did so if she was concerned then something had to be wrong.

That couldn't be right. Crystal made her way back to her station. "What's the alert level?"

"Low, but it's coming from the battery room."

That made less sense. The team that operated the battery room knew to report even the slightest issue to the bridge. As the primary source of power to the ship's life support system, they were constantly monitored. Crystal pulled up the schematic for the battery room on her main screen. She couldn't find the source of the alert. Everything looked like it was operating at full capacity. Crystal hit a button next to her station, "Bridge to Battery, this is Commander Wolf."

"Battery Room. This is Chief Wong."

"Chief we are picking up a low-level alert coming from there. Are you seeing anything unusual on your end?"

"We've noticed that battery three is taking longer than the others to charge," Wong answered, "but it's with in the operating standards."

"Thank you." Crystal closed the line and zoomed her monitor in on battery three. She couldn't find anything in the wiring to suggest why it was taking longer to recharge. That's when she saw that it wasn't even maintaining full power. It was hovering at ninety-eight percent. Just above the set point for the alarms. Crystal hit a few buttons and her screen changed so that she could see everything on the ship that pulled energy from battery three. Given that they were just hovering outside of the colony, battery three shouldn't even been engaged, since batteries one and two provided more than enough energy to power the ship when they weren't moving.

There was only one thing drawing power from battery three. Crystal studied the screen for a second longer before reaching over and hitting the intercom button again. "Ensign Price, report to the bridge immediately."

Crystal watched the orange dot on her screen while she waited for Tyler. She hoped that it would disappear once she had called him, but it stayed. A tiny imperfection on her otherwise flawless screen.

"Commander Wolf?" Tyler walked over to her, slightly out of breath.

"What's this?" She pointed at her screen.

Tyler leaned over her chair to get a better look at her screen. "I have no idea."

"Something in your quarters is pulling energy from the batteries at a steady rate. Do you have any systems running?" As *Journey's* head computer programmer, Tyler's room was filled with computer equipment. It wasn't outside the realm of possibility that he had something running she wasn't aware of using the extra power.

"No, everything's powered down." Tyler cupped his chin as he thought.

"Commander, we're transmitting a data message," Stiner said.

"I didn't authorize that." Something in Crystal's head clicked. She looked at Tyler in horror. He seemed to reach the same conclusion a second later.

"Shit." Tyler turned and ran off the bridge.

Crystal jumped to her feet. "Stiner, do whatever you need to in order to stop that transmission. Jam every frequency in the area if you have to. Command is yours." Crystal ran after Tyler.

Tyler was frantically scanning his room when Crystal arrived. He drove at his bunk where his laptop was laying harmlessly. He nearly broke off the screen as he pulled it open. Crystal tried to read the expression on his face as his eyes darted over the screen, but she couldn't tell how bad the situation was.

"Damn it, damn it, damn it," he muttered under his breath. He turned toward the desk that divided the room and smashed his computer on it repeatedly. Bits of plastic and letters keys flew into the air. Crystal had to duck to miss being hit in the head by a large section of the screen.

"What was that?" she asked shock.

"I'm sorry." He dropped the remains of his computer on the desk. "I don't know how I missed it. The virus left a ghost copy on my hard drive. It can reanimate itself at any time. This was the only way to stop the transmission and keep it from spreading to the rest of ship."

"Are you sure it didn't spread to the rest of the ship's systems?" Crystal's mind ran wild with the possibilities of Teria getting detailed data on *Journey*. Almost every scenario that ran through her mind ended with *Journey's* entire crew dead.

"From what I saw, the virus had only gathered data from my computer. I'll need to do a deep drive into the ship's mainframe to be sure though." Tyler ran his hand through his hair as he looked at the mess. "I'm going to need to requisition a new computer, by the way."

"You think?" Crystal rolled her eyes. She was about to head back to the bridge when a dark thought crossed her mind. She felt like all the air had been sucked from her lungs. "Tyler, if the virus is self-replicating doesn't that mean it's still on the colony's servers?"

Tyler turned to look at her, dread filling his eyes. "Yes, it does."

"Rank could reactive it at any time and kill everyone there in a matter of seconds if he wanted. If he reversed the fans on the atmosphere generator, he could suck all the breathable air out into the ocean. What can we do?"

"I can install some firewalls to slow it down while I work to dismantle it, but it could take weeks to get through the code." Tyler pulled out a chair from his desk and sat down.

"We need to come up with a better solution." Crystal paced in front of the door. She always seemed to think more clearly when she was moving.

"Young must have an encryption code on it that would shut it down."

Crystal nodded and turned toward the door. "Let's go."

"Where are we going?" Tyler got up and followed her out of the room.

"I'm going to get that encryption code out of Young, and then we're going to save the colony all over again."

Crystal entered City Hall alone. The rest of the team had been adamantly against it, but she knew she wouldn't get any useful information out of Young if they were there. Justin had been sent to get Ben, though Crystal didn't wait for him to arrive. There wasn't time to waste arguing with him. The virus could be triggered at any time and kill them all. Rank wouldn't hesitate to sacrifice Ryan if it meant he got what he wanted in the end.

Stapleton Farm's lone security guard stood as she entered. Crystal couldn't help but smirk as she recalled

Flint describing him as having more muscles than brains. It was an accurate description. Crystal quickly looked him up and down. Despite the muscle mass, she doubted he would be very effective if Ryan broke out again. She estimated she could take him down in less than a minute if she really wanted to. "I need to speak with the prisoner."

"Why?" The guard stood in front of the door leading back to the cell where Ryan was being held.

"Because I do. Now get out of my way."

The guard turned and tapped on the window in the door. He stepped aside to let Cortez see Crystal. She nodded to the guard.

"You'll have to leave your weapon out here." The guard nodded toward the gun on her hip.

Crystal didn't like it, but there wasn't time to argue. She removed her gun and placed it on the table in front of the guard. He stuck it in a drawer and locked it before opening the door leading to the cell.

"Well, well, I was wondering when you were going to pay me visit," Ryan said languidly. "I'm a little hurt it took this long." He was stretched out on the bed, looking perfectly relaxed despite his current situation.

Crystal ignored him. Instead she walked over to her security team. "Give us a minute."

"Yes ma'am," they said in unison before leaving the room.

Crystal waited till the door had closed behind them before turning around to face Ryan. "We know about the ghost copy of the virus on the colony's computer system. How soon after we left were you going to activate it?"

Ryan got up from the bed and walked up to the front of the cell where Crystal was. He looked genuinely pleased to see her. It was unnerving. "I was going to wait until they felt safe again."

"When did you become so cruel? Why not simply overthrow the colony like you have with every other place Teria has taken over?"

"Come on Crystal. Do you really think no one would oppose that? Stapleton Farms produces food for all the major countries on the planet except Teria. We couldn't take them over unchallenged." Ryan casually weaved his arms through the bars of his cell. Crystal fought the urge to step out of his reach. She wouldn't let him intimidate her.

"How would killing everyone change that?"

"Someone would have to come pick up the pieces after everyone was dead, and who better to do that than beloved colony leader Ian McFarland?" Ryan said gesturing to himself. "And since I'd be the only one left, I'd need help getting this place back up and running. Teria could swoop in and save the day at that point. We would be heroes."

Crystal fought the urge to throw up. "You're sick." What had happened to Ryan over the years to make him so cold hearted? He had been so kind while they were at the Academy.

"It's a smart plan, and you know it."

"What's the encryption code Ryan?" They had gotten too far off track. She couldn't let Ryan draw her in.

"Why in the world would I tell you that?" He was laughing at her.

"Rank is going to get tired of waiting for you to act. Would he even think twice about activating the virus while you're still locked up here? You would die right along with rest of us."

"You underestimate my importance to Teria, but if it comes to that, I'm willing to make the sacrifice." Ryan was much too confident. He had always been the ultimate survivalist. Crystal expected him to at least consider his self-preservation instincts. Something wasn't right. Was there some kind of failsafe in place so that Ryan was the only one that could relaunch the virus? She hoped that was the case; at least they would have more time then.

"We'll figure it out eventfully, even without your help. You're only prolonging things."

"You really think Ben is going to grant you access to all the confidential servers where the virus is housed? He's too stubborn for that. Like you. How was reuniting with your dear old dad again? Was it everything you had dreamed it would be?" There was a false friendliness in his voice that gave her goose bumps.

"How long have you known?" Crystal knew he was just trying to mess with her. She knew she should ignore the comment and move on, but she couldn't help herself.

"I figured it out a couple of months after I got here. I had seen his pictures thousands of times in your room at school."

"Why didn't you tell anyone? Why didn't you tell me?" The question had been gnawing at her since she first realized that Ryan was involved. He claimed to have loved her. Even with all the bad blood currently between them, didn't he at least owe her that much?

"How would I have done that, even if I had wanted to? We aren't a team anymore. You ended that a long time ago." Ryan's posture changed. He was standing straighter, his muscles in his arm tensed. She had found a crack in his defensives.

"I might have been the one to end things, but you killed our relationship when you chose the Purification Movement over me." Crystal wasn't sure why she was getting so defensive. She had thought all of this was behind her. They had barely spoken to each other after she ended their relationship. Were they finally going to have the fight they should have had five years ago? She dreaded the thought, but if that's what it took to get Ryan to give her the code, she would do it.

"I never chose them over you," he said bitterly. "You couldn't accept who I was anymore. My involvement with the Movement never changed the way I felt about you. You're the one that chose your distorted sense of morals over us. Not me. I didn't owe you anything after that." Ryan pointed at her accusingly through the bars of his cell. She could see the veins popping from his throat as he spoke.

Crystal wasn't prepared for the anger in his voice. Had he really been holding on to it all these years? Or was he trying to get into her head and build some sympathy for himself? "At the very least you could have given me some clue that he was still alive when we were on Soupionia last month. There was plenty of time when you had me tied to a chair that it was just the two of us. No one would have even overheard you."

"And risk blowing my cover at Stapleton Farms?" he scoffed, shaking his head, muscles still tense with anger. "Besides you're better off without him. He's weak and selfish."

"That's not for you to decide. I know we're on opposite sides now, and that you don't have feelings for me anymore, and that's fine. But you should have told me, if for no other reason than you claimed to have loved me at one point." She huffed out a breath, just barely keeping herself from turning and pacing. "Why do you think I took the time to tell you that your mother was dying last month while you had a gun to my head? I know you still love her, even if you deny it. I gave you the chance to say goodbye."

"I haven't spoken to Carolynn in years." Ryan turned away from her for the first time. She was starting to get to him.

"I know you sent her flowers and candy. She passed peacefully with them by her bedside." Crystal watched him carefully as she spoke.

"She's gone?" His voice caught in the back of his throat. Crystal assumed he had known. It had gotten decent coverage from the press. It wasn't every day that the wife of LAWON's most decorated admirals died.

"She died in her sleep," Crystal confirmed gently. "Almost three weeks ago."

Ryan's face flooded with sudden disbelief. It was only there a second as he forced his usual cocky smile on his face. "It makes no difference to me."

In that moment, Crystal knew what the encryption code was. It was the same code he used for his locker at the Academy, and to unlock his computer, and his gun safe. It was the date that Carolynn picked him up from the orphanage. The day she became his mother. "Thank you, Ryan. I know how to stop the virus." Crystal walked straight out of the holding area. The rest of the team was waiting for her in hallway. "The encryption code is the date he was adopted."

"Are you sure?" Tyler asked.

"Positive."

Tyler nodded and then took off toward the server room with Ben following in his wake. Crystal wondered if he had put up much of a fight while the others kept him out of the interrogation room, though she was too tired to ask. She just wanted this whole situation to be over so that things could go back to normal.

"What do you do now?" Justin asked.

"I guess now we wait." Crystal leaned against the wall. Confronting Ryan had taken a lot out of her.

"For what?" Grady crossed his arms in front of him.

"A decision about Young, an all-clear from Price, a call to The Board, take your pick," Flint said.

"Well if we're going to wait, we might as well eat while we're doing it," Grady said. "Anyone up for a trip to the diner?"

"I'm in." Flint raised her hand as if Grady was taking attendance.

"What do you want to do?" Justin turned to Crystal.

"I think I'd like to be alone for a while. Clear my head a little and recharge. You should go with them." Crystal nodded toward Flint and Grady. Justin squeezed her hands once and then followed Flint and Grady down the hall and out to the lobby.

# Chapter 18

Crystal hung back in the lobby until she was sure the others had gone before leaving City Hall. The main street was crowded. School had just let out, and it looked like most of the students were hanging around before heading home. Crystal scanned the crowd quickly for Leo. She wouldn't be rude if he spotted her and wanted to talk, but she would rather avoid it if possible. It was nothing against him, she just wasn't sure she had the emotional strength for any more today. Not seeing Leo, she quickly ducked down a side alley.

The corridor between the two buildings was narrow, but at least Crystal was alone. There was a service drive that ran behind the buildings connecting the fields and the launch bay on the other side of the colony. Crystal turned toward the fields. As she passed along the back of City Hall, she noticed one of the emergency exit doors was ajar. Ben really needed to start taking security more seriously. She went over to closed it when she noticed the wire to the door's alarm had been cut. She pulled the door open and saw that it led to the holding area.

Crystal's stomach turned to ice. She nearly tripped over the door frame as she ran inside. Cortez and the other guard from *Journey* were lying motionless on the floor outside the empty jail cell. She quickly scanned the room to make sure Ryan wasn't still there, but there was nowhere for him to hide. She rushed over to one of her people. She couldn't find a pulse.

"Damn it, Ryan." She grabbed her communicator. "I need medical assistance at the jail. Two men down. The prisoner has escaped."

Crystal didn't wait to for a response. It was hard to say exactly how long it had been since Ryan had escaped, and time was essential here. If he made it off the colony, they would have no hope of catching him again. She ran out of the back door, trusting that her team would be along shortly to provide back up.

She didn't head back to the main street. He wouldn't have gone that way. He would need to keep a low profile. Word of his betrayal had spread fast through Stapleton Farms, and the citizens were out for blood. If he was spotted, he was done for. She headed toward the nearest field. There would be a hatch at the end of it to offload crops. Crystal would bet her life that Ryan had a launch waiting there.

She saw him as soon as she got to the field. He hadn't gotten too much of a head start. She was surprised to see that he wasn't alone. She should have suspected that he had someone inside the colony helping him. It had been the main reason Flint had left members of their team to guard Ryan. Two team members whose families she would need to write letters to.

Crystal moved closer, careful to keep herself low to the ground so that the half-grown corn stalk kept her hidden. She needed to get a better assessment of the situation so she could figure out a plan. It looked like Ryan was pushing the person in front of him. They were not the willing accomplice she'd thought. She hurried to the end of the row to try to cut them off. Ryan got there first. She finally got a good look at his hostage. It was Leo. Ryan had a gun to his back.

All thoughts of waiting for backup were dashed from her head. She felt an urge to protect like she had never felt before. No one went after her family. Without thinking she ran out of the crops. "Let him go, Ryan," she yelled at his back.

Ryan turned and laughed at her. "Oh sure, since you asked so nicely."

Crystal reached for her gun, but it's place on her hip was empty. She thought back to the last time she had it: in the jail, before she had gone to see him. She had been so focused on getting the encryption code to Tyler that she had forgotten to go back for it.

"Thanks for this by the way." He waved her gun at her. He had to have taken it from the desk before escaping.

"You don't need him." Crystal held her hands up, maintaining eye contact with Ryan. Leo was frozen with fear.

"Sure, I do. Leo and I are old friends. He doesn't mind coming with me," Ryan said. Leo struggled to free himself, but Ryan squeezed his arm tighter.

"Take me instead," Crystal offered. "We both know I'm the bigger prize." She was afraid to make a move. If she wasn't fast enough, Ryan could kill Leo before she ever reached him. She wanted to believe Ryan wouldn't hurt an innocent kid, but in her gut, she knew that wasn't true. Ryan was desperate, and desperate people were capable of doing terrible things.

"I have a better idea," Ryan said, digging Crystal's gun into Leo's back. Leo winced. "How about I take both you back to Teria with me?"

"That's not going to happen." Crystal took a step forward but stopped as soon as she saw Leo rise up on his tiptoes as Ryan increased the pressure.

"You're not the one in charge," Ryan spat. "I'm the one with the gun, so I'll be the one giving the orders." Ryan aimed the gun at her. At least it wasn't pointed at Leo for a moment.

"If you have me, why do you even need him?" Crystal asked, keeping her voice steady. "I'm more than enough leverage to get you out of here and back in Rank's good graces." If Crystal could just keep him talking long enough for the rest of her team to get here, none of this would matter.

"I agree," Ryan said, "but you have this problem doing what you're told. So, Leo here will be my assurance that you won't do anything stupid."

"Run Crystal! I'll be fine," Leo yelled as he struggled to free himself again. Crystal admired his bravery, but he didn't have any idea what he was dealing with. He would be dead the second they set foot on Teria.

Crystal wouldn't let that happen. "I'm not going anywhere."

"This is sweet and all, but I'm getting bored." Ryan nodded to someone behind Crystal. She turned just in time to see the security guard from the jail swinging a shovel at her head. She heard the metal connect with her skull as it vibrated inside her. Her vision went black, and a buzzing noise filled her ears.

"You could have shot her with your stun gun," Ryan said, a hint of anger in his voice. It was the last thing Crystal heard before she hit the ground.

Desi grabbed her communicator the second Wolf's message started to play. The entire diner got quiet as it echoed around them. She looked at Grady and Justin in horror. It was like they were all frozen in time, unable to do anything except take in Wolf's words "I need medical assistance at the jail. Two men down. The prisoner has escaped."

They were on their feet the second the communication ended, nearly overturning their table in the process. The remains of their meal scattered across the restaurant's floor. People moved out of their way as they ran down the street to City Hall. Price and Ben were already at the police station when they arrived.

"Where's Wolf?" Desi looked over her two fallen men. There wasn't any sign of a struggle. Young had taken them out quickly.

"She's not here," Price said. There was no sign of Wolf or Young anywhere in the alley.

"She went after him." Grady was standing in the back doorway. He waited for Desi's nod before he took off, after only a moment's hesitation, toward the right. Desi had no choice but to follow him into the nearest field.

"I don't see them." Justin's voice was panicked.

"There," Ben pointed to a broken stalk. "Someone cut through here."

Desi took off running through the field, following the trail of broken stalks. Desi wasn't sure why Ben was still there, but she didn't have time to fight with him. Wolf could be in trouble.

"There they are," Price pointed across the field. Desi was shocked he had been the first to spot them, since he spent most of his time glued to a screen inches away from his face.

They were about five hundred meters away. Desi tried to make out the tiny blob of people moving on the other side of the field. "Is one of them carrying something?"

"It looks like a body," Justin yelled.

"It's Crystal." Grady pushed past her at a full sprint. There was no use trying to keep up with him.

"What's up there? Where are they heading?" She yelled over her shoulder to Ben. If he was going to be here, then he might as well be useful.

"There's nothing over there, except…" Ben's voice trailed off causing Desi to stop and face him.

"Except what?"

"A loading hatch for the crops."

Desi cursed under her breath. If Young reached that hatch, they didn't stand a chance at getting Wolf back. "Grady, they're heading toward a loading hatch. We can't let them get to it!" she yelled and started running again. She would have given just about anything for the headset that came standard issue with their combat gear. To bad it was all safely stored back on *Journey.*

Grady responded by pulling out his gun. He had closed the gap considerably. He fired wildly in their direction. Young's team stopped momentarily. There was a second when Desi thought they might give up, but it didn't last. Young turned and returned fire. It was only then that they saw that Young was using Leo as a shield.

"Leo!" Ben's voice echoed off of the glass dome.

"Dad!" Leo's desperate plea reached them as little more than a whisper.

Grady continued to fire, though his shots were hitting further and further away. Between Young hiding behind Leo and Wolf's limp body slung over the shoulder of the other guy, they couldn't get a clean shot. The best they could hope for was to keep firing and hold them in place until help arrived.

Young wasn't taking the same precautions. She heard Price stifle a groan next to her. She looked over to see him clutching his arm. "Price's been hit," she yelled to her team.

"I'm fine! Barely grazed me," Price said. "We have to move—they're getting away!"

Young used the moment of distraction to take off running, pushing Leo in front of him as they went. It was too risky to fire at them now. Desi's team reached the hatch just as it closed behind Young.

"Can you stop them?" Desi asked.

"No, they've shot out the controls." Justin examined the smoking remains of the control panel.

"We need to get to *Journey*." Desi said.

"There's another shuttle docked at the next hatch," Ben said.

"Take us there." Desi followed Ben, allowing him to take the lead.

# Chapter 19

Metal grating pressed into Crystal's face. Its vibrations helped bring her back to consciousness. She didn't know where she was, but she knew they were moving. That and the splitting pain in her head were all she was sure of at the moment. She laid there with her eyes closed while she tried to remember what happened. Someone had hit her over the head with a shovel. Where was she that there was a shovel handy?

Everything came flooding back. Ryan had taken her and Leo hostage as he escaped the colony. Leo. Where was he? Was he hurt?

Her eyes flew open. She was laying on the dirty floor of a shuttle. The other side was lined with metal crates full of potatoes. She did a quick check; they were all secured to the shuttle wall. At least she wouldn't have to worry about potatoes shifting and crushing her. She tried to pull herself up, but her hands were chained to the bar at the bottom of the bench seat. "Leo?" she whispered, hoping he was close enough to hear her over the noise of the shuttle's engines.

Leo was by her side in an instant. "Crystal are you all right?" His voice was laced with fear.

"Yeah," she said, despite the pain in her head. She was pretty sure she had a concussion, but it wouldn't do any good to tell him that. Besides, a concussion would be the least of their problems if Rank got his hands on them. She had to keep Leo calm so that he could help her get them out of this mess. "Could you help me sit up?" With Leo's help, Crystal was able to work her way into a seated position. Her arms were stretched to one side at an uncomfortable angle, but it was better than lying on the floor. "Did they hurt you?"

"No, I'm fine."

"Good." Now that she was sitting, she could see up the small ladder and into the shuttle's cockpit. Ryan was driving, and the guard was sitting next to him. Thankfully, neither of them paid any attention to what was going on in the back of the shuttle. She suspected that might change once they realized she was awake. "We need a way to defend ourselves. See if you can find anything we can use as a weapon, but be careful. We don't want to attract any attention."

Leo moved slowly along the seat, searching the compartments along it. "How about this?" Leo held up a rusted box cutter. It was better than nothing.

"Let me see." Leo handed it to her. She ran her finger over the dull blade. Crystal longed for her combat gear, especially the gun Flint had given her to hide in her boot. Two shots and she would have control of the shuttle. Instead, she had a box cutter she wasn't even sure would pierce skin. She contorted her wrist to try to work the blade into the lock securing the chains around her hands.

Crystal glanced up at Leo. He was on the verge of breaking down. She needed to something. "Tell me what you know about that guy." Crystal nodded at Ryan's copilot while she tried to pick the lock.

"His name is Vince. I don't know much about him expcet that he's kind of a jerk," Leo said with a shrug, relaxing as he talked. Good. "He came to the colony about a year ago. He works out in the fields mostly. We don't have a lot of work for security guards. I don't think he has any family at the colony."

"Do you know if he is Sertex or Aquienin?" For a second Crystal thought she was getting somewhere with the lock when the box cutter slipped from her hand. She stretched her fingers to try to get it again.

"Both I think, but I don't know for sure. I've seen him out swimming without any gear once to twice." Leo stared at the cockpit, as if he was reading Vince's history off of the back of his head.

It took Crystal a few seconds to process what Leo had told her. Her brain wasn't working as it normally did. If Leo was right and Vince wasn't a pure blood Sertex, then he wouldn't be seen as a valued member of Teria's society. Why would he go there only to be treated as a second-rate citizen? What had Ryan offered him to convince Vince to break him out? "Listen, I'm not going to lie to you," she said quietly. "We're not in a great situation right now. No matter what happens I want you to stay near me. I'll do whatever I can to protect you."

Leo turned back to look at her. She could see the effort he was making to hold back tears. "Are we going to be able to get out of this?"

"I don't know. I don't even know if the rest of my team knows what happened to us."

"They do," Leo said with a little more confidence in his voice.

Crystal's heart leapt in her chest. "What do you

mean?"

"They chased us out of the colony."

This was great news. If her team knew Ryan had them, there was a chance. Crystal's mind raced through the possibilities of what their next move would be. It took her a lot longer than normal to come up with an answer. "Leo, strap yourself in. Now!" There was only one-way *Journey* would be able to stop their shuttle from reaching Teria.

"Why?" Leo moved to the seat next to her and began to put on the safety harness.

"*Journey* will probably try to disable our sub, and I don't want you to get hurt." Crystal had worked the box cutter back up to the palm of her hand. She gave up hope of using it to pick the lock. Instead she clutched it in her hand. Maybe she would be able to use it against Ryan.

"What about you?"

"I'll be fine. It's not like I'm going anywhere." Crystal lightly clanged her chains against the bar and smiled. She had to keep Leo calm.

Desi was out of her seat the second the shuttle arrived at *Journey*. She didn't wait for the hatch doors to finish opening before she slipped out and raced to the next launch bay, where her subfighter was waiting for her. She jumped into the seat and was halfway through securing her harness when she realized Grady was doing the same thing in the sub next to her.

There was only one thing that mattered now. They needed to stop Young before he made it to Teria's water. If he managed to do that, Crystal and Leo would be lost forever. "Bridge, this is Flint. I'm ready to launch," Desi said as she adjusted her headset.

"Flint, you are clear to launch," Dewite responded.

Desi pulled out of the ship with Dewite's voice still echoing in her ear. The subfighters were fast, but they needed to make up a lot of ground. Every second would matter. "Give me some guidance here people," Desi said. She had a general idea of where Young was heading, but she needed to do better than that.

"I'm sending coordinates to you now," said Stiner.

A second later, a route appeared on Desi's monitor. It led directly to Young's shuttle. She was roughly two kilometers behind him. She would need to be a lot closer before she could get a clear shot off. "Grady, are you with me?"

"Right behind you."

"Flint, Grady," Reed's voice filled Desi's sub. "There's a small uninhabited island about five kilometers to Young's port. See if you can force him to land there. The goal is to disable the sub, but if you need to open direct fire, you are cleared to do so. We'll have a recovery team standing by."

Desi didn't like the sound of that. A recovery team wasn't for survivors. She turned off her connection to the bridge. "Hey Jim."

"Yeah."

"I don't think I can destroy the shuttle." Her confession shook her to the core. She had never questioned an order to destroy before, even if there was the possibility of civilians getting hurt. It was always a necessary risk. Had her time on Neophia made her soft?

"Then let's make sure we don't have to." Grady's voice echoed in her ear. She knew that if it came down to it, she would have to be the one to destroy the sub. Grady would never be able to take it down with Wolf onboard.

Desi nodded even though no one could see her and switched on her connection to the bridge. They were gaining on Young. He was still speeding straight ahead, but he would realize they were on him any second and begin evasive maneuvers.

"What's the fire power on that thing anyway?" Grady asked.

"It's a standard crop hauler." Desi was shocked to hear Ben's voice coming through the channel. How had he wormed his way onto the bridge? "It has a decent laser, but nothing else."

"He's turning starboard," Grady said.

"Cut him off and try to get him to come back to me."

"No problem." Grady took off at full speed. He came within inches of colliding with the crop hauler, forcing Young to turn abruptly. Desi prayed that Wolf and Leo were strapped in. A few moves like that, and it might not matter it they disabled the ship or not.

Desi got into position. She would try to take out Young's rudder. She powered her laser to forty percent and fired. Young made another abrupt turn and her shot missed. She cursed wildly into her headset, completely forgetting that her words were being broadcasted to everyone on the bridge.

They had managed to get Young's shuttle within five hundred meters of the island. If they were going to disable the ship, now was the best time to do it. Desi was lining up to take another shot when Young's ship looped around and fired at her. Desi was so shocked to see the bulky sub preform the maneuver, she didn't react quickly enough. Young's laser hit the side of her ship. The lights on the control panel flashed, then went dead. She smacked the panel in a fruitless effort to bring it back to life. Her sub slowed until it was drifting helplessly in the water. "I'm hit," she said into her headset.

"Are you hurt?" Reed asked.

"No sir, but the subfighter's toast. It's all on you now, Grady"

"I'm on it." Grady's ship sped past her. He had been hanging back to keep Young from turning back toward Teria's water. Desi watched in frustration as Grady and Young exchanged fire, each weaving and swerving to avoid being hit. The longer the dance went on, the angrier Desi got. She hated not being able to help.

Grady pulled his subfighter directly behind the shuttle. As much as Young tried, he wasn't able to shake him. Grady was perfectly aligned when he fired. Pieces of the propulsion system floated through the water. "The shuttle had been disabled," Grady reported.

"Grady, get Flint and return to *Journey,*" Reed ordered. "I don't want to engage with Young until he reaches the surface. The shuttle's too confined, and if we push him before he surfaces, he's likely to destroy them all. Let's not forget we have a civilian kid on that ship."

"Yes sir."

Desi felt the clang of Grady's grappling hook attach to her sub and pull her back toward the ship. Wolf was going to be pissed that Desi broke her ship—that is, if they were able to get her back.

# Chapter 20

Crystal could feel bruises forming all over her body. She had tried her best to hold on during the fight, but her attempts had been useless. She had been slammed into the floor and bench repeatedly. To make matters worse, several dozen potatoes had come loose and flown directly at her. The force of the shot that took them down sent her flying toward the wall headfirst. Stars burst into her eyes, but she was able to blink them away. At least Leo wasn't hurt.

"Those bastards took out our whole propulsion system," Ryan yelled, bringing a smile to Crystal's face. With the engine dead, their voices could easily be heard throughout the shuttle.

"What does that mean?" Vince asked.

"It means the ship is useless," Ryan said through gritted teeth.

"What do we do now?"

"We can either wait here for *Journey* to capture us, or we can try to make it to that island and hope that by some miracle we can overpower the team they send to rescue those two." Ryan pointed over his shoulder without turning away from the console.

"I say we fight," Vince said.

"Of course you do," Ryan said under his breath. "Go make sure they're still alive back there. I'm going to try to get us to the surface."

Vince sauntered back to Crystal. She sensed the danger immediately. Given their current situation, he should be showing some signs of concern; Ryan certainly was, and yet Vince still seemed completely confident. It might be the concussion, but Crystal was pretty sure Vince was enjoying this whole thing way too much. She clutched at the box cutter, only to find it was no longer in her hand. She must have lost it during the attack, though she couldn't remember when.

"Are you still breathing down there you little piece of shit?" Vince kicked her upper thigh.

Crystal winced. She was usually so much better at hiding her pain, but her brain was operating in slow motion. Crystal glanced over at Leo. He looked like he was about to say something, but Crystal shook her head. She didn't want him to draw any unnecessary attention to himself. As long as Vince was focused on her, Leo would be safe. "Why are you helping him?" she groaned.

"Do you honestly think I'd help you?" Vince spit at her.

Crystal's anger flared, but she fought to push it back down. Keep his attention, keep Leo safe. She repeated it over and over in her head as she forced herself to focus on what she needed to do. "He tried to kill you."

"When?" Could Vince really be that stupid?

"He was responsible for the virus that took out Stapleton Farms life support system. You would have died along with everyone else if it hadn't been for my team. Do you honestly think Young would have given you a second thought as he stepped over your cold dead body?" Crystal struggled to sit up again. She didn't like the feeling of Vince standing over her while she lay on the shuttle floor unable to move.

"You sure do think you're tough shit, don't you?" Vince crouched down next to her.

"I do actually." Keep his attention, keep Leo safe, she repeated in her mind. A wicked smile formed on Vince's lips as his eyes slid from her face to her wrists. It was only then that Crystal realized that a warm liquid was running down her arm. She strained to look up at where her wrists were chained to see everything covered in blood. The box cutter must have sliced her wrist open before she lost hold of it. She was surprised it had been sharp enough to break the skin.

"Well, well, it looks like you got blood all over my nice clean shuttle. What are we going to do about that?"

"I think we have different definitions of clean."

Crystal watched as his face turned a deep shade of red. He reached out and grabbed her throat. She coughed and gasped as he squeezed her throat tighter, cutting off her windpipe. She fought to escape his grip, but with her hands still chained to the bench, there was little she could do. Out of the corner of her eye she saw Leo fumbling to get out of his restraints. He fought to pull Vince's arm away, but it didn't do any good. Vince only squeezed her throat tighter, laughing at them the whole time. Her eyes started to go black, but she fought to remain conscious. If she passed out, she wouldn't be able to protect Leo.

"What's going on back there?" Ryan demanded. He finished what he was doing at the helm before getting up. Then he rushed at Vince, knocking Leo back into the bench before pulling Vince off of Crystal. "What the fuck is wrong with you? She's no good to me dead."

"I figured we had the kid to use as leverage." Vince gestured toward Leo. "I didn't see a reason why we needed them both."

"You don't get to kill anyone without my permission. Is that understood?" Ryan stood between Crystal and Vince. It was almost like he wanted to protect her.

"Yeah, sure, whatever you say." Vince shrugged his shoulders and leaned back against the shuttle wall.

"Go get the kid ready to move. We'll be at the surface soon." Ryan turned toward Crystal, who was still gasping for breath. He crouched down next to her, removing the bloody chains from her wrists.

"What rock did you find that guy under anyway?" Crystal's voice was horse. The throbbing in her throat was starting to overshadow the pain in her head. She was pretty sure the imprint of Vince's fingers would be visible on her neck for days. She looked over Ryan's shoulder to check on Leo. Vince hadn't come near him yet. He seemed to be too busy examining a length of rope to secure Leo's hands. At least that's what she hoped his plan was. Crystal wasn't sure she had the strength to get past Ryan and stop Vince if he tried to hurt Leo, though she would use every last ounce of her energy trying if it came down to that.

"I didn't have a lot to work with." Ryan glanced back at Vince and shrugged his shoulders. "Are you all right?"

Crystal's attention was snapped back to Ryan. His voice was soft and tender. It was the same way he had spoken to her as he held her after each of her grandparent's funerals. "Why do you care?"

"I don't," Ryan said a little too quickly. "If you try anything Leo will be the one to pay the price. Do you understand?"

Crystal nodded. They both knew she wouldn't do anything that would put Leo at risk. Ryan removed the last loop of the chains, freeing her. Crystal brought her arms close to her body and pressed the palm of her hand against the cut on her wrist. It was bleeding a lot faster than she realized. She applied as much pressure as she could to try to slow it down.

"Hey, watch it," Leo yelled. Vince was pulling Leo off the bench by the collar of his shirt. Crystal jumped to her feet, but a waved of dizziness washed over her. She started to fall forward, but Ryan caught her. He pushed her down onto the bench. Crystal regained some semblance of balance just as Vince slammed Leo's back into the wall.

Crystal watched as Leo changed his stance. He was getting ready to fight back. "Leo, no," she called, but it was too late. He was already mid swing. His fist connected to Vince's jaw with surprising accuracy. Crystal felt a moment of pride. That was until Vince turned his head back and laughed.

"You don't know who you're dealing with you spoiled little punk." Vince punched Leo in the gut with enough force to send him to his knees. Crystal lunged at Vince, but Ryan put out his arm to stop her. In one swift movement, he pulled out his gun and fired. Vince fell to the shuttle floor with a resounding thud. Crystal caught a glimpse of the gun's setting indicator as Ryan returned it to his side. It was set at level four. Vince was dead.

"What?" Ryan answered her look of shock. "I was going to have to kill him eventually. It's not like I was really going to take him back to Teria to live a life of ease," he said with a humorless laugh. "You can't tell me you don't think he deserved it,"

"The guy was a violent jerk, but that doesn't mean you had to kill him," Crystal protested. She looked past Ryan to Leo. He was staring down at Vince's body with his mouth slightly open. Honestly he was handling it better than she expected. "There are other ways to handle it." At least the numbers were back on her side. All she needed to do was work up the strength to fight.

"Yeah but this was easier." Ryan shrugged his shoulders. "Leo, see if you can find a first aid kit."

Leo stood frozen in place, his eyes glued to Vince's body. "It's ok, Leo," Crystal said with what she hoped was a reassuring smile. She couldn't afford for him to lose it now. She would need his help to get them out of this. She'd already been having a hard time focusing before cutting open her wrist. She took a couple of deep breaths to push the dizziness from her head. It didn't really work.

Leo gingerly stepped over Vince's body. He opened one of the overhead compartments, pulled out an old battered box, and handed it to Ryan without a word.

"Let me see your wrist," Ryan told Crystal. He rummaged through the box and pulled out several items.

Crystal hesitated a moment before holding her arm out to him. The tenderness in his touch confused her. She blamed the concussion for dampening her senses. He used medical tape to help close the wound before cleaning the area. Every touch was gentle. It reminded her of how he used to absentmindedly run his fingers over her palm after they had made love. Crystal wasn't sure if it was his touch or the blood loss that was making her stomach flutter.

"Why are you doing this?" She studied his face as he concentrated on her wound.

"I can't have you bleeding to death before I get you back to Teria, can I?" He pulled out a roll of gauze and began to wrap it tightly around her wrist. His fingers lingered on her palm for a few seconds after he secured the gauze. It was like he was reading her mind. Crystal felt the ship start to bob. They had reached the surface.

"Time to go." Ryan patted her wound a few times, causing her to flinch. Had she only imagined the tenderness? He got up, grabbed Leo by the arm and pulled out Crystal's gun. "Let's move."

Crystal stumbled as she got to her feet. She closed her eyes to try to regain her balance. She couldn't let her lightheadedness get the better of her. She forced herself to focus. Leo needed her at her best. She slowly climbed up the ladder to the top hatch and, after a few tries, was able to open it with her good hand. The life raft had automatically deployed as soon as they reached the surface. She climbed in and tried to position herself so that she would be next to Ryan. She would need to act fast if he tried to do anything to Leo. They were only a hundred meters from shore.

Ryan pulled out his communicator, making sure his gun was fixed on Leo. "This is General Young. I need an emergency evac from my current location for myself and two passengers."

"Yes, sir," crackled a voice on the other end. "A helicopter will be at your location in ten minutes." Young put his communicator away and started the life raft's engine.

They must have been standing by, waiting for him to make his escape. Crystal looked down at her wrist. The bleeding had slowed substantially, though she could already see red seeping through the bandage. She needed to come up with a plan fast if she was going to have any chance of getting Leo out of this. If Ryan still had them when that helicopter showed up, they were as good as dead. Crystal just hoped she would be able to hold on that long.

Justin and Price were already prepping the launch when Desi and Grady arrived back at the ship. The rest of the combat team was still back on Stapleton Farms. "What's Young's status?" Desi grabbed the gear Price had brought for her. She didn't have time to change, but was glad to at least have her vest, headset, and weapon.

"He's surfacing," Justin said as he handed Grady his gear.

"Good." At least things were going according to plan, even if Desi would have killed to have a few more people on the landing party.

"Lieutenant Flint, we're intercepting a transmission from Young," Dewite's voice came through the shuttle's intercom. "I'm putting it through to you now."

"Finishing prepping the shuttle. We need to get moving," Desi said to Justin. He nodded and made his way back to the helm.

Desi listened carefully while Young's distress call played over the shuttle's speakers. She was shocked to hear that his helicopter would be there in ten minutes. Desi set a timer on her wrist computer. She gave them eight minutes to get to the island, save their people, capture Young, and get the shuttle back in the water before that helicopter was in firing range.

"Why aren't we moving yet?" Desi made her way up the helm. The shuttle started to move before she made it there. She was about to sit down in the copilot seat only to find it was occupied. "What the hell are you doing here?"

"Those are my kids up there. I couldn't sit back and do nothing." Ben said.

Justin shot her an apologetic look from the pilot's seat, but it didn't help. Desi was furious. She wanted to stop the shuttle and throw Ben off, but there wasn't time. He did have military training, even if she thought he was little more than a coward. "Stay out of the way, or I'll shoot you myself." She turned and headed toward the back of the shuttle where Grady and Price were waiting. She glanced down at her wrist. Seven minutes and forty-five seconds left.

Crystal watched the surface of the water with such intensity, she was sure Ryan would be able to tell what she was planning. She knew backup was coming; the only question was if they would get here in time. Ryan's attention was drawn to the sky. It would come down to who arrived first.

Now that they were standing on the shore, Ryan had taken to holding Leo's arm again. It complicated things. Crystal repeated her plan over and over in her mind. Wait for a sign that backup had arrived, get between Ryan and Leo, distract Ryan, give Leo time to run for safety. It wasn't a complicated plan, but she was still having a hard time keeping it in her head. All she really wanted to do was lie down on the sand and close her eyes for a few minutes. Instead she tried to pump herself up for the fight she knew was coming. If she could get her adrenaline flowing, she would be able to focus better.

A small disturbance appeared in the water. It could have easily been a fish trying to catch a bug on the surface, but it was good enough for Crystal. They were running out of time. If she didn't act now, she doubted she would get another chance. She dove at Ryan. She hit him slightly off center but was still able to knock all three of them to the ground. She fought her way between Ryan and Leo. The spinning sensation in her head was getting worse, but she ignored it. She tried to punch him, but she felt weak, dizzy, and she knew that she didn't have her usual force behind her.

Instead she focused everything she had on his gun. It was still set to level four, so if he shot either of them it would be fatal. She tried to wrestle it out of his hand, but she wasn't able to break his grip with any of her normal tricks. She smirked to herself as she realized this entire fight was taking place with them rolling on the ground. Not her normal style, but it seemed to be working ok. She grabbed the handle of the gun with her bad hand. Ryan pulled it away, sending a stray shot into the air.

A weight lifted behind her. Leo had finally managed to untangle himself and get to his feet. "Run, Leo!" she yelled, trying to keep Ryan distracted.

"I can help you!" Leo called.

"Go! I got this." Crystal rolled so that her whole body was lying on top of Ryan. His fists and elbows flew at her. She tried to dodge them, but her body wasn't responding as it should. She made the mistake of glancing over her shoulder to make sure Leo had listened to her. It was all Ryan needed to overpower her. He threw her off of him and rose to his feet.

He started to run after Leo, his gun pointed at his back. Crystal wasn't entirely sure if Ryan was trying to recapture Leo or kill him. She could hear faint voices in the distance. Her people were here. They would get Leo and make sure he was safe, she just needed to buy him a little more time. She scrambled across the sand and made a wild grab for Ryan's ankle. He twisted around as he fell. He landed on his back, sending another shot down the beach. Crystal was sure that shot had been meant for her.

Crystal fought to get to her feet, but once she did it was a struggle to stay there. The whole beach was moving around her, but she only concerned herself with one thing: Ryan. He was focused on something down the beach. She couldn't tell what it was, but it didn't really matter. The only thing she knew was that he wouldn't reach his target. She stepped directly in front of him. Their eyes locked. Ryan leveled the gun directly over her heart. She watched him pull back the trigger as if it was in slow motion. She braced for the shot. At least her last action would be one she could be proud of. She had saved her brother.

# Chapter 21

Desi glanced at her wrist computer as she bounced on the balls of her feet. It was taking way too long to surface. If they landed even a few hundred meters away from where Young had, they might miss their chance to save Wolf and Leo. She could feel the adrenaline coursing through her. This was what she was good at.

"Impact with the shore in three, two, one," Justin called from the helm.

The shuttle crashed onto the beach. Desi didn't wait for any of the usual safety calls before opening the hatch. There wasn't time. Besides, they were on the surface; it wasn't like she would flood the shuttle. She climbed out and jumped down to the beach.

Her heart skipped a beat. She didn't see Young. They had come up in the wrong spot. She was about to start cursing when she saw Leo racing down the beach toward them. He had managed to get away. Desi was afraid to think what that would mean for Wolf. Were they already too late?

The rest of the team was on the beach. They ran to

close the distance between them and Leo. "Where's Wolf?" Desi yelled.

"Back there." Leo paused to catch his breath. Ben was at his side in an instant. "Dad, she's hurt pretty bad."

Desi looked down the beach. Wolf and Young were rolling on the ground. Leo said she was hurt, but at least she was still putting up a fight. Desi took that as a good sign. She took off running down the beach.

A misfired shot came at them. Desi dove to the ground to avoid being hit. That's when she noticed Ben was with them. She had assumed he would stay behind with Leo. Desi scrambled to her feet. She had to admit, the old man was fast.

Young had broken free and was pointing his gun toward them. She tried to follow the line of sight to figure out where he was aiming. The best she could tell, he was pointing it at Justin's head. She didn't question why he had chosen to target Justin out of everyone on the team. "Anderson, look out," Desi called, but it didn't matter. Wolf had gotten to her feet and stepped directly in front of the gun.

Desi watched as Ryan shifted the gun from Justin to Wolf. They were so close—why couldn't she have held him off a little longer? She knew this wouldn't be like the last time. Young wasn't putting on a show. If he managed to get the shot off, Wolf would be dead. She pushed herself to run faster, but she knew she wasn't going to make it in time. She tried to get a shot at Young, but Wolf was blocking the way.

"Wolf, hit the deck," Desi yelled as she ran. Wolf didn't even flinch. It was like she couldn't hear her.

Desi felt the shot more than she heard it. She now had a clear line of sight to Young. She planted her feet and fired three times. She knew she only needed one shot to take him down, but the anger inside her erased any self-restraint she had. Her first shot hit him square in the chest, stunning him.

Young dealt with, she raced toward Wolf. Part of her was afraid to look. It took her a second to register that there was more than one body on the ground. She made it over to Wolf as Justin and Grady rolled Ben off her. Desi had been so focused on Young, she hadn't seen how close Ben had gotten to the fight. He must have thrown himself on Wolf. She prayed he had been quick enough.

"Crystal! Crystal!" The panic in Justin's voice cut Desi like a knife.

"I'm fine." Wolf held a hand to her forehead as she slowly sat up. Wolf gave a small smile as her balance wavered, and Justin knelt next to her to hold her steady. "Not fine. But not dead." Desi had never been more relieved in her life. "Ben?" Wolf turned to look at him lying in the sand next to her, Grady at his side. He wasn't moving. "Dad."

Grady was searching him for a pulse. He hesitated, just an instant. "He's dead."

Wolf sat in silence, a look of intense concentration on her face. "There's a helicopter. We have to go."

Desi looked down at her computer. Wolf was right; they had just over a minute to get back in the water. She couldn't see the helicopter yet, but the thumping of its rotating blades was beginning to cut through the air. "Right. Price, Grady, get Young. Anderson and I will get Ben." She turned to Wolf who still hadn't gotten to her feet. "Are you going to be ok on your own?"

"I'll manage." Crystal got up and started to make her way toward the shuttle. Desi noticed that she wasn't moving in a straight line, but her general direction was good. It was the best she could hope for at the moment.

She grabbed Ben's shoulders while Justin grabbed his feet and together they ran back to the shuttle.

Leo was waiting for them. Crystal wasn't sure how she was going to face him. He had lost his father and didn't even know it yet. The worse part was that it was all her fault. She never should have gone after Ryan alone. Why hadn't she waited for back up?

"Crystal, you're alright!" Leo ran over to her and threw his arms around her neck, nearly knocking her to the ground again.

"Yeah, I'm fine." She struggled to regain her equilibrium. Something that was getting harder to do with every passing second.

"I thought for sure..." Leo's voice trailed off as he hugged her.

Crystal didn't know what to say. Leo would be so disappointed when he realized that she had survived at the expense of their father. A thumping sound filled her ears. For a moment she thought it was the sound of her heartbeat, but it was much too loud. The helicopter. She broke away from Leo and turned around. The dark speck in the sky was growing larger every second. "We need to get in the shuttle." Crystal grabbed Leo's hand and started to pull him toward it.

"We need to wait for dad." Leo didn't move, his eyes were fixed down the beach.

"Please, Leo." Crystal pulled at his sleeve, certain that she was dragging him toward the shuttle. But it was too late. Leo had seen Flint and Justin carrying Ben's body.

"Dad!" Leo broke free of Crystal's grip and ran to them.

"Leo, no! That's the wrong way." Crystal stumbled

after him.

Leo stood frozen as Flint and Justin neared. "Crystal, why are they carrying him? Is he hurt? What happened?"

"He's dead." She probably could have found a gentler way to deliver the news, but she was having a hard time putting coherent thoughts together without worrying how they came across.

"No. That's not possible. I just saw him." Leo took a few more steps away from the shuttle. Crystal grabbed him and tried to pull him back. That was her job. Get Leo on the shuttle. She managed to bring him back a few steps, before her energy started to fade. She noticed his sleeve was covered in blood and she started to panic. She was certain she had protected him better than that. When had he gotten hurt? That's when she felt blood running down her arm. The bandage was completely soaked. Her wound must have reopened at some point. The quick patch job Ryan had done wasn't meant to hold up against all this movement.

"Get him in the shuttle, they're almost here," Flint yelled as she ran past with Ben's body.

"That's what I'm doing."

At the sight of Ben's body, Leo collapsed to his knees. At least he wasn't fighting her any more, though he still wasn't moving in the direction she needed him to go. Crystal dug deep inside herself, tapping into an energy reserve she wasn't entirely sure was there. She grabbed ahold of him under his arms and lifted him to his feet. He didn't fight her, but he wasn't doing anything to help her either. She wrapped one of his arms around her neck. She started to drag him toward the shuttle but had to stop. Her field of vision was narrowing. She pushed it aside. She would not lose anyone else today.

"I got him. Go." Grady grabbed Leo from her. Where had he come from? Now that Leo was gone, she wasn't sure what to do with herself, so she just stood there and watched Grady running toward the shuttle, dragging Leo along with him. "Crystal, run!" Grady yelled over his shoulder.

Crystal nodded and started to move toward the shuttle. She was pretty sure she was making amazing time, though somehow the shuttle kept getting farther and farther away. Grady had already gotten Leo up the ladder and into the shuttle and she was still several hundred meters away. She saw Grady hanging off the ladder looking for her. Crystal tried to motion to him to go on, leave her behind. At this rate she was never going to make it in time. She noticed that sand had mixed with the blood on her arm. When had she fallen? She could have sworn she was still running toward the shuttle. It didn't matter. She would be fine here. It was warm in the sun. Crystal rolled to her back and closed her eyes.

"Damn it kid, come on." Grady scooped her up in his arms. She rested her face against his chest as he ran. The sound of him breathing was like a lullaby. She felt herself drifting away, but was suddenly jerked back as he threw her over his shoulder and started to climb the ladder to the shuttle's hatch. Crystal let out a giggle as she watched the beach become the sky. "You're delirious," Grady muttered as he jumped through the hatch and deposited her into one of the seats. He secured her safety belt, before taking the seat next to her.

"Anderson, get us the hell out of here," Desi yelled.

"Do we have everyone? Did Crystal make it?"

"Yes, now go!"

Crystal was vaguely aware of the shuttle reentering the water. She knew she should be concerned, but she couldn't seem to remember why. She leaned back in her chair and closed her eyes.

"No you don't," Grady said while gently tapping her face. Crystal swatted at his hand. "Give me your arm." Crystal lifted her arm a few inches "Not that one, the one that's covered in blood." He reached over and grabbed her other hand.

"What's wrong with her?" Flint was sitting on the other side of the shuttle. She seemed worried. Crystal wondered if there was something going on she should be worried about too.

"Could be anything really. Concussion, blood loss, shock over her father dying on top of her. Or maybe she was really looking forward to going back to Teria with me and is upset you ruined our plans," Ryan said.

Crystal looked over to the corner of the shuttle where Ryan was sitting. She didn't remember him getting on the shuttle. "Ryan we can't go to Teria. We have an exam in the morning, and we're supposed to spend the night studying."

"That's outstanding."

Crystal couldn't understand why Ryan was laughing at her.

"I'd stop talking if you want to live," Grady said through gritted teeth. "I have no problem delivering your dead body back to Rank."

Why was Grady talking about Rank? That reminded her—why had Ryan said her father died on top of her? She wasn't there when he died. That's when she noticed someone laying on the floor of the shuttle. Ben. Her father. He had pushed her out of the way and now he was dead. Why hadn't anyone bothered to cover him up? She looked up at Leo, who was sitting across from her. Tears streamed down his face as he looked down at

Ben. She really should try to comfort him. She started to undo her harness, but Grady stopped her. She looks at him confused. "I need to help Leo," she said in a harsh whisper.

"You need to stop moving and let me bandage your arm before you bleed to death." Grady produced a roll of gauze and started to wrap it around her arm.

"And then I can help Leo?"

"No," Grady ordered. "Did you forget there is a Teria helicopter coming to try to blow us out of the water? Now is not the time to be moving around the shuttle."

"Oh," was all Crystal could manage. That seemed like something she should have remembered. She heard Ryan snickering in the corner. Grady released her arm long enough to reach over and punch him. "That wasn't very nice."

"Trust me, he deserves much worse than that." Grady continued to squeeze her arm, even though he had finished wrapping it. Crystal focused on the pressure as she tried to stay in the present, rather than get lost in memories again.

"Everyone, hold on," Tyler called from the helm. "Torpedo in the water."

Crystal felt the shuttle lurch suddenly. It was a good thing she hadn't gotten up. The shuttle weaved back and forth as Justin tried to confuse the tracking on the missile heading for them. Crystal should have felt something—fear, adrenaline, sadness—but she was numb. A loud explosion rattled the ship. The torpedo had struck something close, but she was pretty sure it hadn't hit them. At least, there wasn't water leaking into the shuttle. She felt her ears pop as they dove deeper.

"Second torpedo in the water," Tyler called again.

"Don't these people care that we have their general

onboard?" Flint said.

Crystal felt like she was watching a movie. She squeezed her eyes shut and shook her head. The fog cleared slightly. "It's easier to kill him." She leaned forward to look Ryan in the eye. She still didn't really understand what he was doing here, but at least she knew he was the enemy.

"She's not wrong. Rank would probably even blame it on LAWON." Ryan winked at her and smiled. Maybe he wasn't the enemy after all. Maybe this was all a cover, and he would get them both out of here any second? It wasn't like she really knew the people on the other side of the shuttle. Or did she?

"You need to lean back and relax." Grady gently pushed her back into her seat. If Grady was here then she knew she didn't have anything to worry about. There was no one on the planet she trusted more. She leaned her head against his shoulder and closed her eyes.

Grady nudged her off. "I said relax, not sleep."

"I'm just so tired."

"I know you are, but you have to hang on a little while longer. You can sleep once we get you back to the ship."

Crystal nodded. She put her head back on his shoulder. "Hey Jim."

"Yeah," he said softly.

"Thanks for coming back for me. I'd be lost without you." She stretched her neck toward him. It hurt, but she didn't care. She gave him a small kiss on the cheek. She was safe with Grady. He always took care of her. She closed her eyes for the third time.

"Justin, get us back to *Journey* fast. I'm losing her back here." There was a panic in Grady's voice that she didn't understand, but she didn't let it bother her as she finally allowed herself to drift off into nothingness.

# Chapter 22

Desi had never seen the launch bay this empty. She had sent the entire launch bay crew away as they prepared to move Young from the shuttle to brig. She knew Young would capitalize on any moment of confusion, and the last thing they needed was him loose on the ship. She and Grady had spent the last fifteen minutes securing the route to the brig, making sure to post guards at every intersection. The brig was two levels down on the other side of the ship. Desi had never given its location any thought before. She would have to ask Wolf why she had placed it so far from the launch bay.

She tried not to think about Wolf. She was so pale by the time they arrived back at *Journey*. Justin had panicked the second he saw her. She knew Grady had done what he could to stop the bleeding, but by the look of his clothes, Desi wasn't sure Wolf had any blood left in her. The urgency of the medical team that was waiting in the launch bay didn't put any of them at ease, but Desi couldn't worry about that now. She still had a job to do.

"Commander, what are you doing here?" Desi was surprised to see Dewite waiting at the entrance of the shuttle.

"The captain assigned me to oversee the move of the prisoner while he is attending to Leo." Dewite took a couple of steps toward them.

"I know Young is dangerous, but I'm sure we can handle him."

"I'm not sure it's your safety Reed is concerned about."

"Then whose safety is he worried about?" Grady cocked an eyebrow at Dewite.

"Young's. Given Lieutenant Commander Wolf's current condition, it's safe to assume you're both a little on edge. Maybe a little angry. I'm here to make sure you don't take any of that anger out on Young."

"It's not like he wouldn't deserve it." Desi put her hand on the butt of her gun.

"And that is exactly why I'm here," Dewite reiterated. "Taking Young in is already a risk. We don't want to strain relations with Teria any more than necessary. A press release with Young's bruised face plastered on it wouldn't do LAWON any favors," Dewite said.

Desi didn't bother to hide her scowl. "He killed four people—two of them our guys—and nearly killed Wolf, and you're concerned about how it will play in the press?" Desi waved her hand toward the shuttle where Young was waiting with several armed guards who were ordered to shoot if he so much as flinched.

"I don't like it any more than you do, but that's the way it works."

"How is Crystal?" Grady asked.

Dewite hesitated, obviously wondering if the news would make them angrier. "They're starting her on blood transfusions now," he said. "Dr. Emerson doesn't think there will be any lasting damage, but we won't know for sure until she wakes up." Dewite's posture softened as he talked. He might be here to keep them in line, but Desi knew he was just as angry as they were.

Desi nodded. "Let's go take out the garbage." She led the way into the shuttle. Young was still lounging in the corner. He didn't seem to care about the two guards pointing their weapons at him. "Time to move you to your new home." She pulled him up from his seat and checked the restraints securing his hands behind his back.

"Wonderful," Ryan said cheerfully. Bastard. "I'm dying to see the ship. Crystal has been talking about it since we were at the Academy. I used to sneak into her room when her roommate was on the night shift. We would lay in her bed all night, and she would go on and on about it. It wasn't the most romantic pillow talk, but it got the job done." Young looked at Grady the whole time.

Grady made a move as if he was going to punch Young again, but Dewite stopped him. Maybe they really did need a chaperone. Desi knew she wouldn't have stopped Grady if it had been up to her. Especially given how Young was snickering at them. She wanted to be the one to smack the smile off his face. She settled on twisting his arm a little, as she pushed him toward Grady.

"Sorry to disappoint you, but you won't see one inch of this ship except for the brig," Grady said, his voice on the edge of a growl. "We can't have you running back to Rank and telling him what you saw." Grady produced a black cloth sack they used to store their combat gear in. It had been Grady's idea, so Desi had agreed to let him do the honors. She was afraid Dewite would stop them, but he remained silent as Grady threw the sack over Young's head. She could have sworn she saw a small smile cross Dewite's face.

The walk to the brig was uneventful. The safety measures they had set up ahead of time ensured that the path was clear, and Young didn't put up any kind of resistance. Desi pushed Young into the cell, removed his restraints, and pulled the sack off his head. "I hope you enjoy your accommodations." She walked out of the cell and locked the door behind her. It felt good to finally have Young under her control.

"I truly enjoyed your company." Ryan gently rubbed his wrist as he surveyed the cell. "Now, I understand why you can't stay and talk. Please give Crystal my warm wishes when you see her. Especially you, Lieutenant Grady. I knew you two were close, but I never realized how close until I saw that kiss in the shuttle. I guess I was wrong to think she was with the pilot. At least you two being together make sense, unlike that weak pathetic human," Young said.

Desi stopped in her tracks and fought the urge to turn around. She wanted so badly to question Young, but she resisted. She knew that's what he wanted, and she wouldn't give him the satisfaction of knowing he had gotten to her. She continued to the door where Grady was waiting for her. Dewite must have already returned to the bridge. Good, she didn't need rumors of Crystal kissing Grady to get back to Justin. Not that Dewite would talk, but she couldn't be too careful. Now she just had to deal with Grady. "What was Young talking about?" Her voice was harsher than she intended as she shut the door behind them.

"How should I know?" Grady said.

"Did you kiss Wolf? You know she's with Justin. Why would you do something like that?"

"I didn't kiss Crystal."

"Then why did Young say you did?" She wasn't going to let Grady off that easily.

"Probably to mess you." Grady turned to leave, but Desi reached out and stopped him.

"So, nothing happened between you and Wolf?"

"Nothing like what you're thinking," Grady said. "She kissed me on the cheek seconds before passing out. It was completely innocent. You saw how messed up she was in the shuttle."

"You're sure that's all it was?" Desi pressed. "Because I like you Jim, but Justin's family. If you hurt him, I'd have to kill you." Desi folded her arms across her chest.

"You say Justin's your family? Well Crystal's mine." Grady's expression was serious; no anger, no joking, just pure honesty. "We've been through a lot together. I'm alive today because of her. I care about her, probably more than I care about anyone else, but that doesn't mean there's any kind of romantic relationship between us. She's like my sister. I want her to be happy, and if Justin can make her happy, then great. But like you said, if he hurts her, then he's a dead man."

Still, Desi had to press one more time. "So it meant nothing."

"It meant we're family," Grady reiterated. He blew out a hard breath and offered Desi a humorless smirk, as if he knew how she was feeling, even if he didn't like her accusations. "Don't let Young get into your head," he said, and gave a short nod. Message received. "Now, if we're done, I'm going to go see if Crystal's awake." Grady walked away, shaking his head.

Crystal felt something soft under her head. She tried to remember where she was. Everything from the last couple of hours was fuzzy. She remembered being in the shuttle, and Grady was with her. Was she lying on him? She was pretty sure he wasn't that soft. Either way she didn't think she was in the shuttle anymore. Slowly she opened her eyes. She recognized the steel beams on the ceiling immediately. She had been the one to put them there, after all. She was on *Journey*. Out of the corner of her eye, she saw a bag of blood hanging next to her bed. She followed the IV line down to her arm. She expected to feel something, especially when she saw the large bandage around her wrist, but she felt nothing. She was completely numb, inside and out.

"Welcome back." Justin leaned forward in his chair next to her bed.

"What happened?" Her words came out in a horse whisper.

"You passed out before we made it back to the ship. You lost a lot of blood." Justin gently took her uninjured hand in his.

Crystal lifted her wrist again. She tried to remember how she had gotten hurt. An image of the rusty box cutter floated in her mind. "I'm probably going to need a tetanus shot."

"I'll be sure to let Dr. Emerson know," Justin said with a small laugh.

"How long have I been here?"

"A couple of hours. You have a pretty bad concussion, a bunch of stitches in your wrist, bruising in your throat and on your neck, but no permeant damage."

Crystal appreciated Justin running down her injuries. It helped her to work through it all, as if she was studying a repair list. Crystal repeated the list over and over as she tried to recall how she had gotten each one. "Vince hit me over the head with a shovel."

"A shovel? That's a new one." Justin gently ran his thumb over the back of her hand.

"Well, we were at a farming colony. Did they recover Vince's body? Ryan shot him," Crystal said as she slowly pieced together what had happened.

"Everything's taken care of," Justin promised her. "You don't worry about anything except getting your strength back."

"And my father? Is he dead?" Crystal wasn't sure she wanted to hear the answer, but deep down she knew it was true.

"I'm so sorry, Crystal." There wasn't anything else to say.

"Where's Leo? Is he ok?" She turned her head from one side to the other to see if Leo was lying in one of the beds next to her. She had a vague memory of him covered in blood. The motion caused her head to spin.

"Relax, he's not here." Justin stood up and gently stroked Crystal's hair as she eased back into the pillows. "He wasn't hurt. He's with Captain Reed now. I think Tyler's with them."

Crystal wanted to go find him, but it was probably best that she wasn't able to rush to his side. She had no idea what to say to him, anyway. She expected to feel something at the confirmation of her father's death, but she felt nothing. She had grieved for him a long time ago. Maybe she couldn't do it again. Maybe you only got to grieve for a person once in your life, and her father had already used up his quota.

"What happened to Ryan?" She needed to change the subject before she started to overanalyze her feelings, or lack thereof, and got lost in deep sea of guilt.

"He's in the brig with multiple guards. He won't be able to hurt you now." It was sweet that Justin thought that was what she was concerned about. Despite everything that had happened, she wasn't afraid of Ryan.

"How did they take him there? What route did they take?" Depending on which way they went, Ryan could have seen some design detail of *Journey* he could exploit in the future. He wasn't an engineer, but she had taught him enough about ship design to know what to look for.

"Don't worry, I put a sack over his head while we were moving him," Grady said from outside of her vision. "He didn't see anything." She turned her head slowly and saw Grady moving from the doorway to her bed with a huge smile on his face.

Crystal was shocked to see his face, chest, and arms covered in blood. She shot up in her bed, an action she immediately regretted, and was glad that Justin was there to steady her. "Are you hurt.?"

"Lie back down, I'm fine. All of this is yours." Grady gestured to his blood-soaked uniform. Crystal had lost a lot more blood than she realized. "How are you feeling?"

"Better, I think. It would be really great if the room could stop spinning though." She leaned on Justin and carefully eased herself back down onto the pillows.

"I'll go find Dr. Emerson and see if she can get you some pain medicine." Justin kissed her forehead and walked away. So, the numbness she was feeling wasn't chemically induced like she had hoped. Maybe her heart really was dead.

"You sure you're all right kid?" Grady sat down on the foot of her bed.

"Of course, I am. I wouldn't let a little scratch take me

out." Crystal tried to smile, but her head was throbbing.

"This is the second time I've had to carry your blood-soaked, lifeless body away from a mission," he reminded her. "I'd really like to not have to do it again."

"I make no promises." Crystal closed her eyes to try to get the pain in her head under control. "Were you able to keep it together?" Grady had gone off the deep end at just the suggestion of Ryan hurting her. She was afraid that seeing her like that would have pushed him over the edge again.

"Of course. You needed me," Grady said in a soft voice.

"Good."

"Besides we're even now. You saved my life and now I've saved yours."

"There's no way we're even," Crystal ribbed. "I took a bullet for you and spent four months in rehab. You're just going to have to take a shower and wash your uniform. I still win."

"That's my girl. Get some rest kid." Grady got up, and patted her leg.

Justin was back with Dr. Emerson, who was adding something to one of the IVs. She felt her whole body grow heavy as the drugs took effect, and she drifted off into darkness.

# Chapter 23

Crystal was released from the Med Bay the next morning with strict orders not to engage in any kind of physical activity. For once, Crystal didn't push back. She would be leaving the ship in a few hours, anyway, and the chances of anyone attacking her while she was away were slim. There was someone she needed to talk to before she left, though.

If the guards outside the brig were surprised to see her, they didn't let on. She placed her hand on the scanner, and two metal doors slid open without a sound. She walked past the two empty cells to the one in the corner where Ryan was being held.

He didn't get up from the metal bench as she approached. "Glad to see you've recovered." There wasn't any malice in his voice. If anything, he sounded distracted.

"You killed my father," Crystal said.

Ryan let out a single laugh. "You can't honestly be upset about that. That man lied to you your entire life. He didn't even care enough to come back for you. You should be thanking me."

"Is that why you did it?" she demanded. "Some kind of sick payback for how he treated me?"

"No, I was aiming for you. He just got in the way." Ryan got up from the bench and walked over to where she was standing. Crystal didn't step away.

"I wasn't your original target though, was I?" The events of the day before had been coming back to her slowly. "Who were you planning on shooting? Was it Leo?"

"What kind of monster do you think I am? I wouldn't shoot an unarmed kid in the back. You know me better than that." Ryan seemed truly offended at the suggestion. Crystal wasn't sure why; he had done nothing but threaten Leo to keep Crystal in line the whole time he had them. Was it really that far of a stretch to think he would follow through on his threats?

"I thought I did," she said, "but that was a long time ago. I don't know what you would do now. You've been living undercover for the last three years, trying to gain peoples' trust just so you could turn around and kill them. There were innocent, unarmed kids at Stapleton Farms when you turned off their life support systems."

"That was different," Ryan said, as though it didn't count. "That was an order. Rank needed me to take over the colony once everyone was dead and annex it to Teria. Those deaths would have served a purpose. Shooting Leo at that point wouldn't have achieved anything."

"Then who were you aiming at?" Crystal closed her eyes and squeezed the bridge of her nose to keep the headache that was developing from getting any worse.

"The human," Ryan said with a smirk.

It took a Crystal a few minutes to fully comprehend what Ryan meant. She took her hand away from her face so she could glare at him. "You are a monster."

"Come on, you don't mean that." The smile he wore was the same one she remembered from when they were dating. Her heart skipped a beat. Part of her still longed for that Ryan, even if she would never admit it. She couldn't let him get to her.

"I do. The only reason to target Justin would be to hurt me." Crystal pointed at herself for emphasis.

"The pleasure of killing your new boyfriend would have been an added bonus," he said with a shrug. "I targeted him because he's human and he doesn't belong here. Besides he was pointing his gun at me, and you don't seem real broken up about that." Ryan waved his hand through the bar, as if they were discussing dinner options instead of who was trying to kill whom.

"He wouldn't have killed you."

"Then he's just as weak as I thought he was."

Crystal shook her head. She shouldn't have come here. Talking to Ryan would do her no good. She wouldn't find closure. She wanted so badly to believe that there was some good left in him, that the man she once loved was still in there somewhere, but every chance she gave him to show it, he only disappointed her. She turned away from him and started to walk out of the room.

"Crystal, wait."

She stopped but didn't turn around. "What?"

"Did you mean what you said when we were at Soupionia?" The usual cockiness was gone. The hint of desperation in his voice was enough to make her turn around.

"About what?"

"About the two of us running off together. About helping me hide from Rank and the assassins he would send after me if I left Teria?"

"Yeah, I did," she said without hesitation. There was no use denying it. Ryan had always been able to tell when she was lying.

"Then let's do it. You and me against it all." The glint in his eye broke her heart.

"No." There was a time she would have given anything to have her Ryan back. She would have given up her career, her dreams, to be with him again. But too much had changed. He wasn't the same person he had been when they were at the Academy, and he had proven that to her time and again. Besides she had a new family now, she didn't need Ryan the way she did back then.

"No?" He sounded hurt, and she was relieved to find she didn't feel any guilt at that.

"It's too late," she said. "You killed my father, kidnapped my younger brother at gunpoint and used him to manipulate me—not to mention the fact that you tried to wipe out a whole colony." She shook her head, slowly, to avoid rattling her brain and amplifying the growing headache. "I can't help you out of this one. You're going to have to face what you've done."

"We both know that's not going to happen. I'll spend two or three days in LAWON custody and then be released with a full apology." Ryan's cockiness was back. She knew it was too good to last. At least she hadn't let herself fall prey to his mind games.

"What make you so sure Rank will save you this time? He's not going to be thrilled with how this played out, and he's not known for his forgiveness."

"I was in charge of his personal security team for years," Ryan said. "I know things about him that he wouldn't want to be made public. I've seen the lengths he's willing to go to keep his secrets safe. He isn't going to allow LAWON to hold me for long."

Crystal wasn't sure if Ryan was trying to trick her again, or if he was telling the truth this time. He always was one to broadcast his accomplishments as widely as he could, and he seemed like he was itching to tell her something big. "Why doesn't he kill you and eliminate the risk?"

"I'm smarter than that. If he were to kill me, the information would be broadcast before my body hit the ground. He can't touch me." What kind of information could Ryan have that would make him so sure Rank would save him? It would have to be something that would destroy Rank. He wouldn't keep Ryan around to avoid some minor embarrassment. Especially after Ryan had failed him so many times.

"Then why do you stay? You clearly don't need me to keep you safe from Rank."

"Because I have a good life in Teria. I have money, power, an entire military at my disposal—why would I leave? Besides I agree with everything Rank's trying to do. He's going to rid Neophia of the human infestation, and I want to be on the right side of history when that happens."

"Goodbye, Ryan." Crystal turned and walked away. There was nothing more she wanted to hear from him. Nothing of the Ryan she once loved was left. She didn't know the man in the cell behind her.

Desi knocked on Reed's door. This was the first time Reed had asked to see her in his quarters, and she wasn't sure what to expect. She waited for Reed to acknowledge her before opening the door. "You wanted to see me, sir?"

"Yes. Have a seat." Reed was sitting at a small round table with Commander Dewite. Desi racked her brain to try to figure out what she could have done that would warrant a private meeting with the both them. She hadn't caused any problems lately—at least not any that she was aware of.

"We wanted to discuss the argument you were preparing for The Board," Dewite said.

Desi breathed a sigh of relief and joined them at the table. "Of course, though I didn't think we would need it now that Young is in our custody."

"We don't need it to seize control of Stapleton Farms, but you made some very valid points that LAWON needs to start looking into if we want to get ahead of Teria." Reed had bags under his eyes. Desi wondered if he had gotten any sleep, or if he had been up all night dealing with Ben's death.

"How much evidence were you able to pull together?" Dewite asked.

"I think we were able to put together a pretty tight argument around what we know of Teria's recent movements. When you look at the big picture, I think it would be hard to deny what Rank's intentions are." Desi was confident that her theory was correct; she just hoped she would be able to explain it well enough that the higher ups would take her seriously.

"Good. I'm placing the call to Admiral Craft." Reed punched a few buttons on the keypad in front of him. Desi sat up a little straighter as she rehearsed her arguments in her mind. She really wished she had her computer with her. She didn't want to forget anything. Wolf had told her it was going to be a hard sell, even with all the evidence they had. No one wanted to believe that another war was possible.

"Captain Reed." Craft's face appeared on the screen in front of the table. "Commander Dewite, Lieutenant Flint." He nodded to each of them. "Are you calling me with good news or bad news?"

"We have apprehended Young; however he killed Ben Martin before we were able to stop him. We will be arriving back at Stapleton Farms shortly to return the body," Reed said.

"I can have a helicopter waiting at the nearest piece of land to bring Young back to Headquarters to await sentencing."

Desi watched Craft closely. She knew that Young was his son, though it was rarely mentioned. She wondered what must be going through his head. From what Wolf had told her, it had been years since the two had been in the same room. Craft must have taken some lessons on emotional control from Wolf, because he didn't react at all at the mention of Young.

"Commander Wolf has requested some leave and would like to return to Kincaron with Young if possible," Dewite said. Desi looked at him in shock. She hadn't been aware that Wolf had requested leave. From the way people talked, she hadn't taken any time off in years. Why did she need it now?

"That shouldn't be a problem. How is she?" Craft's face softened when he talked about Wolf. Desi always forgot that they had a connection outside of the chain of command. A connection that she had locked up in the brig.

"She's handling the situation as well as can be expected," Reed said.

"Well if there's nothing else, I'll let you get back to work." Craft leaned forward as if to close the line.

"Sir," Desi said quickly before he could end the call. They hadn't even gotten to the real reason for the call.

"Was there something else?"

"Yes," said Reed. "While investigating the incident at Stapleton Farms, Lieutenant Flint uncovered something we feel you need to hear." Reed turned to Desi.

She took a deep breath and jumped right in. There was no use wasting anyone's time sugar coating things. "Sir, I believe that President Rank is preparing Teria for war."

A smirk flitted across Craft's face before he regained his composure. "With all due respect to Lieutenant Flint, it is not possible that Rank is preparing to declare war on anyone. Having only been on Neophia for two months, I'm sure you don't fully comprehend how things work here yet."

Desi choked back her anger; it wouldn't help her argument. "With all due respect sir, I know I'm right. I might not fully understand all the political complexities of Neophia, but I do know what war looks like. Probably better than anyone else on the planet."

"If Rank was preparing for war," Craft said, "our intelligence agencies would have picked up on something and they haven't."

"Then they aren't looking at the right information." Desi pressed the palms of her hands on the table. It was taking all of her willpower to keep her anger in check.

"If you take a look at the information Flint has put together, I think you'll see that she's onto something," Dewite said.

"I'm a busy man Commander. I don't have time to look into every crazy theory that comes across my desk. Especially when it's something as unlikely as this." Craft waved his hand at the screen.

Desi started to rise out of her seat, but Reed put his hand out to stop her. "Admiral Craft, this isn't some conspiracy theory. I believe Lieutenant Flint is right about this, and if you're smart you will too."

Craft took a deep breath. "Johnathan, do you hear what you're saying? If you push this and you're wrong, it will be the end of your careers."

"And if we're right, think of all the lives we could save," Reed countered. "Alan, just look at the evidence. I've already had it uploaded to your secure server."

"Fine. I'll take a look, but I'm not promising anything. Out." The screen went black.

"Well that was…" Dewite started.

"Condescending and infuriating?" Desi offered. She started to pace next to the table. How naive could Craft be? Given everything he knew about Rank, why couldn't he believe that Rank would want to start another war?

"I was going to say easier than expected," Dewite finished with a chuckle.

Desi stopped mid-pace. "You're kidding, right?"

"Craft agreed to look at the evidence," Reed said. "That's the best that we can hope for at this point."

"And if that's not enough?" Desi asked. "Do we just sit back and wait for Rank to declare war?"

"We keep gathering evidence until they don't have any choice but to believe us," Reed said.

"I just hope we aren't too late." Desi didn't wait to be dismissed. Why had they even bothered to bring her to this planet if they weren't going to listen to her?

Crystal sat on the steps in Launch Bay One with her bag at her feet. She would be leaving for Kincaron soon, but she needed to talk to Leo before he left. She hadn't seen him since they were rescued, and she needed to see for herself that he was ok before she said goodbye. She wouldn't be going back to Stapleton Farms with him for Ben's funeral, and she felt that she owed him an explanation.

She stood up when she heard people approaching. Two nurses were wheeling in Ben's body to be loaded onto the shuttle before anyone else arrived. She walked over to them. They didn't stop her from unzipping the body bag so that she could see him one last time.

There was so much she wanted to ask him. She still didn't understand why he had done it. Why he had given up everything to save her? Ben had this whole other life waiting for him. He should have gone back to it. Sacrifice was part of her job, a part she willingly accepted. And if he was going to risk himself to save her, why hadn't he come back for her in the first place? He could have protected her growing up. It didn't make sense. She had him back for such a short time, and she had wasted so much of it being angry.

That's what bothered her the most. Not that he was gone. He had been gone her whole life. Nothing would really change for her. It would be Leo and Gina who would feel this. The pain belonged to them, not her. She wouldn't steal that from them. "Thank you," she whispered and carefully zipped the bag shut. She stepped back to allow the nurses to finish loading him into the shuttle.

Leo and Tyler walked in a few seconds later. She was glad she hadn't held the nurses up longer. The last thing Leo needed to see was them moving Ben's body. To Crystal's surprise, Leo ran up to her and gave her a hug. The physical contact paralyzed her for a moment, but she saw Tyler smirking at her. She cautiously wrapped her good arm around Leo and patted him on the back.

"I wasn't sure you were going to be well enough to come with us." Leo released her and looked her up and down to assess her condition for himself.

Guilt shot through her. She really should have just written Leo a letter to explain things; that would have been easier. She took a deep breath. "I'm not coming to the funeral."

Leo's face fell at once. "What do you mean? You have to be there."

"I'm sorry. I can't. I've already attended his funeral once. I can't do it again." Crystal sat back down on the steps leading to the shuttle. Her head was starting to throb again.

"I don't understand."

"I don't expect you to."

"If you aren't coming with us, then where are you going?" Leo waved at the bag at her feet.

"Ben made a lot of mistakes in his life, and I want to try to make some of them right." She looked up at Leo from where she was sitting, not minding that he was looming above her. "I know that's what he would want me to do. To fix part of his legacy."

"Can't you do that another time?" Leo demanded. "I mean it's your fault he's dead. The least you can do is show up to his funeral." Leo stormed past her and into the shuttle.

"Well that went great." Crystal pressed the palms of her hands to her eyes.

"He's hurting. He didn't mean that." Tyler came over and sat down next to her. His arm was in a sling while he recovered from the gun shot wound he'd gotten from Ryan.

"He's not wrong," Crystal argued. "If I had waited for

back up, instead of going after Young alone, Ben might still be alive."

"Or we could have lost Leo," Tyler pointed out. "You can't blame yourself for this. You weren't the one that pull the trigger."

"I know." Crystal nodded. She wasn't sure if she was trying to convince herself or Tyler.

"I have the information you asked for." Tyler pulled a computer chip from his pocket and handed it to her.

"Thanks Ty." Crystal carefully placed it in her bag.

"I wish you would let me come with you."

"You need to go to the funeral," she said. "I know that's what you want to do. You never got the chance to say goodbye to him like I did. Besides this is my responsibility. I'm the only one that can set the record straight."

"Lieutenant Commander Wolf, please report to Launch Bay Two." They both looked up at the speaker.

"I should go." Crystal got up and grabbed her bag. "I'll be back in week."

"Good luck." Tyler got to his feet. He squeezed her hand before climbing in the shuttle that would take him back to Stapleton Farms.

# Chapter 24

Crystal's motorcycle was waiting for her when she arrived at the base. She had managed to avoid Ryan during the trip. She was straddling the bike checking things when Ryan was escorted off the transport. She wondered what he was feeling now that he was back. Was he scared at all? He certainly wasn't showing any signs of fear as he walked confidently across the tarmac. Whatever information he had on President Rank must be pretty damaging to give him that kind of confidence. He looked over at her and smiled. Crystal wouldn't let herself get drawn in. She wasn't here for him. She put down the visor on her helmet and pulled away.

She really should go get settled into her room on the base. She had a lot of meetings lined up over the next two days she needed to get ready for, but there was a stop she needed to make first. The drive to the military memorial park where her mother's ashes were was a short one. Had it been any longer, Crystal might have had second thoughts and turned around.

It had been years since she had been there. Even though she had been working down the road building *Journey* for the past year, she never seemed to find the time to come here. Someone had been keeping up the memorial though. The plaque bearing her mother's name was as shiny as it was when it was first put up. The small vase at the base of the plaque was full of fresh flowers. She wondered who had placed them there.

The plaque next to it bore the name Jedidiah Wolf. Crystal removed a roll of white duct tape from her bag and used it cover the name. She wrote Ensign Elias Patterson on it with a thick black marker. It didn't look great, but at least it finally honored the person whose ashes were really behind it. It was her first small step in making things right.

Crystal turned back to her mother's name. "I'm sorry I haven't been here in a while." She placed her hand over the engraved letters on the stone. It was cool to the touch. "Thank you for your message. I can't tell you how much it meant to me to be able to hear your voice again. I only wished I had gotten it sooner." Crystal turned away and sat on the ground with her back pressed against the stone. "I wish a lot of things had been different, but there's no good in looking back. I can't change what's already happened, I can only change what's ahead of me. You taught me that."

Crystal took a deep breath and stared out over the horizon. The sun was starting to set. The soft light brought out hits of metallic green in the rocks along the shore line "I hope you would be proud of me if you were here. I've always wanted to live up to the legacy you left behind. To be the hero you were. I always thought it was the best way to honor you and dad. Only I wasn't really honoring him, was I?" She remembered his pressure on her shoulders as he pushed her out of the way, then blinked back the memory. "He did sacrifice himself for me in the end, so I guess that counts for something."

Crystal watched the waves crashing against the shore. Her mother would have liked it here, where the ocean met the land. A ship sailed across the horizon. Her heart skipped a beat at the sight of it. She longed to be back at sea, even though she had only been away for a few hours. She knew the military was where she belonged. She wasn't doing this to make her parents proud, or to live up to their legacy. She was doing this for herself.

The last two days had gone by in a blur of conference rooms, well-appointed offices, and unfamiliar faces. Crystal had talked to every department head she could, using the notoriety of her family name to secure her meetings with higher ups who otherwise wouldn't have glanced in her direction. She told her story over and over until it felt rehearsed on her tongue. She was determined to right the wrongs of her father, and for the most part, she had. At least as far as the official record went. Correcting the public's view of him would be a lot more challenging, but that was a task for another day. Now came the part she had been dreading the most.

The address Tyler had given her for the Patterson family was about a five-hour drive inland. The sun was warm, and the sky was clear as she drove through the wooded forests and grassy fields of her home country. Having grown up in one of her nation's underwater colonies, she didn't get to see its beauty as much as she would have liked to.

She was a few hours into her drive when a call came through. She had connected her helmet to her communicator so she could take the calls without stopping. She had been fielding questions and updates from her engineering team, even though she was technically on leave. She was about to answer the call when she saw it was from Admiral Craft. She pulled off to the side of the road in order to give the call her full attention.

"Admiral Craft, what's going on?" she asked without preamble. "Did something happen to *Journey?*"

"Crystal, your ship is fine," Craft said with a chuckle. "This is a personal call."

"Oh, ok. Then hi, I guess. How are you?" She had been close to Craft when she had been dating Ryan, but never once had he called her for personal reasons. Crystal didn't know what to expect. She was glad she had pulled over; otherwise she might have crashed her bike.

"I wanted you to hear this from me before the news got out."

"Ok."

"Ryan is being released back to Teria."

Crystal wasn't surprised. After what Ryan had told her, she knew they wouldn't be able to hold him for long, let alone actually try him for any of his crimes. She had hoped that LAWON would be able to hold him for more than a couple of days, though.

"When does the apology come out?" She hoped she managed to keep the disgust out of her voice. Personal call or not, Craft was still her Admiral.

"No apology. Both sides have agreed to call it an arranged meeting between Teria and LAWON."

"That's insane." The words slipped out of her mouth before she realized what she was saying. "What did Rank threaten us with this time to get The Board to agree to that?"

"I don't know," Craft said. Did she imagine the frustration in his voice? "Given my relationship to Ryan, everyone thought it would be best if I wasn't involved."

"Did you at least get to see him?" she asked gently. The last time Craft had seen his son was at their Academy graduation ceremony five years ago.

"Briefly." The long pause made Crystal wonder if he'd continue. "He wouldn't even look at me," Craft said finally. "It was like I was nothing to him."

"I'm sorry, sir. I'm sure it was an act. I know he still loves you," Crystal lied. She knew Ryan hated his father with every fiber of his being, but she couldn't tell Craft that.

"Thank you, Crystal. That means a lot coming from you." There was another pause, and when Craft continued, his voice was more professional, back to Admiral instead of wounded father. "As I said, I wanted to let you know that Ryan is being released, but he is being sent directly back to Teria, so you shouldn't have to worry about any kind of retaliation."

"Thank you, sir." The thought of Ryan coming after her on LAWON soil had never even crossed her mind. He wasn't stupid enough to risk it. No, he would come after her when he was certain that he would win. Crystal ended the call and pulled back on the road. She still had a few more hours to drive.

Crystal pulled up in front of a small house in a poor neighborhood. She took out her tablet to make sure she had the right place. The address on the front of the house matched the one Tyler had given her. She had hoped she was wrong, that she had gotten turned around somewhere. She wanted the Patterson family to have had a good life, despite not getting what the military owed them. She would have felt a lot less guilt that way. Nothing seemed to be going her way lately.

She took a deep breath and got off her bike. She took her time crossing the street and climbing the steps to the front door. This would be one of the hardest things Crystal ever had to do. She knocked. It took a while, but eventually a teenage boy answered the door. He looked at her for a moment before starting to close the door on her.

"Please," Crystal said. "Wait."

"We've had enough with the military," the boy said

angrily. The second teenage boy to yell at her that week. "There's nothing you can say to us that we haven't heard before. Can't you people leave my family in peace?"

"Oliver, who's at the door?" A woman appeared next to the teen. Her hair was disheveled, and her waitress uniform was covered in other peoples' food. It made Crystal feel self-conscious in her crisp clean military uniform. Maybe she should have worn her civilian clothing.

"It's no one," Oliver said. "They were just leaving." Oliver went to close the door on Crystal again.

"I know what happened to Elias Patterson," Crystal said. "Please just let me talk to you for minute." The door stopped closing, but didn't open again. Crystal heard a whispered argument on the other side, but she couldn't tell who was winning. A few seconds later the door opened with only the woman on the other side.

"Are you Mrs. Patterson?"

"Yes, I am. And you are?"

"I'm Lieutenant Commander Crystal Wolf." This was not going at all how she planned.

"If you are here to answer our latest request by telling me that all the evidence points to Eli abandoning us, I don't want to hear it." There was a learned coldness in her voice.

"I'm not. I know what really happened to him." Crystal looked down at her hands. "Please, I just want to make things right."

Mrs. Patterson stepped out of the way to let Crystal into the house. Crystal followed her into the kitchen, where two people in wheelchairs were sitting at the table doing a puzzle. "These are Eli's parents," she said to Crystal. "Mom, Dad, this is Lieutenant Commander Wolf. She's here to tell us what happened to Eli," she yelled as she touched each of their arms. The old couple looked up at Crystal confused, but as soon as they saw her uniform a cold expression formed on each of their faces. Crystal couldn't blame them. The military hadn't treated them very well over the years. They all looked at her expectantly.

"I've recently uncovered new information that confirms that Elias Patterson was killed in action during the war." This was even harder than she thought it would be.

Mrs. Patterson pulled out a chair from the kitchen table and collapsed into it. She held her hand over her heart. "I always knew that he wouldn't abandon us." Oliver walked over from where he had been standing in the doorway and placed his hands on his mother's shoulders. Crystal hadn't noticed him standing there. A few tears rolled down Mrs. Patterson's face as she took in the news. After a few moments, she wiped them away and patted her son's hand. "Go out back and get your brother. He should be here for this." The boy nodded and headed out the back door. "I always knew he was dead. It was the only thing that made sense. It's just hard to hear it confirmed." She wiped at her tears. "I guess I always held out hope that one day he would find his way back to us."

Crystal wanted to tell her that it wasn't any easier to think someone was dead your whole life, only to find out that they had been alive. She wanted to say that the pain and anger she would have felt would have overshadowed any joy she might find in the moment. But she didn't. This wasn't about her. "I'm sorry for your loss."

"Please, tell me how my son died," said Eli's father. The twins had returned, so now the whole family was watching her.

She pulled a tablet from her bag, cued up the video, and set it down on the table for them to watch. Crystal didn't look at the screen. She had seen the video more times than anyone on the planet. It replayed in her mind every time she closed her eyes.

"Wait a minute, I remember this," Mrs. Patterson said. "This is the execution of the Wolfs. This event was the trigger that ended the war."

"Didn't you say your name was Wolf? Are you related to them?" one of the twins asked while pointing at the screen. Now that they were both here, Crystal couldn't tell them apart. It didn't matter; she wouldn't be here much longer.

"Yes," she said. "That's my mother and, up until a week ago, I believed that was my father."

"What does this have to do with Eli?" Mrs. Patterson asked.

"That is Ensign Elias Patterson."

"How is that possible?" the other twin asked.

"It was recently discovered that Jedidiah Wolf has been living under an alias since the end of the war. His cover was blown on a mission, and rather than abort the mission all together, Ensign Patterson volunteered to take his place. None of this was ever documented, so when that happened," Crystal motioned toward the tablet, "the Kincaron military assumed it was Lieutenant Wolf."

"I want to talk to him. I want to hear this for myself," Mrs. Patterson said.

"I'm sorry, but he was killed last week," Crystal said numbly. "I was able to record his statement prior to his death, and a copy of the recording is on the tablet when you're ready to watch it. I've spoken to several officials at LAWON Headquarters and they are in the process of updating Eli's file to reflect what actually happened. His dishonorable discharge will be removed, and his record will reflect that he died in action. You will retroactively receive all the benefits you should have as his surviving family."

Crystal watched as they listened, but she wasn't finished. "I've also had all the money I received in my father's name transferred to your account. Eli's ashes are at the National War Memorial Park. They are waiting for your call. You can have him removed and placed somewhere closer to you if you like, or you can leave him there and they will have a new plaque up tomorrow. It's a really beautiful spot overlooking the ocean. He's right next to my mother." The words spilled out of Crystal's mouth until everything had been said.

The Patterson family looked at Crystal in shock. She knew it was a lot of information to throw at them. It would probably take them days to process it. "All the information you need is on the tablet," she said, stumbling now that the rehearsed portion was out of the way. "If anyone gives you a hard time, tell them to contact me. I'll leave you alone now. Again, I'm sorry for everything my family has put you through." Crystal turned and left the kitchen. She had reached the front door when she heard a voice behind her.

"Why are you doing all of this?" Mrs. Patterson asked.

"Your family has suffered so much because of my father, I had to try to make it right," she said, the truth of it burning away her uneasiness. "Eli was the one that died a hero, not Jedidiah Wolf. The world should know that."

"Thank you," Mrs. Patterson said, more tears waiting to fall. "You have no idea what all of this means to my family. And it's not about the money, no matter what the officials at LAWON think. It was always about his honor."

"I know," Crystal said with a warm smile. "Oh, there's one last thing." Crystal pulled the computer chip she had taken from Ben's office out of her pocket. She wasn't sure if it was the nerves or the effects of the concussion that had made her forget about it. "Eli recorded this before his last mission. I'm sorry it's taken so long to find its way home to you."

Crystal left the house quickly. She didn't want to be there when Mrs. Patterson watched the recording. She jumped on her motorcycle and took off. She needed to get back to *Journey*. She needed to get back to her family.

# Acknowledgements

I was in elementary school when my family got its first computer. Home computers were just starting to becoming popular, so it was really exciting to be one of the first families I knew to have one. It was set up in my parent's bedroom and while dialup internet was a thing, we didn't have it. What we did have was Mavis Beacon typing, some underwater game with a talking dolphin, and most importantly a word processor. That computer was a game changer for me. I would spend hours in there after school and on the weekend with my Walkman writing stories. When I'd get stuck, I'd stand in front of the mirror on their dresser making facing to try better describe my characters facial expressions. It was my sanctuary, expect for the fact that it was still my parent's bedroom.

So, one day I asked my parents for a laptop. I'm sure I had been not so subtly hinting at it for a long time before I finally asked. It was big deal. Laptops were fairly new technology and crazy expensive. I would dream about owning one in the future someday when I was a successful writer making all kinds of money. Well one day my dad came home with a refurbished laptop. I don't think it was for any kind of special occasion, or even if it was technically for me, but I'm pretty sure I was the only one that used it. It was massive, slow, with external CD and floppy disk drives you had to swap out, and the only program it had was a word processor. I loved it. I could now write in the privacy of my room whenever I wanted.

My parents have always been supportive of my writing. My mom has always been my first, and sometimes only reader. I cringe looking about at some of the things I gave her to read, but she always encouraged me to keep going. I wouldn't be the writer I am today if it wasn't for the unwavering support and allowing me the freedom to spend hours locked in my room, or theirs, typing away.

This book also wouldn't be possible without the support and encouragement of all my fellow Cabin in the Woods writers. They keep me going when I don't think I'll ever be able to write again. You are my tribe, my circle, my writing family and I love each and every one of you!

A huge thank you to my critique partner M K Marteens. I would be absolutely lost without your insight. I feel so lucky that we found each other on the NaNo forums all those years ago.

And as always, a special thank you to my husband Mike who goes out of his way to make sure I have the time I need to get Crystal and Desi's story out of my head and onto paper so I can share it with all of you. I love you.

Made in the USA
Columbia, SC
12 August 2021